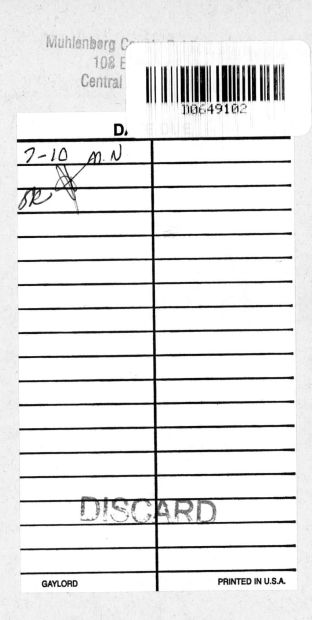

Looking for a Love Story

Looking for a Love Story

a novel

LOUISE SHAFFER

BALLANTINE BOOKS TRADE PAPERBACKS
NEW YORK

A Ballantine Books Trade Paperback Original

Copyright © 2010 by Louise Shaffer
Reading group guide copyright © 2010 by Random House, Inc.

Published in the United States by Ballantine Books,
an imprint of The Random House Publishing Group,
a division of Random House, Inc., New York.

BALLANTINE and colophon are registered
trademarks of Random House, Inc.
RANDOM HOUSE READER'S CIRCLE & Design
is a registered trademark of Random House, Inc.

LIBRARY OF CONGRESS CATALOGING-IN-PUBLICATION DATA

Shaffer, Louise.
Looking for a love story : a novel / Louise Shaffer.
p.   cm.
ISBN 978-0-345-50210-0
1. Women authors—Fiction. 2. Intergenerational relations—Fiction. 3.
Self-realization in women—Fiction. I. Title.
PS3569.H3112L66   2010   813'.54—dc22   2010001578

Printed in the United States of America

www.randomhousereaderscircle.com

2 4 6 8 9 7 5 3 1

For Mama and Roger, with all the love and gratitude for the two pillars of my life

Looking for a Love Story

CHAPTER 1

Okay, here's one of those life lessons I think we all know. When someone looks you in the eye, takes a deep breath, and says, "We have to talk," nothing good is going to come from it. People do not feel they have to warn you when they are about to pay you a compliment or give you that gold bangle you've been angling for. But when you hear the word *talk*, especially from one of your nearest and dearest, the correct response is to do pretty much what my dog, Annie, does when someone says *bath* in her presence. You run. You swallow back the sick feeling in your stomach, and you ignore the ice sliding down the back of your neck, and you take off. Because even those of us who insist that oh, no, we had no clue what was coming, we never dreamed of it . . . well, somewhere deep down we *did* know. We just couldn't face it. So we pretend we didn't hear the T word, and we run. At least, that's what I did when my husband, Jake, said those fateful words on a peaceful Saturday in Manhattan, when we were sitting around not doing much of anything. I immediately got to my feet.

"I think I'll go for a run," I chirped. I always get chirpy when I'm in denial about something. "It's a perfect day for it, and I'm doing so well with the diet, I'll just take a quick jog around the park."

Jake and I both knew I didn't jog anymore. Not since I'd gained thirty-two pounds. For the record, the two of us also knew my diet wasn't going all that well either, but that was one of the things we didn't discuss—one of the many things, I realized later, when I looked back on it. "I've lost another two pounds," I lied gaily.

"Terrific, Francesca," said Jake with a big fake smile. I'd been seeing a lot of that fake smile recently.

"Britney Spears, move over," I said inanely. She was the only pop reference I could think of at a moment's notice. My husband liked it when we sprinkled our conversation with pop references, because he thought it made us seem hip. And if we could claim a personal relationship to the pop reference—no matter how distant—he was really happy, because that made us seem successful. Being successful is very important to Jake. But I'd been slipping up on my pop culture lately—the damn stuff moves so fast—because I'd been busy battling the writer's block from hell. Which is not a good thing when you write books for a living. But I'm getting ahead of my story.

Jake knew the names of so many of those interchangeable young blond starlets who career back and forth between rehab and multimillion-dollar movie deals because he was a photographer, and he'd taken pictures of quite a few of them back when they were still living in Manhattan, waiting tables and trying to make it as serious actresses. Before they wised up and moved to Los Angeles, the starlet's natural habitat.

"I'm going to go change into my running clothes," I went on in my chirpy voice, as I started out of the living room. But then I couldn't resist going back to plant a little kiss on the top of his head. "Love you," I said, and raced out before he could come up with an answer—or avoid coming up with one. Like I said, we all know what it means when a Talk is looming. But instead of heading for our bedroom, I took a quick detour to the kitchen to grab one of the cocoa-flavored diet bars I substitute for breakfast every morning—except when I sneak one after breakfast because we don't have any real chocolate in the house. And yes, I know all the clichés about eating sweets when you're stressed. But chocolate helps. A lot. That's another life lesson I've learned.

Jake has always told me I fell in love with him because he's shallow. "You married me because I gave you permission to be shallow too," he said, after we'd exchanged our vows at City Hall. We both laughed, and I thought how lucky I was to be married to a man who had such a terrific self-deprecating sense of humor. I mean, most guys take themselves so seriously. And the truth was, Jake isn't shallow, he's just not as intense as I am, which puts him in the same category with almost everyone except a couple of religious fanatics and my mother, the Feminist Icon. I felt blessed beyond my wildest dreams to have snagged a gem like Jake. Not that I ever shared that mushy sentiment with him. Jake and I were into snappy patter.

Of course, it doesn't hurt that Jake is gorgeous. The man has these fabulous green eyes, a great mouth, cheekbones that balance his square jaw perfectly, and dark wavy hair that hugs the back of his head in a way that makes you want to kiss it. On top of everything else, his hair is frosted ever so slightly with gray—Jake is a few years older than I am—and it looks fabulous on him, so you know he's going to age beautifully. He's slim but well built and about six feet tall.

But it really was the you-married-me-because-I-gave-you-permission-to-be-shallow line that got me. And he did give me permission—maybe not to be shallow but to have fun. *Fun* was a four-letter word to me before Jake came into my life. (See above reference to intensity.) That probably sounds weird, since I was in my thirties when we met and should have been past needing permission for anything. But I was a late bloomer—seriously late. And while I've read enough self-help books to know that we all have to take responsibility for our own emotional growth, I will say that my early years were not exactly conducive to blooming.

AS I MADE my way down the hall to our bedroom, I looked out the wide window that fronts Central Park. The condo Jake and I lived in was on the Upper East Side, almost directly across the park from the co-op my mother used to own, where I spent what I guess you could say were my formative years. I'm one of those rare creatures who were born and bred in Manhattan, except for two years when my family lived up in Rye. Since that hiatus probably caused—or at least heavily contributed to—the breakup of my parents' marriage, I'm a little ambivalent about the suburbs. Although, to be fair, I'm ambivalent about most things. Deep down, at my core, where it really counts, I'm marshmallow fluff. And someday, damn it, I'm going to figure out how to be proud of that. Or reconciled to it.

My mother's West Side apartment was in one of those buildings noted for their prewar charm and dicey plumbing, and since she had zilch interest in domesticity it was never really decorated, or even painted, as I recall. When Jake and I bought our condo we opted for a brand-new building and a wildly expensive decorator to "create our environment." As far as I was concerned, the result—except for our bedroom, where I'd prevailed—was terrifyingly sleek, and the place was as inviting as the lobby of a high-end insurance company. Our chairs, tables, and sofas were limited editions designed by a sculptor in some Nordic country where the sun doesn't shine much. And the pièce de résistance, which Jake just had to have, was a high-tech clock in the foyer. The thing cost as much as a car—a cheap one, but still a car. It was hooked up to an international satellite system so it could tell you the time in Borneo and the weather in Tanzania; I think it could also launch rockets. I was always afraid that one night it would go rogue and start a war.

Naturally this haute furniture cost a fortune, and even though the decorator swore we were buying investment pieces that would hold their value, I would have balked at the price. But Jake loved it all—and I've always thought it was *because* of the price.

I told myself I understood. Jake had grown up as the only child of a hardworking single mother who held down two jobs so her talented son could go to the city's best art school and study photography. If he was into pricey and showy, it was understandable. Besides, I wasn't sure what *I* was into—there's that ambivalent thing again—although I knew my taste was cozier than Jake's. But I wanted him to be happy. When Jake is happy, it's like having a ringside seat at the best Fourth of July fireworks ever. Sparks of pleasure just seem to fly off him. What woman wouldn't want to be around that, especially if she felt she'd caused it? And our new condo had produced a Vesuvius of sparks from Jake. In the beginning, anyway.

So we had those glitzy big windows overlooking the park and a large-for-Manhattan gourmet kitchen we never used, and the building itself had a professionally equipped exercise room and a roof garden. Jake and I had everything we needed, except closet space. We used to have enough of that before I had three wardrobes: sizes four, ten, and fourteen. Jake was always telling me to dump either the clothes that didn't fit or the pounds.

"You're just torturing yourself, Francesca," he'd say, as I stood in front of the jammed racks trying to find the one skirt that actually fit me. "Why do you want to be miserable?"

Well, I didn't, of course. But I still hung on to the size fours—also known as my Happy Clothes—and I haven't met a woman who can't relate. (If such a woman does exist, I propose that we shoot her.) I fought to get into those minuscule garments—for eight months I ate five hundred calories a day, supplemented with vitamin B shots, and I almost passed out twice in Barnes & Noble—and I knew I could get back down to that weight again. I just had to change a lifetime of bad eating habits, stop trying to solve all my problems with chocolate, and become someone who likes to jog—or, at least, walk fast. But if I packed up the tiny jeans and the itsy-bitsy skirts and sent them to Goodwill, I'd be admitting defeat—or, okay, accepting reality. I'm not a big fan of reality.

On the Saturday in question, I couldn't make myself open the closet door. I lay down on our bed and closed my eyes. There was a snuffling noise somewhere in the vicinity of my right ear.

"Go away, Annie," I murmured.

The snuffling was followed by a couple of snorts. I gave up and opened my eyes to face my dog. Annie was a rescue, so her ancestry has always been a mystery; it's clear that several large breeds were involved in her family tree, and at least a few of them were mega-shedders. Coal-black mega-shedders. We had to dump the decorator's favorite white rug after only a couple of weeks because of Annie. However, Annie has a beautiful face, a terrific dog smile, and a heavy-duty work ethic about her gig as Francesca's Best Friend. Part of that job, as she sees it, is to keep me in line, which is why she was nosing me to get off the bed. It was at least six hours before I was supposed to call it quits for the day, and Annie is a stickler about my schedule. I finally managed to convince her to lie down next to me by bribing her with the dog cookies I keep in my nightstand. Annie will do anything for a cookie; she's my dog, after all. Once she settled down, I closed my eyes again.

One reason I didn't want to open the closet was the new gown—a size sixteen—that was hanging on the special rack our closet consultant (yes, I know, I know) had installed for my party clothes back in the days when I still told myself I loved going to parties. I'd bought the gown because Jake and I were going to an awards dinner that night; the honoree was a friend of ours named Andrea Grace. Andy, as she is known to her intimates, is a television producer. She'd worked for the Big Three (that would be CBS, NBC, and ABC), as well as Lifetime and Hallmark, and now she was striking out on her own as an independent. That's why the National Academy of Women in Film decided to give her a dinner and, probably, a really ugly little plaque. Jake had been asked to say a few words to introduce her acceptance speech, because he and Andy were working together on several of her new projects. I'd also been invited—as Jake's date, of course.

That's what I'd become, the wife who was also invited. It hadn't always been that way. As I mentioned before, I'm an author, and my debut novel was hailed as a success by everyone. But, as I've also mentioned, I'd been having a little trouble with writer's block. . . . Okay, let me rephrase. I'd been wrestling with the mother of all writer's blocks for three years, and there were times when I found it depressing to hang out with people who were getting awards—or people who were merely functioning, for that matter. I wasn't proud of this, but it was the reason I'd backed out of a couple of social events in recent months. No one wants to talk to a depressed person at a cocktail party; eating finger food without getting arugula caught in your teeth is enough of a challenge. Besides, I knew Jake was okay with going to these shindigs on his own, he could talk better to all the successful folk if he didn't have to keep including me in the conversation. It was actually a nice thing I was doing for Jake when I stayed home—or so I told myself.

I shifted on the bed so I could cuddle closer to Annie. She actually hates cuddling, but some rule in the Good Dog Manual decrees that she has to allow it when she knows I'm feeling needy. There was a part of me that wanted to run back to the living room and scream at Jake, *I just said I love you, damn it! Say something back! I know, even though you're ten years older than I am, that you look better than I do. But you're supposed to cherish me anyway. The vows didn't say "for better or for better" when we got married.* But I don't scream. A shrink I once saw told me it's because I heard too much screaming growing up. And besides, fighting with Jake was sure to bring on the Talk. My stomach lurched just thinking about that. I hopped off the bed, and Annie heaved a sigh of relief.

I opened the dreaded closet, found the jogging suit with the top that was long enough to cover my hips, and pulled it on. Then I forced myself to look in the mirror. Even when I'm slim, I'm built like one of those heroines in old-fashioned novels everyone describes as *sturdy*. No one has ever been able to explain why I am this way. My father's family, the Sewells, are tall lanky WASPs. My mother's father was Greek American, and the women on his side were all downright skinny. The wild card in my genetic mix is my maternal grandmother. I'm not sure what her original heritage was, since she died when my mother was three and no one talks about her much. But I figure someone in her family tree must have had child-bearing hips. And sturdy thighs.

From my mother I get red-brown hair that has a tendency to frizz, a mouth that is too full, a nose that is definitely on the long side, and blue eyes, which I actually like. For years I thought I was homely, to use an old-fashioned word, but then I finally learned how to put on makeup. I'll never be the kind of natural beauty who can just hop out of bed in the morning and glow, but I can do a lot with the right shade of blush and properly applied eyeliner. When I want to. When I remember to do it.

I went into the bathroom, flicked on the professional stage lights that surround my vanity, and suddenly I saw it. *It* was a problem our friend Andy had hinted about a few months earlier: my chin. To be honest, the hinting hadn't been all that subtle. "You need to get your chin done, Francesca," was what she'd said. "You've developed a little pouf of flab right under the jaw since you gained weight. You probably haven't noticed it because you look at yourself every day, but I haven't seen you for a couple of months." Andy lives in LA, but she flies in and out of Manhattan all the time. "If you take care of it right now, you probably won't need anything more than a little nip and tuck."

I have to admit I was pissed. Especially when I told Jake about the conversation afterward and waited for him to say something like never in a million years would he let anyone touch my chin, because he adored me just the way I was. Jake didn't open his mouth. That was when I had to face the fact that my husband had probably noticed the damn pouf of flab himself. I already knew he was less than thrilled about my weight gain. Well, why wouldn't he be? It is hardwired into the brain of every American male that skinny is sexy, and my guy was not one to buck trends. To be fair, he'd never said anything about it, but I'd really wanted him to jump to my defense—and that of my flabby chin. When he didn't, I went into a riff about elective surgery being a temptation to God to hurt you, maybe give you permanent Creepy Android Face. I cited the example of several celebrities whose eyebrows are hanging off their hairlines. I thought I was being really clever, but Jake never cracked a smile, not even his big fake one.

Now that I thought about that moment—and the looming Talk—it seemed to me that he'd started pulling away from me right after that.

So I took another look at my chin in my mirror. Andy was right. If I didn't have it done in another year—or maybe sooner—I'd have to start hiding it. Or I'd have to become my mother's daughter, not give a damn, and let it all hang out. My mother, Alexandra Karras Sewell, is an old-school feminist who considers it a political statement that she hasn't purchased a tube of lipstick in over thirty years. It would never occur to her to worry about a wobbling chin. But I have never been the woman she is, so I knew the day would come when I'd be shopping for turtlenecks and scarves. When you looked at the situation—and my frigging chin—from that perspective, Jake was actually being supportive. He knew I was letting myself go and he was concerned about it. And, okay, he liked glamorous women, and my jawline and I didn't fit the bill anymore. Come on, the man didn't say he was shallow for no reason.

So why not get a chin job? Yes, there was the issue of pain and danger and maybe looking like a female impersonator—but if it made Jake happy, wasn't it worth it? And if I told him about it right now, and it made him so happy that we avoided the Talk, where was the harm in that? Somewhere in the back of my mind I heard my mother drawing in a big hissing breath of disapproval, but I reminded myself that she'd never been a poster child for hanging on to your man. Of course, there was absolutely no guarantee that surgery would help me hang on to mine, but I wasn't going to dwell on that.

"I'm going to walk into the living room and tell Jake I'm getting rid of the pouf," I said to Annie. "And don't look at me like that, because I'm fine with it." But I would have killed for a big, thick chocolate bar.

Jake had gone out, without leaving a note. I know how this is going to sound, but I was relieved. "Maybe the Talk wasn't all that important," I said to Annie. "Maybe I overreacted. I've got to watch that."

When I'm in denial, I can be a total idiot.

The living room felt empty with Jake gone. "Come, Annie," I said with false cheer. "Go for a walk!"

She gave me a withering look—Annie considers exercise something that happens to dogs who are being punished—and headed back to the bedroom. I threw on my coat and left without her. Exercise isn't my favorite thing either—who do you think Annie learned from?—but I needed some air.

Outside the apartment, I started off, not running exactly but walking briskly toward Central Park. As I walked, my mind went back to the beginning with Jake—to the good times. Suddenly, I realized I'd been doing that a lot in recent weeks. Reminiscing had become my favorite pastime.

Life lesson: When you find yourself frequently strolling down Memory Lane, you're probably in trouble.

CHAPTER 2

I met Jake because of a book I wrote. It was called *Love, Max,* and it was about a divorce as seen through the eyes of the family dog. The family in question was one of those enlightened clans living on the Upper West Side of Manhattan. You know the kind I'm talking about: Each child has a shrink, and a professional mediator is hired to make sure the divorce experience is a positive one for all involved. In my book, only the dog, Max, was pissed off about the loss of his family and his home until the last chapter, when everyone got all emotional and more than a little ugly, but they realized how much they cared. The book reviews included phrases like "a slyly biting commentary on modern mores."

I wrote it because, like Max, I was pissed off. I probably had been ever since my parents went their separate ways when I was a kid. Like my imaginary characters, Mother and Dad had one of the cheeriest divorces on record. This was, in part, due to their liberal ideology, and in part because they were so delighted to be getting away from each other. I don't think it dawned on either of them that anyone—like me—could actually be in mourning for our little family unit. My brother, Peter, who is younger than I am, wasn't. Hell, even our dog, Fierce, was happier when he moved to southern California with my dad. I was the only one who was upset—which didn't make me any less angry about the whole thing.

But it wasn't the actual divorce that led to my writing *Love, Max*. (For one thing, I was only twelve when my parents split.) What did it was my stepmother's remarriage.

I'm not going to argue that I am one of the world's most logical thinkers—Pete says I'm a couple of Brazil nuts shy of a fruitcake, and for the most part I agree. So I'll try to make my admittedly convoluted thinking clear. My father married Sheryl—the woman he'd been sleeping with while he was still unhappily wed to my mother—and moved to the West Coast with her. So, technically speaking, Sheryl was the catalyst for my parents' breakup, and after my father moved to Pasadena I tried to dislike her out of loyalty to my mother. But that was hard to do when my mother so clearly regarded Sheryl as the one-woman cavalry charge that had saved her—my mother—from the burden of having to try to be a wife. Instead, I proved my daughterly loyalty by never using makeup or having a fashion sense, and let myself like Sheryl. I can't imagine anyone actually disliking Sheryl. (Pete managed to pull it off for a while, but eventually even he caved. And he's made of steel.)

Sheryl is kind, generous, and caring. I suppose she would have felt guilty about ending Dad's marriage to my mother if Mother hadn't been so happy about it. Sheryl is the kind of person who wants everyone to be happy. She adored my father, and—an even more radical concept to me at the time—she seemed to think that keeping him content was all the career she needed. She kept her incredible legs in shape with exercise sessions that would have appealed to the boys who cooked up the Spanish Inquisition, because, as she once told me with a giggle, Dad was a leg man. She ran his home in Pasadena like a four-star hotel because that was the way Dad liked it. And, she told me, when he came home from work at the end of the day, she was always as excited as she'd been the time she'd asked Barry Manilow for his autograph after a concert and he'd given her a kiss as well. Sheryl isn't my mother's equal in the brains department—not even close—but my father was blissfully happy with her. So I cast Sheryl in the role of Dad's True Love, a blond California Juliet to his considerably older Romeo. I wanted desperately to believe in Romeo and Juliet. I was already looking for the perfect love story even back then; a romantic tale of love at first sight. And, most importantly, a love that would last forever.

Then Romeo died. It was a heart attack that came out of nowhere, and I still can't talk about it a lot because I start to tear up. He was only fifty-six.

After a year of mourning, Juliet started dating again. I was devastated. It wasn't that I wanted Sheryl to stop living—no matter what Pete said, I didn't expect her to toss herself on Dad's funeral pyre. I accepted the fact that she would develop a new life and new interests; she could have taken up scrapbooking, for example. I would have been fine with that. But I did want her to stay true to Dad's memory forever, and I never *ever* expected her to replace him. Yes, in the kid part of the brain that we can't control, that's how I saw it when, after two years of widowhood, Sheryl got engaged to someone new.

How I reacted to this was . . . unique. I realize that. I joined an adult-ed class called Write Your Bestseller! that was being offered at a college on the Upper East Side. I'd always had a secret yen to write; in college I'd taken a writing run by a failed novelist who probably drank too much. After one particularly blurry session, she'd called me to her office and said, "I never encourage my students, because the last thing the world needs is more lousy fiction, but Francesca, you may just have some talent."

Armed with this somewhat dubious praise, and desperately needing to find an outlet for all the boiling emotions I couldn't admit to because they were way too childish, I signed up for Write Your Bestseller! And spurred on by all those messy emotions, I produced *Love, Max* in two semesters. The book was my answer to the whole concept of divorce as a damn growth experience. And no, thank you, I have no desire to discuss any of this with a good shrink.

I'M SURE YOU'RE wondering what all this history has to do with Jake and me. Hang on, because I'm getting there. But first you need to understand where my life was before I wrote *Love, Max*.

My brilliant mother was one of the nation's major go-to lawyers for women's rights, and I had taken my LSATs after college and failed them twice. I was also the older sister of a genius architect— that would be Pete—who raced around the world designing green housing for the impoverished. While he was collecting awards at the UN for his work as a humanitarian and an environmentalist, I was still living at home—Alexandra's apartment—with a job working as prop person for a lesbian theater group in SoHo. The gig had come through one of Mother's political connections and paid enough to cover my daily round-trip on the subway. To say I had some heavy-duty sibling rivalry going on would be a massive understatement. I probably had a major dose of mommy envy as well. Okay, scratch the word *probably*.

On top of all this, I was usually dating some man who gave new and more poignant meaning to the term Narcissistic Personality Disorder.

Love, Max changed all of that.

CHAPTER 3

I'd been so busy remembering the past that I hadn't noticed that I'd wandered across Central Park. By the time I looked up, I realized I was standing in front of the co-op apartment building where my mother had moved with Pete and me after the divorce. She'd sold the co-op after I moved out—which I did as soon as I had the check for my book advance in my hand—and traded down to a smaller apartment three blocks away, staying in the area because she said she didn't have the time to learn a different neighborhood. My mother never gave a damn about her surroundings; all she ever wanted was a place in her beloved Manhattan that was low-maintenance and had a good Chinese restaurant around the corner. All her apartments looked the same: There were unpacked boxes stacked in the corners—I think some of them were wedding presents she'd never bothered to open—and there was always a roll of paper towels tossed on the side of the bathroom sink instead of a hand towel. Alexandra Karras Sewell was the anti–June Cleaver and proud of it.

There is a bench directly across the street from my childhood apartment. I sat down and went back to thinking about the time— the insane, impossible, miraculous time—when my life had changed forever because of *Love, Max*. And Jake. Yes, I'm still getting to the part about Jake.

IT WAS SHERYL who helped me sell the book. She'd been remarried for a year by the time I finished writing *Love, Max* and there was no way I could stay mad at her for that long. Besides, you've got to focus if you want to carry a grudge, and I was too excited about my book.

I'd already given the final draft of *Love, Max* to the woman who was teaching the Write Your Bestseller! class. She seemed a little stunned when she handed it back to me. "I've never said this to a student before," she'd said in a hushed tone, "but this may actually be publishable."

Secretly, I agreed with her. It was the kind of book I thought I'd like to read. But I knew in the real world people don't take one bogus writing course and produce something that gets published. Real writers have to pay dues. They study the great classics of literature in college and attend prestigious writing seminars, where they grovel at the feet of world-famous mentors. They spend years teaching English 101 at small colleges in dreary New England towns, waking up at four in the morning to work on their masterpieces. I hadn't done any of that. But every instinct I had told me I had a winner on my hands. So—even though my instincts were always wrong—I decided to get a second opinion. Not from Pete, who never read fiction, or from my mother, who was opposed per-

sonally and professionally to girly literature—which *Love, Max*
was. I sent the manuscript to Sheryl.

"I think you were angry when you wrote it," she said, when she
called me from the West Coast.

"So it's no good?" I gulped.

"Oh, no, you're very witty when you're angry."

"Then you liked it?" I told myself I wasn't being pathetic.

"I read it in two days. I stayed up until three in the morning and
I looked like such a wreck I had to get a deep-sea facial. Do you
have an agent?"

"Uh . . . no," I said, stunned. Sheryl was an airhead. Who knew
she was even aware that there were such entities as agents?

"Well, do you remember my friend Sissy Gilbert?"

"She's one of the Girls, right?" Sheryl had more friends than
Bill and Hillary Clinton combined, but her inner circle was a
posse of chums known as the Girls, who had been inseparable
since high school.

"Yes. She was one of my bridesmaids when I married your
father—the chubby one who wouldn't wear yellow, so I went for
pewter, which was much classier and I've always been grateful to
her for that. Her husband's daughter Nancy—she's from Charlie's
first marriage; he's ages older than Sissy—works for an agency in
New York, and I know Sissy said they sell books; what was the
name of it? Stiller . . . something."

"The Stiller and William Agency?" I forced myself not to gen-
uflect. "They're the biggest and the best—"

"Good. I'll put your manuscript in the mail to Nancy today." A
month later I was having lunch in an expensive Manhattan restaurant with Sissy's stepdaughter.

Nancy Gilbert was the kind of woman I'd have wanted as a
friend even if she hadn't been one of the hottest young agents in

the city. She was my age, and we bonded when she asked if we could tell the waiter to take away the bread basket because she needed to lose ten pounds. Then she told me she was dying to be my agent.

"I know there are thousands of readers out there who are going to relate to your book the way I did," she said. "I was eight when my parents divorced, and I swear the only thing that got me through it was my dachshund, Posey. With a fifty percent divorce rate in this country, marketing *Love, Max* is going to be a snap. Plus I don't know of a woman in the civilized world who doesn't have issues about her thighs."

Nancy sold the book in two weeks to a small but prestigious house called Gramercy Publishing. I acquired an editor named Debbie, who took Nancy and me to lunch to discuss book covers and jacket copy, plans for a book tour, and a very few minor rewrites that Debbie suggested oh so gently, while telling me how gifted I was.

When I look back on that time, I wonder if it might have been better for me if it hadn't all been so easy. I'm not complaining, I know what a miracle I was handed and I'm deeply grateful. But I never felt I earned it—you know? It never felt real. And then, to top it all off—there was Jake.

"THE ART DEPARTMENT needs a picture of you for the back of your book jacket," Nancy told me. We were six months away from my pub date—the insider's term for the day when stores start to sell your book and you find out if you've written a dud or a winner. "Do you have any photos of yourself?" Nancy asked.

The choices were not terrific. There was my college graduation portrait, complete with cap and gown, and a few snaps that had been taken during my high school Matriculation Wingding, so named because the progressive school I'd gone to was way too cool for a formal graduation ceremony. In all the shots taken of me since college, I was usually trying to wave the camera away. The truth was, I hated to be photographed. But my publisher needed a recent picture, one in which I was not wearing a cap and gown or sticking out my tongue.

"I know a great photographer named Jake Morris," Nancy said. "Do you remember the model Nina Karsonava? She wrote a beauty book about the benefits of eating borscht—or maybe you were supposed to wash with it, I don't remember. Anyway, it was awful and we all figured it was headed straight for the shredder until we saw the pictures of Nina. They sold that damn book. And Jake Morris is the genius who took them."

I knew I should have been excited about being photographed by a genius. But it made me nervous. No, let's be honest, it made me defensive. So when I called his studio to make my appointment, I had an industrial-sized chip on my shoulder.

THE MORRIS STUDIO was in a former warehouse in what used to be New York's meat-packing district before the city stopped packing its own meat. I paid off my cab, lugged my suitcase to the curb—I'd been instructed to bring at least three changes of clothes for my "shoot"—and looked around. Sometime during the 1990s the humble neighborhood had been reborn as the home of scarily glossy people and hot clubs and businesses. Just looking at the store windows on either side of the Morris Studio was intimidating. The shop on the right called itself a shoe store, which was accurate if you were prepared to spend a thousand bucks on footwear. The shop on the other side was a bakery whose name I recognized as a place that provided designer cakes for celebrities. A garden of spookily real-looking sugar flowers filled the window. I sighed. This was going to be even worse than I had imagined. I rang the doorbell, and for the first time in my life I wished I knew how to pluck my eyebrows.

The waiting room was what I'd expected it would be: lots of chrome, glass, and chairs you can't get out of once you sit. The walls were covered with pictures of famous people, and a ridiculously pretty girl sat behind the front desk Her hair fell to her shoulders in a glossy sheet, and as for her makeup . . . we're talking flawless.

At first, I could tell she was shocked when I told her I'd come to have my picture taken by the master. My un-glam presence seemed to rock her universe. But then she checked her book. "Oh, okay," she said, with a relieved smile, "you're the writer."

That mystery having been solved, she led me out of the waiting room to a large, dark space with high ceilings, a concrete floor, unfinished brick walls, and windows that had been covered with shutters. A white backdrop hung against one wall, surrounded by what looked like a forest of lights. I figured when they were turned on they would generate enough wattage to light up a small nation. From time to time, human figures bustled around in the gloom.

This entire space, my guide informed me, was *the shop*, meaning the area where Jake Morris took his pictures. On the opposite wall, there were three large, well-lit white cubicles.

"That's Makeup and Hair." My guide indicated the first one. "Next to it is Wardrobe, and the last one is Jake's office. I'll take you to see Leeland first."

"Leeland?" I asked.

"Our makeup artist. He'll be doing your face."

For a second it sounded glamorous. But when you live with a mother who regularly gives lectures on the evils of the cosmetics industry, you learn to suppress thoughts like that. "I'm not sure I want anyone doing my face," I said. "I don't wear makeup."

The girl gasped. "Never?" she demanded.

"This is the way I look," I said. "What you see is what you get." But then I heard myself add wistfully, "I *have* used lip gloss." Like I said, at my core I'm marshmallow fluff.

"You can hang your clothes in Wardrobe. I'll tell them you're here," the girl said, and fled, in case whatever madness I suffered from was catching.

I went into the middle cubicle she'd pointed out. It was equipped with an ironing board and iron, a steamer, a sewing machine, a small stool you could stand on while someone pinned up your hem, and an ego-demolishing three-way mirror. Racks of brilliantly colored clothes stood three deep against one wall. Dodging the three-way mirror, I opened my suitcase and hung up my clothes; three mid-calf-length skirts, two crewneck sweaters, one blouse with French cuffs, and three semi-fitted blazers in shades of black, navy, and gray. It was my standard look, and I was determined to be me in this picture. But as I was straightening one of the jackets, I caught sight of myself in the mirror. I was overdue for a haircut, so my frizz was truly impressive, and in the bright light, my complexion looked like I'd died recently. I was wearing a beige crewneck, a brown mid-calf skirt, and a darker brown blazer. I turned away from the mirror with a little shudder. Almost without knowing what I was doing, I walked over and started going through the racks of clothes owned by the Morris Studio. I pulled out a pink ball gown with a huge skirt and puffy sleeves and held it up to myself, as I turned back to the mirror.

"Yeah," said a voice behind me. "That color would be great on you." I whirled around and there he was: Jake. My Jake—although I didn't know it yet. I've already described him, so you can understand why my brain froze.

"I'm Jake Morris," he said. Still clutching the ball gown, I nodded. I couldn't actually say anything because I was afraid if I tried
to talk my teeth would start chattering.

Jake turned to the rack where I'd hung my clothes. "This is it?"
he asked. "This is what you brought to wear?" I nodded again.
"They did tell you the picture was going to be in color, didn't
they?"

"Yes," I managed to whisper. "But I thought I should dress normally. You know, be real."

He shook his head. "It's always the smart ones," he said. Then
he went to the door of the cubicle. "Tommy, come here!" he commanded.

A man materialized out of the darkness. He was probably the
thinnest person I'd ever seen and maybe the tallest, easily six-foot-
seven without the cowboy boots he was wearing. He'd completed
the Wild West motif by dressing in jeans, a plaid work shirt, and
one of those little string ties held together with a silver ring.

"You bellowed?" he asked, as he entered the cubicle. His voice
was soft and tinged with an accent that had originated south of the
Mason-Dixon Line.

"This is Ms. Sewell; she brought the wrong clothes for her
shoot. See if you and Elisa can find something for her to wear."

The tall one moved to me and gently removed the gown from
my grasp. "No, sugar," he murmured. "Not without a tiara."

"Yeah, but she liked the color," said Jake. Then he stared at me.
Something about me—maybe the fact that I was so totally out of
my depth, or it could have been my snazzy beige-on-brown ensemble—seemed to fascinate him. Finally, he spoke: "Is your book
good?" Then he said quickly, "That was a dumb thing to ask. Forget it." He started to go.

But the question had penetrated the mists of lust that had addled my brain. In spite of my libido, I had my pride. "Yes," I called out after him. "It's damn good."

"Then don't blow it by trying to look like your own grand-mother. Even little TV stations in the middle of nowhere would rather book a girl who's cute." And he left.

What happened next is pretty much a blur. Tommy and his as-sistant, Elisa, went through the clothing racks and produced a pink silk wraparound dress that accentuated my cleavage and showed off my waist. The top of me, according to Tommy, was just fine, and I should never wear a baggy sweater again as long as I lived. Elisa stitched a couple of darts in the bodice that made my waistline look even smaller. The full skirt of the dress swished gracefully over my hips and thighs—which Tommy called "that little problem area down under."

The hairdresser piled most of my wild-woman's mane on top of my head, leaving just enough falling down around my face to make me look like I'd recently climbed out of bed. Then Leeland, the makeup artist, went to work with lip liners, false lashes, tweezers, brushes, and blushers to reveal a couple of cheekbones I'd never known were there, a pair of almond-shaped eyes, and a mouth that was still full, but now it was a good thing. In this new face my long nose looked . . . elegant. As a finishing touch, Tommy handed me a pair of high-heeled pumps to wear instead of my sensible shoes. I teetered on them for a minute or two and then, when I had the balance right, I swanned over to the white backdrop where Jake was waiting to take my picture. When he saw me, he clapped. Really. The guy applauded.

"You have a Henry Higgins/George Bernard Shaw/Pygmalion thing going on, don't you?" I asked, because I was feeling shy all of a sudden and I wanted to be funny. But when he looked at me, I realized I'd hit home.

"Yeah, I'm afraid I do," he said.

"Hey, that's a good thing," I said.

"You think?"

"Works for me."

"But I prefer to think of myself as Svengali."

I nodded. "Sounds more exotic."

Then he laughed and said, "Look at you! You're a fox! She's smart, and she's a fox!" And for the first time, I got the full force of Jake Morris in Happiness Mode. Up to that moment I'd been overcome by his looks, and, okay, he was sexy as hell. But when I stood there watching those sparks of pleasure that just seemed to be exploding around him and realized I had caused them . . . that was when I fell in love.

CHAPTER 4

The problem was what to do next. I'd never learned how to flirt. It wasn't a skill that was prized in my home, where the mantra was the old seventies slogan that everyone attributes to Gloria Steinem although she wasn't the one who said it: "A woman without a man is like a fish without a bicycle."

Like most feminists of her era, my mother was determined that her girl child not fall prey to the myths of romantic love that had kept women in shackles for so many generations—her words, not mine. "Just remember, Francesca," she said, when I was five and she was dismissing the entire Disney Girl oeuvre, "Snow White was an idiot who ate an apple without washing it first, and Cinderella jammed her feet into glass slippers, which had to hurt like hell, so she could find a guy to save her from having to scrub toilets. She should have hired a lawyer and taken the bitch stepmother to court. Even better, she should have become a lawyer and fought for herself."

When it came to my mother's romantic life . . . well, *romantic life* wasn't the right term, *sex life* was more accurate. Alexandra preferred to have occasional flings with commitment-phobic men who got out of her hair in the morning before she had to worry about making them coffee—or introducing them to Pete and me. Not that she had to worry about that, because Pete and I were out of the house and in college before our mother started dating again. Alexandra was never quite the free spirit she intended to be. She believed firmly that all women had the same right to sexual fulfillment as men did, but she felt there should be no subterfuge involved. A woman in the throes of a lust like the one I was now feeling for Jake Morris should feel free to express her feelings and ask if they were reciprocated. An enlightened man would respond in kind. Simple.

Well, there was no way in hell I was going to inform Jake that I wanted to tear his clothes off with my teeth. As for a more subtle way of conveying that sentiment—well, that's what flirting is for, and we've already covered my total cluelessness in that department. As I stood in the darkness of his big studio and watched him laugh, I knew I was doomed. After these pictures were taken I was never going to see him again.

He stopped laughing and held out his hand. "Let's get started," he said. "Come sit." He led me to a stool that had been set up in front of the white backdrop and put his hands around my waist to help me onto the seat. Beautiful strong hands with long slim fingers. *I have to do something to keep him*, I thought. But I couldn't think of a damn thing. Jake backed off and picked up his camera.

Now we've all seen the cliché of the Photography Session as Seduction in TV shows and movies. You know the scene I'm talking about: The photographer starts clicking away with his camera while he's urging the model to lean toward him and lick her lips and let herself go, baby. Then she's leaning and licking and letting go while the camera is clicking faster and he's telling her how beautiful and sexy she is, and before you know it, his voice is getting husky and her eyes are getting glazed and they're both really turned on. Well, here's the thing about a lot of clichés: They're based in fact. At least, that was my experience. You have a guy who's drop-dead gorgeous giving you the kind of undivided attention you've never gotten from a man before, and you're following his lead the way Ginger Rogers did with Fred Astaire and . . . I'm sorry to be unenlightened, but that's a turn-on.

I thought—hoped—for a second that Jake was feeling the same thing I was. All of sudden, he stopped shooting pictures, and I was pretty sure our eyes connected. I thought he was having trouble swallowing like I was. And breathing. But then he started taking my picture again. I was so disappointed, tears started welling up.

"What's wrong?" he asked. "Are the lights bothering you?"

I shook my head.

"We can take a break, if your eyes are tired."

I looked at him. He was standing in the dark, but a beam of light had spilled over him as if he were in a spotlight. He looked like a superstar.

I knew the shoot was almost finished. *I have to do something*, I thought. In my desperation I decided to give my mother's approach a whirl. *I'll tell him I'm attracted to him. What have I got to lose besides my pride, dignity, and self-respect?*

"I don't know how you feel . . ." I began; then I stopped. "What I'm trying to say is, I'm very . . ." I stopped again. Because he was staring at me. The studio was dark and we were all alone because his minions had gone out for lunch, and Jake Morris was staring at me. I knew he knew what I'd been about to say next—before I'd chickened out. I waited for him to do something or say something, but he kept on staring. Suddenly I couldn't handle the suspense another second, so I started to sing. Yes, the silence got to me so I sang: "Just you wait, 'enry 'iggins, just you wait!" It's the opening line of one of Eliza Doolittle's songs from the show *My Fair Lady*, which, for those of you who are not up on your American musical-comedy history, was the wildly successful Broadway show based on George Bernard Shaw's *Pygmalion*. I kicked off my high-heeled shoes and attempted a little soft-shoe. Now Jake looked stunned, but not nearly as stunned as I was. I couldn't believe what I was doing; it was like having an out-of-body experience. And I don't know what I would have done next if Jake hadn't started to laugh. Then he put down his camera, walked over, and put his arms around me.

"Smart, foxy, and unhinged," he whispered, into my sexy new hairdo.

"But in a nice way," I added.

Then he kissed me. And while I'm not going to go into details, he was, and is, one hell of a kisser. Personally, I could have kept on with that scenario for a while—like maybe the rest of the day or the rest of my life. But after a second he murmured, "Everyone will be coming back from lunch, but my loft is near here."

"Define *near*," I murmured back.

"Two doors down from this building, on your left, and up one flight. We can be there in five minutes."

"I'm not sure how long it will take me to change."

"Don't bother."

IT TOOK US much less than five minutes to get to Jake's loft. And again, I'm not going into details except to say that we would have stayed there all afternoon if it hadn't been for his five-o'clock photo shoot back at the studio. He raced through it, while I raced

uptown to pick up some clothes and a toothbrush—and congratu-
lated myself because Jake wasn't the kind of man who stocked
spare toothbrushes just in case. In fact, in every way I could think
of, Jake was perfect. I stayed over that night. And every night
afterward until my clean underwear ran out. And, yeah, I was
stunned by that too. I'd never done anything like that before in my
life.

From then on, Jake and I were inseparable. And when I think
about that time, I know it wasn't quite real. Or at least I wasn't. My
book was about to be published and the advance buzz on it was
good, and it seemed like Jake had about a million friends—
acquaintances—who wanted to meet me. We were always going
to drinks or brunch or dinner with someone. I'm not wild about
social stuff but Jake loved every minute of it, and I loved watching
him love it.

Jake asked me to marry him two weeks before my pub date—
when we'd been together for four and a half months. We'd gone to
a party my publisher was throwing to introduce their hot new
writers to the press. The bash was held in the Campbell Apartment in Grand Central Terminal—a space that had been the
wildly luxurious office of a mover and shaker in the twenties and
was reborn as a party venue during the remake of Grand Central.
I'd been so excited I couldn't eat any of the hors d'oeuvres at the
party. That had been happening often—being successful and in
love seemed to kill my appetite, which had resulted in a fifteen-
pound weight loss. I was daring to hope the sturdy thighs were
history. Also, you should know that I had taught myself to put on
false eyelashes. And for this party I'd bought a pink dress that cost
so much I had to breathe into a paper bag when I looked at the bill.
But I can say it without reservation: On that particular night I was
a fox.

After the festivities ended, Jake took me to the food court in

Grand Central so I could eat. While we were standing in line at the Feng Shui Chinese food station he looked at a spot over my head, drew in a deep breath, and said, "I've been married twice."

"Really?" I tried to be casual, but my heart started imitating a trip-hammer. He'd never said the word *married* before. Or anything that even suggested it.

"I bet you want a big wedding." He continued staring at the spot.

"Define *big*," I said carefully. I was concentrating on not passing out.

"More people than two. See, I've had a couple of blowout weddings. The first took place in the Brooklyn Botanic Garden. It cost about as much as the national debt, but less than our divorce. My lawyers added a wing to their office after I got through paying them. I think they have a memorial plaque with my name on it."

"Oh," I said. The food court had stopped spinning, but the trip-hammer in my chest had now gotten so loud I was afraid he'd hear it.

"My second wedding took place in Southampton at my ex-wife's home. Well, her palazzo, really. That divorce was much tamer, but I lost a fully reconstructed 1967 Lincoln convertible in the settlement. I think weddings are jinxed for me." He finally looked at me. "If I were to get married again, I'd want to do it quickly."

"Like when?" I managed.

"Three weeks from now. City Hall. Thursday at eleven-thirty."

So my book hit the stores, and a week later I was married. One thing about me, when I decide to turn my life upside down, I don't mess around.

● ● ●

I'D BEEN SITTING on the bench for my entire stroll down Memory Lane. Now I stood, turned away from the apartment where I'd grown up and started back to the East Side. Remembering the early days with Jake had made me anxious to get home. And to be honest, it also made me just plain anxious in general. For one thing, I wanted to see if Jake was back yet. Not that I was worried—after all, I had the whole Talk thing figured out now—but for some reason I started counting in my head all the times lately that Jake had disappeared without saying where he was going. The number was high, a lot higher than I'd realized. At the entrance to the park I set a nice brisk pace, and as I walked I promised myself I was going to turn over a new leaf. No more sitting at home feeling sorry for myself. Tonight I'd go to Andy's awards dinner with my husband and make him proud of me. I'd be charming and witty and fun. I picked up the pace some more. From now on, I told myself, I was going to start counting my blessings—and top on the list was Jake.

I had to slow down because I was having a little trouble catching my breath. It probably wasn't a great idea to try to power walk through Central Park when I hadn't done anything more strenuous for the past month than take the elevator downstairs to our lobby to get the mail. I checked my watch; it was later than I thought. If I didn't get home soon I wouldn't have time to get dolled up. And I owed Jake that. Since there's no way to hail a cab in the middle of Central Park, I picked up the pace again—a little slower this time.

WHEN I ANNOUNCED to my mother and my brother—who was actually in the country at the time—that I was going to become Mrs. Jake Morris, they were happy that I seemed to have found a man who wasn't: (a) debt ridden, (b) seeing his shrink seven days a week, or (c) an imbecile.

However, on a long-distance call from California, Sheryl asked me a question I have never answered: "Does Jake really know you, Francesca?"

I dodged. "He says he wants to marry me, so he must."

"But your father always used to say that you were . . . high maintenance."

"Daddy said that about me?" I tried not to sound dismayed, but Sheryl picked up on it anyway.

"I think that was the wrong word. What he meant was, you're like your mother."

Oh, please, no.

"You're like her when it comes to serious things like wanting to be a success and being ambitious. But sometimes you get confused about whether you want to be like her or like me. That makes you a little . . . needy. Does Jake know that?"

"Trust me, when you meet Jake, you'll love him as much as I do."

I knew I was ducking her question, but I had no intention of letting Jake see me in Bottomless Pit Mode before we tied the knot. Did Sheryl think I was nuts? I wanted to marry the man, not send him running in the opposite direction.

Meanwhile there had been big changes, both in my mother's life and in Pete's. When I say big, I mean huge. My mother, the lawyer for victimized wives everywhere, was getting married again. His name was Lenny. His politics were impeccable—he'd been a Freedom Rider during the sixties—and he was a fellow workaholic, a shrink who worked in a storefront clinic in a high-risk neighborhood. He had no interest in possessions—including his home—or in having fun. In Alexandra World, he was the perfect man.

"The shrink part is a good thing if he's going to marry me," my mother told Pete and me with a grin. But then she blushed and her eyes filled with tears as she added, "I never thought I'd meet another man who wanted to give me a try. I'm so grateful to him. Isn't that amazing?"

Pete and I both nodded. But I wanted to ask where the hell she'd been keeping this dewy-eyed part of her personality all my life. I mean, while I was running around with boyfriends from the Dark Side it would have been nice if I could have had a chat with my mom about what to look for in a guy. But I'd met Jake, so it had all worked out in the end.

Pete had news of his own. He'd fallen in love with an evolutionary biologist named Bonita who shared his commitment to the environment and the betterment of emerging nations, and since she was two months pregnant they were getting married.

Mother, Pete, and I toasted one another, and I thanked God once more for Jake and *Love, Max*, because if my brilliant, handsome baby brother had found true love and was starting a family while I was still living at home and earning nada, running props at the Well of Loneliness Theater, I would have been suicidal. And yes, I do know how petty and immature that sounds.

The day after Jake and I got engaged, I made a decision about something that had been nagging at me for a while. I hadn't yet shown *Love, Max* to my mother, but now it was due to hit the stores in a couple of weeks. "I have to give Alexandra an advance copy to read," I told Jake. And I could hear the marshmallow fluff coming into my voice.

"What are you so afraid of?" Jake had read the book by then, and he said he thought it would sell big. Back in those days, Jake was all about being supportive.

"I'm afraid she'll think the story is inconsequential," I told him. But that wasn't my only reason for putting off showing it to my mother. I tried to explain my biggest fear to Nancy. "The story isn't about my mother and my father. Not really. Not totally. But—"

"But it's based on them—loosely. And now you're afraid your mother will recognize herself. Trust me, it'll never happen. The only time people think you wrote about them is when you didn't."

Nancy was right—and she wasn't. I gave Alexandra a copy of the book on a Wednesday and, knowing her packed schedule, I didn't expect to hear from her for weeks. On Sunday morning, she showed up at my doorstep carrying what looked like a duffel bag with holes in the side and my book. There were tears in her eyes. "Oh, Francesca, honey," she said. "I'm so sorry." She dropped the duffel bag and held out the book. "I never knew how you felt."

I promised myself that the next time I saw Nancy I was going to strangle her.

"It was a long time ago," I started to say, "and"—but my mother had gotten down on her knees and was unzipping the duffel bag.

"I never knew how much you missed having a dog after ours went with your father to California," said my mother, as a puppy with humongous feet emerged. "I know it's a few years after the fact, but better late than never, right?" she asked hopefully. She beamed down at the puppy. "Lenny and I picked her up in a shelter on Long Island. I couldn't call her Max, because she's a girl, so I named her Annie, after my mother."

I need to take a moment to make it clear what this meant. My mother almost never mentioned her birth mother, but when she was a kid she'd had all these fantasies about Annie. Little Alexandra Karras's dream mommy was a mix of Eleanor Roosevelt, Marie Curie, and Mother Teresa—with a little Wonder Woman thrown in. And although my mother had matured since then, I knew in her heart the dream still lived. In fact, I always thought my mother's career as a female Lone Ranger was a tribute to Annie, who once told her—with great pride—that her name, Alexandra, meant *defender of mankind* in Greek. Mother was three at the time, and Annie died shortly afterward, but the memory was one my mother cherished. When she named my new dog Annie, I knew it was a really big deal. So even though Jake and I had never discussed getting a pet, I said, "Oh Mother, a puppy! She's just what I wanted!" Come on, what would you have done?

CHAPTER 5

Our apartment building came into sight as the sun was just starting to set. I figured by now Jake would be back home getting ready for the awards dinner, so I took out my cell phone and called to tell him I was on my way. There was no answer on our landline. That was a little strange, but I thought maybe he was taking Annie out for her evening potty break. It wasn't something he usually did, since he had agreed to keep her only because I said she was my dog and therefore my responsibility, but he could have decided to surprise me. I called his cell. It was turned off. I wondered if he'd started for the awards ceremony without me. I checked my watch; it was way too early. I started walking faster again. There had been a time—when we were first married—when Jake wouldn't have dreamed of taking off without telling me where he was going and when he would be back. And, come to think of it, I wouldn't have gone wandering through the park without letting him know. We always kissed each other good-bye back then. Back then, when I was a success, and Jake was proud of me.

MY SUCCESS BEGAN before *Love, Max* even went on sale. It started with a phone call from Nancy. I'd been running in the park with Annie—yeah, we both jogged in those days—and I came back to find a message on my machine saying that a Hollywood producer was in town and she wanted to take a breakfast meeting with me to discuss making my book into a TV movie. The phrase *take a meeting* sounded so official and scary that I asked Jake to come along because he had experience with show-business people. That was how we met Andrea Grace. Given everything I'd heard about how young everyone was in the entertainment industry, I expected her to be a baby. But Andy was a year older than Jake, and she was a knockout. Her thick chestnut hair was pulled back into a low bun, and Sheryl would have killed for the name of the genius who'd done her highlights. I would have killed for a figure like hers, without an ounce of fat. Her brown eyes were big and warm, and she was one of those rare women who can make wearing eyeglasses seem chic. When we shook hands she did that two-handed thing that falls somewhere between a shake and a clasp and told us to call her Andy, in a voice that reminded me of old-time movie stars like Greer Garson and Irene Dunne. She asked us to sit.

"If the producing thing doesn't work out for you, I'd say you've got a career in voice-overs, Andy," said my husband. She laughed delightedly. That was another of her skills: She was the kind of person who laughed so genuinely at your jokes that you actually got funnier.

We talked briefly about what happens when a producer options a book. Andy explained that she would put down ten percent of the purchase price—which she would negotiate with Nancy—to secure the rights to *Love, Max*. This option would last for a year, during which time she'd try to sell one of the networks on the idea of making the book into a movie. She'd also try to interest a couple of big-name actors. If none of this worked out, the rights to *Love, Max* would revert to me. If the project was *green-lighted*, Andy would be my new producer.

"Of course I'm not promising anything, because this business is a floating crap game, but I really think I can make this happen, Francesca," she said.

I was already seeing my name on a credit crawl. Maybe I'd get to go to the Emmys.

"Now, tell me how you visualize *Love, Max* the movie," Andy said. "Who do you see as the leads?"

I didn't. For me, the characters were so tied to real people I couldn't imagine anyone playing them. But before I had to admit that, Jake stepped in with a list of names I never would have thought of in a million years. Soon he and Andy were chatting merrily about directors and writers and which actor should do the dog's voice-overs. When the breakfast was over, Andy kissed us both good-bye like we were long-lost relatives. Later, Nancy said she was able to up the option price for the book by twenty-five thousand dollars because Jake did such a good job of charming Andy. Talk about the perfect husband.

Getting optioned by a Hollywood producer was just the beginning for my book. I'm not going to say *Love, Max* was a huge John Grisham–sized success, but it was an impressive debut novel. Everyone agreed on that. And the momentum kept growing. When I went on my book tour, the salespeople in the bookstores told me they couldn't keep it on the shelves. I spoke at libraries where the lists of people who were waiting to take it out were so long they'd had to order more copies.

Everywhere I went, I wore false lashes and piled up my hair

on top of my head with a few sexy tendrils hanging down. And if there were days, even back then, when spending an hour and twenty minutes making up my face, and gluing the damn lashes to my eyelids—not to mention the time I almost glued one to my eyeball—seemed like a total waste of time, and if I got sick of remembering to schlep three different kinds of hair straightener around the country, I told myself it was worth it. Certainly Jake thought it was. He flew to be with me whenever he had a free day, because he said I needed an entourage. I felt like a rock star—most of the time. Sometimes, like I've said, I felt like none of it was real and I was waiting for some cosmic second shoe to drop. But I kept that to myself. (Life lesson: When you're on a roll, no one wants to hear about your angst.)

GRAMERCY PUBLISHING DID six printings of my book. *People* magazine did an article on me. *Love, Max* made the *New York Times* bestseller list for the entire month of August. Grant you, the book never got out of the bottom half, but it was on the list. Gramercy was thrilled with me. Sheryl was thrilled. So were Alexandra and Pete. And Jake couldn't tell me often enough how much he loved me.

Jake sold his loft apartment—it was pretty heavily mortgaged so there was only a tiny profit—and I sold the co-op I'd bought with my advance check for *Love, Max*. We took that money, plus the inheritance from Dad that I'd been saving for a rainy day, and bought our palace on the Upper East Side. Somehow it seemed ungrateful to save for a rainy day when the universe was handing us so many goodies. We ate out almost every night, and we went to lots of parties.

"I feel like I'm in my Sheryl phase," I told my stepmother on the phone.

"But you're not like me," she said.

"Okay, then I'm in my Cheerleader phase."

"You never were the cheerleader type either."

"People change."

I wanted to believe that. Well, maybe I missed the old me sometimes, but mostly I wanted to believe I was part of this sparkly new creature called Jake-and-Francesca. I'm not saying we were one of those high-profile couples who have to fight off the paparazzi at the airport—for one thing, we didn't travel much—but Jake felt we were getting there.

"Getting where?" I asked him on New Year's Eve, when we were dressing for a party at some museum.

"Oh, come on, Francesca, it's a figure of speech. Don't always pick things apart." Jake hated it when I did that.

"I'm serious. What are we aiming for? How far up the food chain do we want to go?"

"As far as we can."

"There will always be someone above us. This is Manhattan."

"You're just bitching because you hate New Year's Eve."

That was true. I'd spent too many years home alone on one of the great date nights of the calendar. December 31 was way too much pressure for my taste. I've always felt the same way about Valentine's Day. But now Jake grabbed me and led me to the mirror. "What do you see?" he demanded.

The couple that smiled back at me was *New York Magazine* glamorous. Jake was wearing a tux and looked like he'd just stepped out of the pages of *GQ*. I'd had my hair and makeup done at the hot salon du jour, and my gown was a flattering pink—I'd settled on pink as my signature color. I knew I was never going to look better than I did at that moment. And if somewhere in the back of my head I heard Alexandra's voice saying that focusing women's attention on their looks was society's way of keeping them chained intellectually, I told the voice to lay off.

"We're pretty spiffy," I said.

"We're going to own this town before we're through." He laughed happily. When Jake laughed like that, I could believe anything.

WE CONTINUED TO do the social whirl. We went to the opening nights of galleries, Broadway shows, and designer boutiques. I became a part of a group of women—all movers and shakers—who got together once a month for dinner in wildly overpriced restaurants.

"I've made some friends," I told Sheryl on the phone, knowing she'd be as surprised as I was. I've never been Miss Popularity.

There were reasons for that. During my teen years, I'd gone to a progressive private high school, and since there were only forty-nine students in the entire school you were either in or you weren't. We had classrooms without walls and called our teachers by their first names, there were no written grades, and the dress code mandated only that we wear shoes every day. Sports were considered deeply uncool; that was the sort of thing kids did who lived in those parts of the country where people voted Republican. This was the kind of thinking that went on in my own home, so it wasn't new to me. However, the other students at my school were mostly from families that successfully did creative things like act and write and paint—which meant they were rich and nuts—and I didn't fit that mold; my mother couldn't afford to send me to Aspen to ski during the Christmas break, and I wasn't doing drugs. I hadn't made one lasting friend, either in high school or in my equally progressive and nutsy small college. As for the years after college, I believe I've mentioned that I worked almost exclusively for my mother's friends.

But I thought all that changed after my marriage and *Love, Max*.

"Now I'm like you and the Girls," I told Sheryl.

"Oh, Francesca, I'm so glad," she said. "I know you have Pete and your mom, but there's nothing like knowing you have a bunch of girlfriends who are there for you."

My new pals did talk about being there for one another; the word *supportive* was tossed around a lot. But it seemed to me that most of the time at dinner was spent detailing all the fabulous moving and shaking they were doing.

"So they share the good stuff instead of boring the hell out of one another with a lot of soul searching," Jake said, when I mentioned it. "Not everyone wants to get all gloomy and introspective."

"But would they really have my back if I needed them?"

"Who says you're going to need someone to have your back? Lighten up, Francesca."

I told myself that he was right, and I just wasn't used to hanging out with the *in* crowd.

"I love my life," I murmured happily to Jake one night as I was drifting off to sleep. "If I ever go back to being me, shoot me."

We were six months into our marriage by then. *Love, Max* had been published six months and a week earlier, and I'd had my run on the *Times* bestseller list. I truly believed that my life was golden and nothing could ever go wrong for me again. Then Nancy took me out to lunch.

"Gramercy has gotten in touch," she said. She was so excited, she'd forgotten to send the breadbasket back and was inhaling a hunk of focaccia. "They'd like to buy another book from you. Do you know what you want to write next?"

I didn't have a clue. My brain—and I could actually visualize this as I sat there—was like an empty room with nothing in it but a few dust bunnies in the corners. But Nancy was licking focaccia crumbs off her fingers and waiting for me to speak. I couldn't admit I had nothing.

"Well, I thought maybe I'd write about Max again."

"A sequel!" Nancy said. "Oh, God, you don't know how happy I am that you said that. Gramercy will be over the moon."

"Really?"

"Sequels sell. Big-time."

Well, it made sense. People would want to read about the characters they already knew they loved. And I wanted to write a book that would sell even better than my first one. No way I wanted to lose my shiny new success. "That's what I want to write," I said. "A sequel."

Nancy leaned forward eagerly. "What's the story?" she asked.

I was back to dust bunnies in the brain. "I have a couple of . . . thoughts . . . and themes . . . that interest me," I improvised. "Let me go home and put something down on paper."

It wasn't that I didn't have any ideas, I reassured myself, it was just that I hadn't thought seriously about writing a second book. I'd been too busy running around, sparkling and getting manicures. Once I got back into work mode, I was sure to come up with something.

The trouble with me being in work mode was, frankly, there were times when it wasn't pretty. When I was writing *Love, Max*, there were days when I got so absorbed I forgot to brush my hair—let alone curl it fetchingly on top of my head. Hell, there were times when I forgot to brush my teeth. I didn't go out of the house for three weeks while I was rewriting the first draft except to grab food and chocolate. I walked into walls and talked to myself when I was working out plot points. No way I was going to expose Jake to this side of Francesca.

I told myself I could continue the active social life Jake enjoyed so much even though I was working. It would just take a little discipline. I'd put myself on a schedule—check into my office from nine to five like anyone else with a job. I'd still have my weekends free to get my hair straightened. I could still do my makeup every morning.

It took me three weeks to figure out that story ideas do not come on command. At least mine didn't. I sat in my office wearing my itchy false lashes for eight frustrating, terrifying hours a day and came up with nothing. I eighty-sixed the damn lashes. I also canceled a couple of brunches and a hair appointment. Finally, I managed to concoct a plot that even I knew was too vague to show to Nancy.

Meanwhile, Jake watched me thrash around and became increasingly bewildered. "Don't you have a deadline for finishing this proposal?" he asked me.

"Not a specific one, but Nancy says the sooner the better."

"Why don't you just write it?" It was the first time I'd had to remind myself of all the reasons why I loved him.

The good news was, Jake was going to Tuscany for a week to do a shoot with a young Italian starlet—a gig he'd gotten on Andy's recommendation—and he wanted me to go with him so I had a reprieve.

"We didn't have a honeymoon, so this will be like one," I said to Nancy. "I'll get that book proposal to you as soon as I get back."

"Great. Because they're hot for Francesca Sewell's next novel, and we don't want to let them cool down," she said, thereby ensuring that I spent every morning of my belated honeymoon hunched over my computer trying to force sentences out of my brain and into the keyboard. In the afternoons, I joined Jake and the starlet and Andy, who had flown over to see how the shoot was going. We drank cappuccinos in little cafés, and I tried to pretend that I was paying attention to all the laughing and fun chat that was swirling around me, while the computer back in the hotel room haunted me.

Andy was the one who noticed how distracted I was. "Go up to the room and work," she'd say, with her warm laugh. "You know that's what you want to do. We can entertain ourselves."

By the time we were back in the States, I had finally written a proposal of sorts. Nancy took me out for a drink and I showed it to her. She read it and paused a really long time before she said, "Well, we all know it's the details that make the story." Then she added, "Why don't you write up a few chapters to flesh this out before we send it to Gramercy?"

"No problem," I said cheerily. Then I went home and threw up.

But I was still determined not to disappoint Jake. I continued going to gallery openings and fancy dinners held to raise money for research on obscure diseases—Jake and I never got invitations for A-list illnesses like cancer—but I was crying a lot, and I'd gained ten pounds.

Jake tried to help. "Why don't you join a gym?" he suggested. "It'll get you out of the house and away from that damn computer for a couple of hours." I tried to explain that I needed concentrated time—blocks of it—to do my kind of work. "Okay," he said, and he gave me a little kiss. "But it's so depressing to watch you."

For the next few days, I did my damnedest not to be depressing. I swear I tried. But it seemed like every time I might be getting a handle on my story, I had to quit to get dressed up so Jake and I could go somewhere and hang out with a friend who suddenly seemed to me to have the IQ of an avocado.

"When did you become antisocial?" Jake asked angrily, as we were going home in a cab one night. I didn't have an answer for him.

I wrote and deleted the first chapters of my book five times.

And I learned the painful difference between writing a book you love and throwing words at a book you wish you wanted to write. I started being afraid it would be like this for the rest of my life.

I told Jake I had to take a rain check when he asked me to go out to California. He had impressed the starlet from Italy and was in negotiations with her people to work as the director of a documentary about endangered species for her wildlife charity.

"This could be the start of a whole new career for me, Francesca," he said. "I've been a cinematographer before, but this is my first shot at directing. I'd like you to be with me. I went with you on your book tour."

"Please try to understand," I begged. "I just need to get an outline on paper."

"You've been saying that for months."

"Weeks," I corrected, with what I hoped was a cute grin.

Jake didn't grin back.

"It just seems longer."

"You can say that again."

"I don't know why this book is so hard. I didn't have this kind of trouble with *Love, Max.*"

"Stop worrying. Just sit down and get it done. This is getting frustrating."

I FINALLY ADMITTED my problem to Nancy, who told me in soothing tones that what I was suffering from was called Second Book Syndrome. "It happens all the time," she said. "When you have a hit with a first book, the expectations can be so great that you freeze. You'll work your way out of it."

But it didn't feel like I was working my way out of it. It felt like I was drowning.

At the same time Jake was out in LA, where he was being wined and dined by the starlet and her people. And of course he hung out with our pal Andy—who had some bad news to report. She hadn't been able to sell *Love, Max* to the television people.

"She said to tell you it has nothing to do with the book," Jake said on the phone. "Lifetime has too many projects in the pipeline already, and Hallmark is putting everything into turnaround because of budget problems. The Big Three aren't doing long form anymore, and the actor Andy pitched, the one with the deal at Fox, said he didn't want to play second fiddle to a dog."

"Wow, it's impressive how you do Hollywood-speak," I said.

"Francesca, you don't have to try to be funny. I know you've got to be feeling a little disappointed."

That was like saying someone who has just been through a tsunami is feeling a little waterlogged. What I was was numb. "Have you had a chance to meet Sheryl?" I asked, so we wouldn't have to dwell on me and my feelings.

"She's a sweetheart," he said.

Sheryl was a little more cryptic about Jake. "I think he's the kind of man who doesn't like to be alone," she said. Then she paused, and I could feel her picking her words carefully. "He's so . . . outgoing. And I don't think he really understands how important your writing is to you, Francesca."

When Jake came back, I tried to explain it. "I feel like I'm fighting for my life!"

"Don't you think that's a little over the top? It's just a book, Francesca." He gave me a kiss—was it my imagination, or was it the kind of kiss you'd give your mother?

"I can't seem to do all the running around we do and work. I need to lie low—just for a little while."

"How long?"

As long as it takes! I wanted to scream at him. "Give me a few months."

"You've already had months."

The point of telling you all of this is: There were signs. But I was so busy trying to beat Second Book Syndrome, I didn't pick up on them. No, let me be really honest: I didn't want to. I should have known better. I *did* know better. I'd learned that lesson the hard way when I was a kid.

CHAPTER 6

I'd finally reached our apartment building. I checked the clock in the lobby; it was still too early for Jake to have left for Andy's awards dinner. It wouldn't take me more than five minutes to get ready if I dressed fast.

"When did my husband get in?" I asked the doorman, as I walked by him.

"I don't think he's back yet, Ms. Morris."

That stopped me for a second. But doormen working at big New York City apartment buildings don't always see everyone who goes in and out. This guy could have been on the phone when Jake came in; there were dozens of other possible scenarios. I got into the elevator and went up.

None of the lights were on. I was greeted at the door by Annie, who made a frantic break for the hallway. Clearly she hadn't had her evening potty break yet, which meant the doorman was right; my husband hadn't come back home. I called out, "Jake, are you here?" just to make sure. There was no answer. I grabbed Annie's leash and the pooper-scooper—Annie and I are good citizens— and we hurried outside so she could do her thing.

A part of me expected to see Jake in the lobby when I walked out of the elevator. He'd be pressing the button anxiously, and he'd say he was sorry he had worried me. But he wasn't there. When Annie and I went outside, I couldn't help waiting for him to come up the street, running because he was so late. I promised myself I wouldn't get mad or demand to know where he'd been. I'd just be grateful that he was back. But Jake didn't rush up to me on the street with his hair mussed, breathing hard. Jake wasn't anywhere.

And now the memories that were flooding through my mind were getting scary. I stood next to the curb outside my apartment building, while Annie sniffed around for that one perfect spot, and tried to block them, to stop remembering what I'd done—and hadn't done—during the time when I was trying so desperately to recapture the lightning in a bottle that was *Love, Max*. But memory is a pesky thing; once you start it rolling it's almost impossible to turn it off.

IT TOOK ME a year, but I finally finished the first half of my new book—at least, I hoped that was what I'd done—but after my editor, Debbie, read it she didn't seem happy.

"Why did the dog get so mean?" she asked.

Because I got desperate.

"He was funny the first time, but he's not anymore, Francesca."

Well, neither am I.

I took another six months, rewrote the first half of the book without the dog, and showed it to Nancy.

"It's not any fun without Max," she said.

I decided to abandon the book I clearly couldn't write and start over with a brand-new one. "I've always loved the Victorians," I told Nancy. "I think I'll try my hand at a historical novel." I bought dozens of history books and spent months doing research in the library. I sketched out a plot and worked feverishly at it for a few more months before I had to admit to myself that, when you got to know them, the Victorians were unpleasantly smug and their personal hygiene left a lot to be desired. Plus, my heroine was a self-righteous pill. I dumped the historical novel. "I'm going to do a courtroom thriller," I told everyone I knew. "After all, I wanted to be a lawyer once." It only took me a couple of months of research to remember why I hadn't followed up on my legal career. The good news was, I never started writing that book. The bad news? I gained another ten pounds. Oh, yeah, and I still didn't have a new book for Gramercy Publishing.

Pete suggested I take a break from writing and do some other kind of work. Sheryl suggested that I go to Weight Watchers. Alexandra suggested that I try my hand at nonfiction. But I was a novelist—one who'd had an impressive debut. I kept on going into my home office every day to sit in front of my computer and stare at the blank screen. I'd write opening lines I would read and immediately delete. And eat chocolate.

Once, I tried to tell my new gal pals about my writer's block. "Actually it's not so much a block as a boulder," I said, with what I hoped was a light little chuckle. A shudder ran around the table. I translated that to mean I had their sympathy. Maybe even their compassion. "I'm so afraid I can't do this," I confessed. "I'm afraid I'm going to fail."

You'd have thought I was announcing that I had a terminal, highly contagious disease. I could actually feel them backing away.

"Oh, God," someone finally said. "This is so depressing. Let's change the subject."

Andy was in town to work with Jake on one of their projects, and when I told her about the incident she shrugged. "What did you expect, Francesca? Those women are all swimming with sharks—the last thing they need is you reminding them of what happens when there's blood in the water. You want my advice?"

I nodded eagerly.

"Get your toes done."

"Excuse me?"

"Get a great pedicure, buy a really expensive pair of sandals, and go out to lunch. No one will know you're having writer's block."

"But I *am*."

"People don't want to know that. Look like a winner, Francesca."

That particular chunk of wisdom reminded me of one of Jake's favorite Hollywood stories; it was about some actor and his wife who had been big TV stars but their show had been canceled, and after several years of not working they were broke. When they finally landed a network meeting, they took out a second mortgage on the house, emptied what was left in the bank account, raided the kids' college fund, and bought a huge diamond ring for the wife to wear. I'm sure you can write the ending to this story. The wife flashed the bling, the network suits were so impressed they figured no way the couple was all washed up, contracts were signed and . . . huzzah! The couple were back on the tube and back on top! "It's all about appearances," Jake used to crow at the end of this little tale. "To hell with the real you." Which was pretty much what Andy had said to me. She and Jake were totally on the same page when it came to the importance of appearances.

By now Jake had officially had it with Francesca the Suffering Artiste. "Screw your work," he said. "I have some free time, and we need a vacation. Stop driving yourself crazy, and let's have some fun."

Fun? How the hell could I have fun when I was terrified that I couldn't write another book? I had to keep on fighting until I'd proved to myself that I could do it. "Why don't you go by yourself for a couple of weeks?" I said. "I think I'm close to a breakthrough." That was the thing—I always thought I was close to a breakthrough. Each morning when I got up I was sure that this was the day.

Jake looked at me for a long time. "I don't like all this drama, Francesca," he said. "I'm Shallow Guy, remember?"

"I just want to write a book again. I just want that feeling you get when everything is flowing."

"And I want to have a life. Everything can't stop dead for your creative muse."

But writing was the only thing I'd ever done well. I'd loved the feeling of being good at something. And yeah, I'd loved the applause afterward. I'd gotten hooked on that.

Jake went to a resort in Mexico by himself. And our buddy Andy flew down to hang out with him for a day. And yes, I know how that sounds—how it probably would have sounded to me if I'd been paying attention. If I hadn't been so busy failing as a writer. But when Jake called to tell me how much fun they'd had, and Andy got on the phone to tell me a funny story about Jake trying to bargain in the local market for a hat he wanted to bring me—or maybe it was a handbag—it seemed perfectly innocent. I mean, a man can have a woman friend, can't he? We're all adults here, right?

So Jake went to Mexico and came back. And I was still beating my brains out trying to come up with a new idea. I reread books

I'd loved and rented old movies, telling myself I was looking for inspiration. Finally I stopped lying to myself and admitted I was hoping to find a story I could cannibalize. But I couldn't even do that. Nothing worked.

Meanwhile, my loved ones were getting on with life. My brother was given a grant by a prestigious foundation to design the definitive green city someplace where there was perpetual sunshine—I forget the country. His wife had her own grant to work with him on the ecological and environmental components. Their little daughter, who was now two, was already speaking both English and Spanish, and her parents were talking about starting her on a third language. My mother was profiled in a college textbook about influential women of the late twentieth century. I tried to be pleased for them, but to be honest, the fact that they had all gone into super-achiever mode was driving me nuts.

Then, just to put the cherry on the Misery Sundae, Nancy announced that she was quitting the business. "I'm adopting a little girl from China," she told me, at the last of our lunches, "and I need some time off. So I'm going back to California to be near my mother."

"But you're one of the best agents in the city."

"I'm not getting any younger, Francesca. I've always wanted to be a mom, and it's now or never."

She was two years younger than I was—that was the first thing I thought. Then I wailed, "What'll I do without you? Who's going to sell my books?"

Nancy's eyes met mine and we had one of those awkward moments. The words *What books?* hung in the air. That was when I realized it had been three years since I published *Love, Max*.

"Congratulations on the adoption," I said, in my chirpiest voice. "If this is what you want, I'm so happy for you!"

"Me too." Then she drew a breath. "Francesca? I still believe in you."

I managed not to cry then. It wasn't until I was standing on the subway platform on my way home, and this guy pulled out his violin and started playing it after putting his hat on the ground in front of him for tips, that I started to sob. I'm pretty sure we all know what the life lesson here is. When you start weeping because someone is playing "Ave Maria"—very badly—in the subway station, you've got a big problem.

I finally gave up my fight to write a book. I haven't looked at the computer in four months. I wish I could say that I've taken a vacation with Jake and had some fun. Or at least that I joined Weight Watchers. But I wasn't sure they'd understand about chocolate. And lately, every time I've suggested that Jake and I take off and go somewhere, he's been busy. As I said, he and Andy have joined forces to work together, and they've been bouncing back and forth between LA and New York, rounding up the funding for their first project. In fact, they just got the final chunk of it last week. So the awards dinner for Andy that Jake and I were attending that night—the one where Jake was going to introduce her as his friend and partner—it was going to be like a celebration for both of them.

ANNIE FINISHED HER business and there was still no sign of Jake. I told myself not to get upset. Somehow, some way, Jake had gotten past me and gone upstairs. I raced into the building and up to my apartment, but it was still dark. And quiet. And empty.

I remembered that we still had an answering machine hooked up to the phone in my office. Now that we had cell phones, it didn't get a lot of use, but sometimes Jake liked to leave messages the old-fashioned way. I rushed to the office and, sure enough, the red light on the machine was blinking. I pushed the button.

"Francesca?" Jake's voice said. "Look, I know you're probably going to blow off Andy's dinner tonight the way you always do. . . ." He trailed off. Then he spoke again. "We need to talk, Francesca," he said. As if I hadn't heard him when he said it earlier.

Annie was jabbing her nose into my stomach, which is her way of telling me that it's past her dinnertime, and since I have an opposable thumb and she doesn't, I'm the one to get busy with the can opener. I went into the kitchen, fed her, and tried to think rationally. According to our big clock in the foyer, it was seven. The awards dinner started at seven-thirty and the hotel ballroom where they were holding it was on the other side of town. No way Jake was coming home this late, he was probably at the hotel already. He'd gone there directly from . . . wherever he'd been for the last couple of hours. And whoever he'd been with.

Because suddenly I knew Jake hadn't been alone. This was his night to celebrate his new partnership with Andy. After he'd had his Talk with me. But I'd screwed up that timetable by taking off for the park. So Jake had gone for a little advance celebration with his partner, which had lasted a bit longer than he'd thought it would. I wondered if he had a spare tux in her hotel suite—the awards dinner was black-tie, and Jake would rather chew glass than screw up a dress code.

And I had been a fool. Probably for a long time.

Here's the thing about being in denial: When you stop, it's like you've been living in a kind of half darkness and suddenly someone turns on every light in the house. All those little nooks and crannies you couldn't quite see but knew were there are all of a sudden brightly, glaringly visible. And you start to think. You realize you have no way of knowing if your husband and his dear pal—and yours—spent one day together in Mexico or two weeks. You don't know if he booked a hotel room for one or for two when they were traveling together, rounding up funding for their new partnership. You don't really know where he stayed all those times when he was in Los Angeles—where she has that roomy old house in Los Feliz. And you sure as hell don't know what he was doing when she was in New York and they were having business meetings that lasted until two in the morning.

That's when you hack into his private email account and read the last message he received before he took off for the day. The one he didn't bother to delete because he never knew you had his password. The message is from his pal. His new business partner. Who is suggesting doing things to him when they're alone in her hotel room that you've never even imagined. And you pride yourself on your creativity.

I changed into my gown, skipped the makeup and hair drill, grabbed my purse, and headed out.

THE HOTEL BALLROOM was decorated in black, red, and silver. Red-and-silver trellises had been attached to the walls and live black roses—I guess they were dyed—were threaded through them. The room was jammed with small round tables that were covered with red tablecloths, black china, and silver-rimmed glasses. The centerpieces featured black roses floating in big bowls of water tinted red with silver flecks drifting around. Very festive—if you could get past the feeling that there was something creepy about roses that were black. Personally, I couldn't. But then no one had asked me.

There was a long table on a dais at the end of the room. I scanned it, looking for Jake. I knew he'd be sitting on the dais because he was giving the introduction. I spotted him right away, seated in the center of the table in front of the microphone. He

was properly attired in black tie. So there *was* an Alternate Plan
Tux. Like the woman who was seated next to him, the fun, successful pal who had been offering him an alternative to his not-
fun, not-successful wife. His partner, who was glowing like a
teenager—probably because she'd spent the last couple of hours
with him doing all those things she'd outlined in her email. Andy.
My friend.

The first course had already been served by the time I arrived.
I'd been to enough awards dinners to know that they wouldn't be
starting the speeches while people were still munching on their
salads, so I moved up to the dais, planning to—well, at that point,
I didn't have a plan. I was winging it. Jake was chatting with someone on his right. On his left, Andy was staring at a bowl of ugly
black roses. She looked pensive. Was she having second thoughts
about breaking up my marriage? No, that was too much to ask.
She turned to Jake with her glowing smile and joined his conversation. I was a little less than a foot away from her. It only took a
second to step in and dump the red water over her perfectly
coiffed head. Black rose petals stuck to her face and shoulders,
looking like polka dots—or a really gross rash. She was drenched
in water the shade of cherry Kool-Aid. Did I mention that the silk
gown she was wearing was beige? Talk about your sweet moments.

Andy shrieked, and Jake looked up. He saw me, jumped to his
feet, and hunched over Andy, trying to shield her from me. I
thought about pointing out that I was the one he'd promised to
protect and cherish, but there was still some water left in the bowl
so I dumped it on him instead. I watched the red liquid run down
his beautiful face and over the place on the back of his neck that I
loved to kiss, and I tried to be as mad at him as I was at her. But he
was Jake, so I couldn't. And that made me even madder.

I started to leave. That was when I noticed that five hundred people were staring at the three of us. Clearly they'd finished their salads—and they were waiting for someone to say something. But Jake was trying to get the silver flecks out of his hair and Andy was still wailing. I clamped my free hand over her mouth and leaned in to the microphone.

"Ladies and gentlemen," I said to the room. "My soon-to-be ex, Jake Morris, was supposed to introduce your honoree tonight, but he's otherwise engaged, so I'm helping out. I give you Andrea Grace, the postmenopausal slut, who has been screwing my husband." Then I strode out.

As I left the ballroom, I tried to feel vindicated. Or satisfied. Or triumphant. But all I could think of was Jake holding me in his arms in a darkened photography studio and whispering into my hair, "Smart, foxy, and unhinged." I thought I was going to start crying then, but I didn't seem to have any tears.

There was a little debate going on when I reached the entrance of the hotel. Several of the hotel's security people wanted to call for a police car and send me to central booking. The dissenters— from the hotel's public-relations department—argued that the publicity would be bad for business, and they wanted to put me in a cab and send me home. I was on their side, but I was too wiped out to join the fight. Because all of a sudden I was tired in a way that I'd never been before in my life. We're talking running-marathons- and-climbing-mountains tired. Not that I've ever done either of those things, but you get the point. Finally, someone summoned the slut and Jake. She didn't want to press charges, and Jake ex- plained to everyone that I'd been having emotional problems. So Team Taxicab won and I got to go home.

But that wasn't the end of the evening's events. Three people with cell phones caught my act and recorded it. I understand that the resulting footage went viral on YouTube, and for a couple of days Andy, Jake, and I were getting almost as many hits as some guy who had trained his dog to use the john. Many, many people got to watch Andy's big night being shot to hell.

The next day, before Jake could come back to the apartment to pack up his clothes, I changed the locks. There were only two things I was sure of: I wasn't going to have a happy divorce, and we weren't going to have the Talk. Okay, there were three things: I was going to miss Jake like hell.

But after I thought about it for a day or two, I realized that it wasn't just Jake I'd lost, it was a vision of myself. Being married to him had also been my shot at being Sheryl, complete with a signature shade of pink. But when my work was at stake, I had morphed into my mother. Alexandra was who I was, whether I wanted to be or not. Alexandra, who hadn't been able to hang on to her man— my daddy. I went into my closet and threw out all my size fours.

"I'm through," I told Annie. "I am never going on another date, and I am never, ever again, going to fall in love. A woman without a man is like a fish without a bicycle. I'm having that embroidered on a hat."

Then I finally started to cry. And I didn't stop for a very long time.

CHAPTER 7

Here's one of the many great things about New York City: If you don't want to leave the house, you don't have to. You can pay someone to walk your dog. You can pay to have hot meals and your newspaper delivered right to your door. You can also pay people to shop for your shampoo, pick up your dry cleaning, and run other errands. Hell, you don't have to get out of bed. I know this because I didn't, for two months.

My divorce had turned out to be depressingly un-bloody. I had wanted to go for the jugular, but I have the wrong DNA for battle. So does Jake. We did have the Talk, however. Or at least we had *a* talk.

"I'm giving up on the Svengali thing," he told me.

"Sorry I was such a disappointment."

"I could say the same thing."

"But I'm not the one who wants out."

"Yes, you do. You just don't know it yet, Francesca."

If I'd been hoping for an apology—and let's face it, you always are, in a situation like that—that was as good as I was going to get from Jake.

The divorce took two months from the time he moved out until we signed the final papers. We didn't fight for the co-op; since almost all of the money we'd put into it was mine, I bought him out of his small share. I didn't hold him up for half of his camera equipment or any of the assets he'd acquired while we were married, and he gave me all our awful furniture. Neither of us asked for alimony.

When Jake and Andy got married minutes after our divorce was final and he took off for California to live with her, I told myself not to think about my dad taking off to be with Sheryl and history repeating itself. After all, this time I got to keep the dog. But then I went to bed and stayed there for eight weeks.

I might still be in bed if I hadn't been hit with a nasty shock—I was running out of money. I know you're asking how come my financial situation came as a surprise to me. I wasn't a kid; I should have done the math and figured out that it had been a long time since I'd earned anything more substantial than the occasional tiny royalty. And by then I had a hefty payroll with all those home deliveries. But I've always had a major math phobia, so when I was married Jake handled our finances. Before him, my parents had taken care of that stuff—and I can't remember ever having a conversation with either one of them about anything as crude as cash. Alexandra's brand of feminism was about marching and self-fulfillment, not the size of her paychecks. And Dad never wanted me to trouble my sweet little head about mundane things like paying the bills. But now I had to. Quickly.

"I'm scared," I wept to Sheryl on the phone. "Thank God, the advance for the Swedish edition of *Love, Max* just came in, but after that's gone I don't know what I'm going to do."

If I'd expected sympathy—and to be honest I'd been begging for it—it wasn't going to happen. "Get a job," Sheryl said, going into problem-solving mode.

"Doing what?" I wailed. "The Well of Loneliness Theater is out of business."

"I saw Nancy and Lan Ying Marigold last week—and I don't care what Sissy says, that name is going to be a problem for that little girl someday—and Nancy told me she knows writers who find freelance work online."

It took me a second to realize that the answer had come back awfully fast. "You saw this coming," I said. "You never liked Jake."

"There are several ways of looking for private work—ghostwriting, I think they call it. That means—"

"Some wannabe hires a professional author to write the novel or whatever they've tried to write and can't," I broke in.

"I can get a list of websites from Nancy and send it to you," said Sheryl.

I wanted to snicker in a really snide way. *No way,* I thought. *I've been on the* New York Times *bestseller list. I had one of the hottest agents in publishing. You think I'm going to try to hire myself out to write vanity projects? Please.*

Sheryl broke into my thoughts. "According to Nancy, you should announce that you're looking for work on your own website and your blog." That idea was even worse than trolling for gigs on other people's websites. My blog and my website had been set up for me by Gramercy's public-relations department when *Love, Max* turned out to be such a success. The idea was to stay in touch with my readers, who would be eager to hear about all my comings and goings, and I'd increase my fan base for the next book—which, as we all know, never materialized. So I'd abandoned the blogging and the staying in touch. To be honest, I'd been too embarrassed to keep it up—I mean, what was I going to say? *I'm now the poster child for writer's block?* But in my golden era, I'd been proud of the website and the blog, and the idea of using them to solicit gigs felt like a huge defeat. On the other hand, there was the maintenance on the co-op to be paid. And I really wasn't ready to do without amenities like food and my phone.

"Great suggestion," I said to Sheryl. "I'll start on the blog entry right away. And if you could send me that list of ghostwriter's websites, that would be very nice."

"I'll email it tonight."

"Thank you."

"And Francesca? Jake isn't a horrible person. He's just all wrong for you."

SO I WROTE a blog entry advertising my availability as a writer, and I posted a notice on my website saying I was now a writer for hire. I tried to sound charming and funny and prayed I hadn't come off as pathetic. Then I joined the horde of freelance writers trying to land a job. Basically, that meant I spent my days sending emails to strangers hoping to convince them that I alone could edit/write/ghostwrite their blog/brochure/Great American Novel. I wrote emails that were breezy and light. Nada. I tried to make my pitch more businesslike. Zilch. I pimped myself shamelessly, sending out copies of my best reviews. Nothing. No one responded to my emails. I didn't get a nibble.

Unfortunately, I understood why. Even I didn't think I was equipped to write an online magazine article about the advantages of eating algae or a daily post about the sexiest hot spots in Brooklyn. I was wondering how much longer I could pay my cable bill when the phone rang.

"Hi," said a masculine voice. "Are you the Francesca Sewell who wrote that book about the dog? Because I'd like to talk to you about a job."

After I scraped myself off the ceiling, I learned that his name was Brandon Bourne. But he wasn't going to be my new boss. Her name was Eleanor Masters. She was in her eighties, and Brandon was an orderly in the assisted-living facility where she resided. "But don't worry," he reassured me. "Ms. Masters is as sharp as a tack. And she's very motivated about this biography she's hiring you to write."

"Terrific," I said, while I racked my brain for the name Masters and drew a blank. "That is so . . . absolutely . . . terrific." Not only was Ms. Masters herself not ringing any bells, this biography had blended into the mass of jobs I'd tried to snag. But now, clearly, I had to identify it. Quickly.

"Um . . . remind me again. Which website did Ms. Masters advertise on?" I ventured. "Was it Ghosts Are Us dot-com?"

"Actually, we responded to the post on your website." The voice on the other end was starting to sound a little perturbed.

"Right, right!" I said enthusiastically, even more in the dark than before. I could have sworn that there weren't any responses. "Of course! And I'm so glad you did. Because I'm sure Ms.—um—Masters and I will have a . . . very productive . . . fun . . . experience, working together."

There was a pause. "I have to tell you, Ms. Masters decided to hire you for this memoir because, when you answered her emails, she felt you had already made a strong emotional investment in the story," Brandon said—a bit severely, I thought.

I struggled to recall whatever College Bullshit 101 I'd slung.

"Well, she sounds like a charmer," I said. Then I could have kicked myself—with my luck, the woman was half gaga.

To my relief, Brandon laughed heartily. "I don't know about that, but she sure is a character," he said.

"Absolutely. That's what I meant," I said, with a hearty laugh of my own. "So remind me, Brandon, how much is she paying again? In all the . . . excitement about her project, I'm afraid I forgot to write down the fee."

"It's fifteen thousand."

It wasn't anywhere near my advance for *Love, Max*, but I'd been trolling for jobs long enough to know that it was generous for a freelance gig. Still, I had to swallow hard. Then I remembered how much I wanted to keep my cable. I'd gotten addicted to the *CSI* shows.

"When do I start?" I asked.

CHAPTER 8

Yorkville House for Senior Living was on the Upper East Side. From the street it looked like one of those inexpensive small hotels that Europeans used to book themselves into when they visited the city—before the global economy did its kamikaze dive.

The Yorkville House lobby was furnished with cushy chairs upholstered in shades of blue and gold; there were brass sconces on the walls and a matching chandelier hanging overhead; and full-length gold drapes hung in the bay windows. You could imagine you really were in an old-world hotel until you saw the wheelchair ramp and the rubber runners laid out on the carpet.

There was a huge desk in the front of the lobby, where a young woman was answering phones, sorting mail, and chatting with an elderly lady with a cane. Somewhere in the background someone was pounding heavily on a piano. It sounded to me like the tune was that ancient standard "Shine On, Harvest Moon." I explained to the multitasker behind the desk that I was looking for Brandon Bourne.

"He's in the crafts room with the Swinging Grandmas," she said. "It's right through there." She pointed me in the direction of the music.

I followed the sound and found myself in a good-sized room with shelves full of art supplies lining the walls. There was a message board near the door announcing a list of classes, speeches, exercise sessions, and field trips to museums and theaters that were available to residents. I tried to tell myself it wasn't sad that adults who had once been contributing members of society were now being entertained like kindergarten children. I also tried to tell myself it wasn't sad that I'd failed so badly that I was here to ghost-write a biography I couldn't remember discussing for one of those aged kindergarteners.

In the far corner of the room was an upright piano; this was where the music was coming from. Half a dozen women, all of them well over sixty, were clustered around it. One of them was in a purple leotard that proved that for some women the legs really are the last thing to go, while the rest had on sweats or jeans, and they were all wearing those shoes with the strap over the arch that you see on dancers. The back of the piano was facing me, and the woman playing it was too short for me to see over the top, but there was a guy turning the pages of the music. His head was shaved, his ears had multiple piercings, and his clingy tank top and stretch pants revealed that he was into serious exercise and body art. He was wearing dancer shoes too.

The guy caught sight of me, smiled, and indicated that I should sit. Meanwhile, the Swinging Grandmas—I assumed that was who they were, although in most cases "Great-Grandma" would have been more accurate—had positioned themselves in a chorus line across the front of the room. A chord chimed out, and a woman's voice, husky and loud, began singing behind the upright. The rest of the troupe joined her in a medley of songs I recognized dimly as a Hit Parade of teen favorites circa 1940. The women weren't exactly on key, but they had presence. And pep, loads of pep. The lead singer at the piano kept the tempo moving along, and, as she swung into a musical bridge, the Grandmas sashayed into a new formation, and the woman in the purple leotard stepped out. She flicked her white Mamie Eisenhower pageboy out of her eyes and began to tap-dance. Purple Leotard had probably been faster a few decades earlier, but from what I could see she wasn't missing a step. Just when I thought she was starting to look a little winded, from behind the piano came the sound of metal taps clicking on the linoleum. Earring Guy was moving front and center. There was nothing slow about him; his feet flew. He danced around Purple Leotard for a couple of minutes while she posed fetchingly—and caught her breath—and then the music went into a rolling arpeggio. This seemed to signal that something special was about to happen. The chorus line shifted into a semicircle, and Earring Guy held out his arm and gave Purple Leotard an encouraging grin. She grabbed his arm, balanced herself, and then seemed to hesitate.

"Let's see those eye-highs, Emmy," called out the voice from behind the piano. "Once a Rockette, always a Rockette!"

Spurred on, Purple Leotard braced herself and executed a series of flawless kicks that actually were eye-high, after which she and her partner blended back into the chorus line, where everyone closed out the performance by singing a song I think Fred Astaire made famous in one of his movies.

I gave them a standing O, and I swear I wasn't doing it to suck up to my potential employer—whoever she was. With their energy and their upbeat 'tude, the Swinging Grandmas were awesome.

The guy dancer broke out of the line and came to me with his hand outstretched. "Brandon Bourne," he said. "You must be Ms. Sewell. Let me introduce you to Ms. Masters."

A Lilliputian emerged from behind the piano and came toward me. She was under five feet tall and maybe ninety pounds soaking wet. Her hair was short and yellow. Not a pale age-appropriate blond; we're talking shiny gold curls that formed a frame around her little heart-shaped face. By far her best features were her round, blue eyes. Even behind a pair of large tortoiseshell glasses they still had a sparkle in them, and they must have been truly lovely when she was young. Her nose was on the large side, and her mouth was surprisingly curvy for someone her age. She'd chosen to wear bright coral lipstick and matching nail polish, her long-sleeved dress was yellow and black, and she'd tossed a black cardigan over her shoulders. How she managed to bang out songs on the piano with such arthritic-looking fingers was beyond me. Ms. Masters waved Brandon aside before he could make any introductions and peered up at me. It felt like she stared at me for an awfully long time; Alexandra's nose was getting special scrutiny. Finally Brandon seemed to think somebody should say something.

"I'm sure you remember that Ms. Sewell is here to—" he began.

"Yes, I remember." The Lilliputian cut him off in her husky growl without taking her eyes off me.

The nonstop gaze was a little unnerving, but I figured what the hell, she could stare at me forever as long as she paid me. "Ms. Masters—" I began, but she stopped me with a vague wave of her hand.

"Call me Chicky," she said. "Everyone does." Then she seemed to break out of her trance. She smiled at me. "I like that face of yours. It's got character." For a moment I thought she was going to reach up and stroke my cheek.

"Uh . . . thank you."

"You're welcome, Doll Face."

I thought about correcting her, but, once again remembering the paychecks she'd be signing, I decided she could call me whatever she wanted. I gestured toward the Swinging Grandmas. "Your group sounds great."

"Doll Face, we sound like shit," she said briskly. "At our age, the wonder is we're hitting any of the notes at all." She waved at the troupe. "Break it up for now, everyone," she said. "Same time tomorrow. Remember we're going to be performing at St. Agnes's Hospital in two weeks."

"You entertain at hospitals?" I said admiringly—and yes, at that point I *was* sucking up—"I think that's so worthy."

"We rehearse this act ten hours a week. You work that hard, you want to be appreciated. Even if you know you've got a captive audience because they can't move on their own." I laughed politely. "That's not a joke, it's a statement of fact," she said. Then she patted my arm gently—almost maternally. "Don't try so hard to please me, Doll Face," she said. "You get to be my age, you develop a pretty good radar for horse pucky."

"Ms. Masters, I didn't mean to—"

"Like I said, it's Chicky. Follow me; we'll talk in my room." She turned to Brandon, who had retrieved a bag of ice out of a tiny refrigerator and was applying it to his leg. "Come on, Show Biz." He straightened up immediately, and the two of us followed the little martinet at a trot through a maze of hallways to the elevator and then up to her room on the seventh floor.

• • •

CHICKY'S ROOM WAS organized like a studio apartment. Along one wall, there was a little galley kitchen consisting of a small fridge, a microwave, a hot plate, and a toaster oven. She wasn't going to be doing any gourmet cooking, but the standard single person's nuked meal was definitely possible. Against a second wall was a daybed that, with bolsters and cushions, served as a sofa. Two comfortable-looking chairs faced it, forming a conversation pit, with a large wooden trunk in the center serving as a coffee table. The trunk looked old and had been varnished to preserve the remnants of what looked like labels for a bunch of theaters; names like the Bardavon Opera House and the Hughes Playhouse were featured. Across the top of the trunk someone had painted the name ORDINARY JOE in large letters.

At one side of the daybed was a low table that I figured served as Chicky's nightstand. There was a lamp on it, a couple of pill bottles, and an iPod—a nice touch, I thought. Above the nightstand on the wall was a sepia-colored photograph of a man and a woman. They were both young, probably in their early twenties. The man was kind of funny looking—as if someone had decided to make a human being out of spare parts and none of them quite fit together. His face was too big for his short, skinny body, his mouth was too wide for his face, and his nose was too big for his mouth. His eyes were round and dark, as was his hair. Even though he wasn't handsome, he did seem to be a natty dresser. I mean, men's fashions at the turn of the last century really weren't my area of expertise, but the guy was wearing spats.

Unlike the man, the woman in the picture had everything going for her in the looks department. Her thick hair had been piled on top of her head, with wings of luxurious waves on either side. Her features were lovely in that patrician way that was so popular a hundred years ago, and she was wearing a dress that was molded to her slender body and revealed just enough of her ankles to suggest that there was nothing wrong with her legs either. Although the picture wasn't in color, I thought her eyes were probably blue, with Chicky's sparkle. Not only was this picture in the place of pride, above Chicky's nightstand, it had been put in an elaborate gilded frame.

"That's Mom and Pop," said Chicky. "Joe and Ellie Masters. Well, it was really Masconi, but back in those days people in the profession thought you needed a British-sounding name. Before she got married, Mom's name was Doran."

In the time since I'd gotten my original phone call from Brandon Bourne, I'd tried to recover the emails we must have exchanged, but when I'd been job hunting I'd usually deleted all cyber correspondence once I thought the gig hadn't worked out. So Mom and Pop were still a mystery to me—as was their profession. I figured they were going to be the protagonists of the biography I was to write, but I still couldn't connect the dots. I stared at the picture, hoping for enlightenment, aware that Chicky was once more watching me with a laserlike focus. Weren't elderly people supposed to be vague and misty?

"Uh . . . your parents look like very interesting people," I said.

"Doll Face—"

"It's Francesca, actually."

"I know, but I like nicknames. I've had several myself, over the years. Chicky was the one that finally stuck."

There didn't seem to be much I could add to that moment of sharing, so I said, "Ah," and hoped it sounded intelligent.

"I give people nicknames all the time," she went on. "It makes me feel like I've got lots of friends—which is a damn good trick at my age. So, Doll Face, you don't know what you're doing here, do you?"

I wanted to say, *No, I don't. Because your ad was like dozens of others I answered, and after a while I stopped trying to keep track. Because the whole thing is humiliating. I don't like begging for a job. I'm a professional writer. No one would ask a doctor or a lawyer to go through hoops the way I have. I deserve a little respect.*

But I was also a professional who had been laid low by Second Book Syndrome, so I was in no position to say anything to anyone. I made myself smile, but I knew it was a lame effort. "Well, Chicky, the thing is—"

She cut off the song-and-dance I was about to do. "You don't know what the hell I want you to write, do you, Doll Face?"

I looked into those blue eyes. "Not a clue," I said.

She seemed delighted. Like I was a not-too-bright toddler who had finally managed to say my first word. "See, that wasn't so hard, was it? I told you, stop trying to con me. You'll never do it. I was always one step ahead of—" She stopped herself. "I'm a smart cookie," she said instead.

She gave me another motherly arm pat.

"Come here," she said, and led me to the gold-framed picture. "Mom and Pop were in show business—vaudeville. You probably don't know anything about vaudeville; no one does anymore. But it was as big as television a hundred years ago. Kids from all over the country—big cities and little tiny towns—who could sing or dance or tell a joke would put an act together and try their luck on talent night at the local vaudeville house." She reached up with an arthritic forefinger and stroked the man's face in the picture. It was the kind of gesture that makes your eyes sting, no matter how tough you're trying to be. "That's how Pop got started. He won a talent contest at an opera house out on Coney Island when he was still in his teens. He had a partner at first, but then he went solo. He was what they called a monologuist back then. It's like a stand-up comic. And he could have been one of the greats." She stroked the picture again. "Pop could have been as big as Jack Benny or Bob Hope."

When she said that, it clicked! I finally remembered the email Brandon Bourne, aka Show Biz, had sent me. "Ms. Masters wants a professional novelist to write a biography of her parents," he'd written. "She wants the world to hear their tale of sacrifice, heartbreak, and triumph. This is a theater story. Joe Masters could have been another Jack Benny or Bob Hope, but he and his wife gave up their dreams for something better."

When I'd read his deathless prose, I'd thought whoever landed the gig was going to need insulin shots—or maybe hard drugs—to write the sticky-sweet tale. But of course I'd pitched for it.

"Chicky felt she could trust you to write her parents' story because of the fabulous job you did on your own book." Brandon had suddenly decided to join the conversation. He'd brought his ice pack along and was sitting in a chair ministering to his leg. Chicky didn't seem to see anything unusual about this, and I figured it wasn't my place to pry.

"You read *Love, Max*?" I asked Chicky. I couldn't imagine how anyone could read that book—which everyone agreed was clever but not exactly warm and fuzzy—and decide I was their choice to write a goopy vanity bio.

"Doll Face, do you think I'd hire someone just because they answered that hokey email Show Biz wrote to you?" She turned to Brandon. "No offense, kiddo, but it did make me want to upchuck." He smiled—obviously nothing she said ever offended him—and Chicky's attention came back to me. "Of course I read your book."

"Great." I did another lame smile: Version Number Two, which is mixed with a dollop of self-deprecating humor.

"For a while after I finished the book I was out of commission—health things—but I never forgot about you. I asked Show Biz to giggle you."

"Google," he corrected.

"We found your website. That was when . . ." She seemed to trail off, but then she regained her train of thought quickly. "I learned a little more about you," she went on. "And after that, I kept track." Now her eyes were gleaming wickedly through her glasses and her mouth was quivering. I thought about asking what was so funny, but then I figured I didn't need to know. I had a contract in my purse that I'd downloaded from one of the ghostwriting sites. As long as she signed it and paid me, she could have all the private little-old-lady jokes she wanted.

"Well, then, I guess we're good to go." I did Lame Smile, Version Number Two again. The smiles were getting to be a specialty of mine.

"Just one question," she said. "What the hell happened to you?"

I felt the lame smile die. "I don't know what you mean." But I was pretty sure I did. "If you're asking why I haven't written anything since *Love, Max*—"

"If you were me, wouldn't you want to know?"

She had a point. But I wasn't sure I wanted to—or could—explain.

"I can give you some privacy," said the ever-helpful Show Biz. The man was like one of those loyal family retainers on a *Masterpiece Theater* series.

"You want to make poor Show Biz go out into the hall?" Chicky asked. "He's got to take care of that knee. As long as he gets ice on it after he dances, it'll be fine. But if he lets it swell up, he'll be limping around here like Quasimodo." She leaned in. "He hurt it a couple of years ago doing a revival of *West Side Story* out at the East Haddam Opera House."

"Paper Mill Playhouse," Show Biz corrected. "A pre-Broadway tryout. The show didn't make it, and neither did my knee."

"The point is, Francesca," Chicky said, "everyone's got something. Me. Brandon." She paused. "And, I'm guessing, so do you."

There was something about the way she said it that got to me. I looked into her smart blue eyes, which had seen so much more than mine had, and I knew there would be no judgments; nothing I could say would surprise or disappoint her. And all of a sudden I found myself telling her how I came to write *Love, Max.* I told her about Second Book Syndrome—and for the first time I didn't try to make a joke of it. And then for absolutely no reason at all I told her about Jake. Except the part where I dumped the water on Andy. I thought that might sound like I was a tad unstable.

"All I ever wanted was to be happy," I summed up.

Chicky looked at me for a long time. "Maybe you need another plan," she said.

"Excuse me?"

"From what you say, you've been trying to be happy for over twenty years, and it hasn't worked out. Maybe you should just stop trying."

"But everyone wants to be happy."

"Nah. If you really listen to people, most of them are after something else . . . like, they want to be successful. Or rich. Or they want other people to need them. Sometimes it's a religious thing; they want to kiss up to God so He'll be on their side. Being happy, when you think about it, is kind of vague. And in my experience, it usually comes as a bonus while you're doing other things. I'd say, pick something different to go for."

"How about—being employed?"

"That's nice and simple."

"But first I need a job."

"You have one . . . even if you didn't remember who the hell I am. I like you, Doll Face." She paused. "I like you as much as I hoped I would."

CHICKY AND I settled the financial arrangements quickly. The helpful ghostwriting site had been very clear about how payments should be structured, and Chicky and I agreed that she would pay me five thousand dollars as an advance, another five thousand after I showed her the first half of the book, and a final five thousand after I completed it to my satisfaction. She had material I could use in my research, including a few pictures of her parents that were taken during their early years.

"And Doll Face, I've got the whole story in my head," she assured me. "I'll tell it to you, and it'll write itself." She went back to the picture on the wall and looked up at it. "All my pop wanted was his moment in the spotlight. I guess a lot of people want that—that's why all those schlubs on reality television are willing to let someone bring a camera into their house and take pictures of them doing things polite folks wouldn't even talk about fifty years ago. The only difference is, my pop earned the right to be downstage center. And Mom was right there with him. They wrote his act together, and she was his stooge in the audience, so it really was the two of them."

"What happened to them?"

"Now you're trying to get ahead of the story." She wagged her finger. "You have to be patient, Doll Face."

She was enjoying this. Too much? It felt like some kind of octogenarian power trip—not that I'd had that much experience with eightysomethings. Whatever. She was the boss.

"Gotcha," I said.

"When I was a kid," she went on, "I promised myself someday I'd make sure Mom and Pop got the spotlight—you know, like they deserved. But I never could figure out how to do it. Then I realized everyone's reading stories about real people nowadays, so why not write a book about them?"

There was a sinking feeling in the bottom of my stomach. I'd been thinking of this project as a personal memento, something she wanted for herself. Maybe she'd give a couple of copies of it as Christmas presents. It had never occurred to me that she was hoping to sell it. "You want to *publish* this . . . book?"

"Absolutely. And now that I've found you, we're going to make it happen. Together."

Anyone with half a brain in her head—in other words, anyone but me—would have said what Chicky wanted to hear, taken her money, and paid their co-op fees. But I'm my mother's daughter. No way I could take a paycheck from a little old lady if she really thought she was going to find a publisher for a story about two long-dead vaudevillians and their equally dead art form. If that was what she was expecting, I was going to have to kiss the fifteen thousand bucks good-bye.

"You need to know," I said, as visions of Annie and me living in a cardboard box raced through my head, "I can't guarantee that this . . . project . . . will actually sell . . ."

"That's so sweet," she murmured. "You're trying to protect me."

"I just don't want you to have any illusions."

"I'd have been dead years ago without 'em, Doll Face."

"What I meant was—"

"I know what you meant. Just you write this story. The rest will take care of itself."

"But—"

"Francesca, sometimes life hands you a gift. You don't question it, you just take it. I have faith in you."

I told myself I'd tried my best to tell her the truth, and it wasn't my fault if she didn't want to hear it. Besides, I liked hearing that someone had faith in me—no matter how misguided. "Okay, then," I said. I took out the contract and we signed it. Then, for good measure, we shook hands. The deal was done.

I have a job! sang my heart. *I'm going to stop at Allie's Chinese Diner on the way home and pick up an order of shredded duck. With extra sauce. Or maybe lobster lo mein. It's been so long since I've had takeout, maybe I'll get both. And something chocolate for dessert.*

"I'll walk you to the lobby," Show Biz said, breaking into my happy reverie. "My shift is over for today."

"Thanks." I turned to my tiny benefactress. "See you tomorrow morning," I said.

"You betcha, Doll Face."

CHAPTER 9

Show Biz was planning to hang around the Upper East Side. "I have a date for dinner, and I live out in Rockland County, so there's no point in going home and then coming all the way back into the city," he explained. "The commute is a pain in the ass."

It had been a long time since I'd been out of my apartment, and all of a sudden I didn't want to go back. "How about a cup of coffee?" I asked. He nodded and we headed for a greasy spoon on the corner. There was a Starbucks that was nearer, but neither of us considered it. Since I believe the invasion of chain restaurants and stores is eroding the soul of Manhattan, I gave us both points for that.

"Chicky seems like a sweet old soul," I said to Show Biz, after we'd ordered our coffees.

"Chicky, sweet?" He gave a little hoot of laughter. "Not exactly."

"She was very nice to me."

"I saw." He frowned a little.

"Was that unusual? She seemed awfully friendly."

"She is—in a way. But total strangers don't usually get a nickname on the first date—if you know what I mean. It took me three weeks to get mine."

"Then I guess I'm honored," I said politely. Show Biz did another frown. "What?"

"I think there's something about you. . . ." He paused. "You know how we found out you were looking for a job?"

"You said you read the post on my website."

"Yeah. But here's the thing. From the moment Chicky read your website, she's been making me check it out for her. Like every couple of months. Just to see what you're doing. She said she wanted to keep up with you because she liked *Love, Max* so much."

"What can I say? It is a fabulous book."

But I had to admit Chicky didn't strike me as the type to become a devoted fan. And there was that feeling I'd had a couple of times—that she wanted more from me than just a business arrangement, which had been a little strange. But when I thought about it, I realized that what we were doing *was* more than mere business. She was trusting me with cherished memories and dreams she'd had for decades. So I wasn't going to dig into it. I had a paycheck and Chinese takeout in my future, and I didn't want to start looking for a job again.

"You're awfully good to Chicky," I said, deftly changing the subject. "She's lucky you're her friend."

"No, I'm the one who's lucky. I wouldn't have my job without Chicky. She pushed for me to get it."

"You knew her before you started working at Yorkville House?"

"Chicky and I met at a rehab center—physical rehab, that is— after I ripped up my knee. We were both in the same boat; I'd just lost my big Broadway shot, and she'd just blown her dream for her golden years. She'd come to New York after living all over the globe, because this was going to be her home for her old age. She told me that this was always her plan, which was why she never put down roots anywhere else. On her first night in her new apart- ment, she went out to shop for groceries. She tripped on a curb and broke her hip. So we both wound up in physical therapy do- ing leg lifts. And we bitched together." He laughed a little at the memory.

"When Chicky was ready to leave the rehabilitation unit at the hospital, she didn't have anyone to help her at home, and they didn't want to release her back to an empty apartment. They were going to send her to a nursing home, which she really didn't want, so I said I'd check up on her every day. I stopped by for six weeks until we were sure the new hip was working."

"Like I said, she was lucky you were around."

He shook his head. "I was in worse shape than she was, I just didn't know it. Chicky's tough. After her fall she realized she shouldn't be on her own, so she moved to Yorkville House because they would look after her. It wasn't what she'd wanted for herself but she was realistic.

"Me, on the other hand? I couldn't admit my dancing days were over. I had a nice apartment in Alphabet City, and a boyfriend who was willing to carry us both until I figured out a new line of work. But there are a lot of doctors in this town who will give you enough pain pills and steroids to get you through anything and I found them. I was three quarters stoned all the time, and even with the meds I was out of my mind with pain because I was insisting on taking dance classes every day.

"My boyfriend walked, which was the only smart thing he

could have done, and since I couldn't last through an entire audition, I wasn't getting any work, so I couldn't pay the rent. Chicky knew all about it and she was worried. So one night I get this phone call." He segued into a really good imitation of Chicky's growl. *"Hey, Show Biz, I've got you a job at the old ladies' home if you want it. Should be right up your alley; you know how good you are with old farts. At least give it a try—for me."* He picked up his coffee cup and smiled down at it. "She'd talked them into hiring me at Yorkville House. I didn't have any training as a health care aide, but she promised them I'd get it." He took a swallow of coffee. "I got the job, quit the dance classes, and canceled my subscription to *Show Business Weekly.* I also stopped the pills. It took me a year to kick them, but I did it."

One look at his eyes told how much it had cost him.

"I moved to Rockland County, where I could afford the rent. And I got the health care training, the way Chicky said I would. Now I'm taking classes at night to get my degree in geriatric social work. My big dream these days? Move back to Manhattan. That's it. I love the city and I hate the frigging train."

"I'm sorry," I said.

"For me? Don't be. Chicky was right: I am good with old farts."

"But you were a dancer on Broadway!" The words slipped out before I could stop them, and I hated myself.

"Excuse me, I am the leading—and, I might add, the only male—Swinging Grandma. I just can't do it for longer than fifteen minutes, and I have to bring my ice bag to performances." He paused. "To paraphrase *Evita,* Don't cry for me, Francesca. I'm in my mid-forties—which is probably why I got hurt in the first place—and the shelf life on my career would have been expiring anyway. Dancers I used to work with are scrambling around trying to figure out what to do next as we speak. I just got a head start on them."

Everything he was saying was responsible and mature. I shivered, just thinking about it. Because what if that was all there was for me—just a Plan B existence I'd have to like because I didn't have a choice?

A vision flashed through my mind. It was the first big charity party Jake and I attended. We stepped out of our rented limo in front of the Museum of Natural History, as photographers' flashes lit up the dark sky. And I heard someone say, "That's Francesca Sewell!"

"I'm still going to write another book of my own," I told Show Biz defiantly.

"Sure. Why not?" he agreed.

"What I'm doing for Chicky is a job. I'll do it as well as I can, but it's not my real work."

"What is?"

"I don't understand."

"Your real work. What's the new book?"

Oh, God. "I can't talk about it yet. That's why I'm doing this biography for Chicky. So I can make enough money to finish my novel." *Or finally start it.*

Show Biz nodded knowledgeably. "Yeah, when you're doing your creative thing, you've got to have a day job to cover the bills."

That was when I realized Chicky hadn't paid me. I had the contract we'd signed safely tucked away in my purse, but in the flurry of saying good-bye, somehow we'd forgotten my check. I thought about running back to Yorkville House to ask her for it, but that seemed pushy. She'd forgotten it. I knew old people could be touchy about memory loss, and I didn't want to embarrass her. I decided to phone her when I got home and remind her. Very gently.

CHAPTER 10

Chicky wasn't embarrassed at all when I called to remind her that I was not yet a paid employee. "Doll Face, at my age I'm lucky if I can remember the day of the week," she growled over the phone. "I figure I'm ahead of the game if I can come up with the president's name." She paused for dramatic effect. "It's Roosevelt—right?" We both chuckled. Then she said, "Seriously, I'm glad you called. I wanted to say something about the book."

"Of course."

"It's a love story. That's what it's really about."

I sighed. I'm sure there are people less qualified to write a love story than I am—the late Jack the Ripper, for instance, and that vicious guy who judges people on *American Idol*—but I'm definitely in the bottom tenth percentile. I mean, check out my track record.

" 'A love story,' " I repeated. "Thanks for the heads-up. I can't wait to get started."

Right after I go play in the traffic in Times Square.

But after I'd hung up, I lay back on my bed and thought about the time when I was a romantic. Back when I was kid. Back when my parents were still together. I was a true believer back then.

MY PARENTS WERE married when Alexandra was nineteen and Dad was twenty-two. Alexandra was the oldest daughter of a prosperous Greek American family that had moved from the Bronx to Riverdale after World War II. Dad—Nathaniel Townsend Sewell III—was the only son of the impoverished wing of a powerful WASP clan that had migrated from Massachusetts to Manhattan sometime after the War of 1812. Grandpa Karras was a truck driver who built himself a small empire of parking lots, garages, and a fleet of moving vans by working eighty hours a week until a month before he died. Grandpa Sewell lost most of his tiny trust fund playing baccarat and drinking at the Yale Club. What he didn't lose, he took with him when he deserted his wife and son for parts unknown before Dad turned five. There is no record of Grandpa Sewell ever working at anything.

When young Nathaniel hit puberty, the Sewells called the family to an emergency session to discuss what should be done with him. Dad rated this concern because he was the only son of the clan's only son and therefore the sole male left to carry on the Sewell name. It was decided that he must be properly groomed to take his place in the world. In Sewell terms this meant immediate removal from his mother's care—and her dingy East Side apartment—to the school that had been educating Sewell men since the American Revolution: Phillips Academy in Andover, Massachusetts, known simply as Andover to the initiated. Here Nathaniel would pick up the basic tenets of muscular Christianity before proceeding on to Yale—another Sewell tradition—where he would forge the friendships that would guarantee him a well-paying gig upon graduation and entrée into all the right social circles. This was how it had always been done in Dad's family, and no one saw any reason for a change.

There was one hitch in this scheme, however. There was no way Dad's mother, Harriet, could afford this pricey regimen of higher learning on her salary as an elevator girl at Saks. The family, which had totally ignored her financial plight up to that moment, was going to have to provide. Two of Dad's maiden aunts were assigned to pick up his tuition at both Andover and Yale—possibly this punishment was imposed on them for not producing heirs of their own—and it was further decreed that when Dad began his freshman year at college, another cousin would take him to Tripler's on Madison Avenue to purchase the navy blue suit, three white cotton shirts, and two silk ties required by all Sewell males attending Yale. Dad would also be given a small check for the rest of his clothes and told to spend it wisely at the Gentlemen's Resale Shop, also on Madison Avenue. Money for his clubs and fraternity would be sent to him as needed by another, even more distant cousin.

The family made it clear that in return for all this largesse, my father was supposed to avoid following in his father's footsteps. He was to make a success of his years at prep school and college. This meant maintaining grades that did not go too far above or below a gentleman's C—no one wanted either a grind or a dummy in the family—and dating the kind of discreetly well-pedigreed girl who could someday become the mother of another generation of Sewells. Instead, Dad never got less than an A in any of his courses and began going out with my highly unacceptable mother in his junior year of college.

His own mother, Harriet, was responsible for this disaster—not directly; she was a timid soul who would never have dreamed of defying her terrifying in-laws—but she had been the cause all the same. It had happened one warm Saturday in August when she was manning the middle elevator at Saks Fifth Avenue. Just as she had stopped the car and was about to announce Ladies's Lingerie, she felt dizzy—it was probably the heat and the fact that she had skipped breakfast—and passed out. My mother happened to be on the elevator that day, shopping for her college wardrobe. It should probably be noted that this excursion represented a major victory for young Alexandra. She was the first Karras female to go beyond high school, and her father had been against it on the grounds that higher learning would turn her into an old maid. Mother had worn him down in a battle that had lasted over two years. So even though she hadn't yet morphed into a feminist crusader, the signs for the future were clearly there.

And anyone who knew her could have predicted that when the elevator operator—my grandmother Sewell—slid to the floor in front of her, Alexandra would spring into action. Dropping her packages, she knelt next to the woman and administered first aid as she had learned it in a lifesaving class at summer camp. After Harriet had come around, she was still rather wobbly, so Alexandra escorted her to the office of the store's manager and demanded that someone take her home immediately. The manager agreed to give Harriet the rest of the day off, but he drew the line at paying for a taxi. She could take the bus, he said. Furious, Alexandra called for the limo her father always provided for her, when she left the safety of Riverdale for the big city, and insisted on hauling the now totally mortified Harriet back to the apartment she shared with her son.

My father, Nate, was working nights that summer, so he was home when his mother and mine burst through the door of Harriet's small fourth-floor walk-up. When I was a child I liked to picture Alexandra as she must have looked to him at that moment.

She wasn't a pretty woman by the standards of her day—her nose was too long and her mouth was too full—but her blue eyes were gorgeous and, indignant as she was, they must have been shooting fire. Her cheeks would have been flushed to the deep rose color that sets off her eyes perfectly, and her mass of red-brown hair had probably escaped from the combs she used to hold it back. When she's angry, and her cause is righteous, my mother can be compelling in a way that goes beyond mere beauty. And my father—with his hazel eyes, blond hair, and patrician features—was always a knockout. So that was what they saw that first time, a passionate girl and a knockout. When I was a kid I was sure it was love at first sight.

Of course, Pete always said I overdid it. "You're trying to make them into some kind of fantasy," he used to say. But damn it, they *were* one. At least, that's what I wanted to believe.

Their families weren't happy about the relationship. The Sewells held another of their famous summits, this time with Dad in attendance. It was pointed out that the family had invested a considerable amount of cash in him and it had certain expectations, which did not include a girl who did not know it was vulgar to say one was "at Yale," because everyone who was anyone said "in New Haven." Dad's response to that piece of old WASP snottiness was to quit Yale and go to work selling cars. See what I mean about true love? The guy gave up an Ivy diploma for her!

Alexandra's father shouted and threatened, but in the end he gave his daughter a wedding. This time it was his wife who went to the mat with him. The truth was, Alexandra often got her own way in the Karras family because her softhearted stepmother felt so sorry for her. Not only had Alexandra's birth mother died when she was only three, but after her death not one member of the woman's family had attempted to contact Alexandra. What was even sadder—as far as Grandma Karras was concerned—was that the poor little girl didn't even look like the rest of the Karras family.

Alexandra's mother had been fair; she was probably of English or Irish descent, although there might have been some German mixed in, and Alexandra's blue eyes and red-brown hair set her apart from her dark-eyed, dark-haired father, stepmother, and half brothers.

"I'm a mutt!" young Alexandra would weep when she wanted something. "I don't belong in this family. No one understands me!" And Grandma Karras would bend over backward to make her feel loved.

So it should have been no surprise that when my mother announced her intention to marry a man who was not Greek Orthodox and Grandpa Karras threw a tantrum, Grandma Karras fought for Alexandra in a way that she never would have for either of her sons. And Grandma Karras and Alexandra won.

The actual wedding was a simple affair—Grandma Karras believed in quitting when she was ahead. The wardrobe Alexandra had collected for her first year at college became her trousseau. The ceremony was held at her church, and Harriet was the only Sewell to attend the festivities. Even she ducked out before everyone went back to the Karras home for lunch. There are no wedding pictures that I know of. Still, the newlyweds were happy in the beginning. I believed that for years—no matter what Pete said.

I OPENED MY eyes. It was six o'clock, time for dinner. I try to tell myself that I've moved on from my childhood, and in most ways I have. But I guess we never really get past certain things, because the pillow was damp. Which seemed to suggest that I'd been crying. Just a little.

CHAPTER 11

The next day I wanted to get an early start, so I dragged Annie out of the apartment at the crack of dawn. Actually, it was only the crack of dawn for Annie and me because we'd been keeping vampire hours; for the rest of Manhattan it was just morning. Which meant, when we stepped into the elevator, we were sharing it with a nanny, a kid in a stroller, and another woman, who was dressed for work and had a minuscule Yorkie on a leash. The nanny was carrying on a conversation sotto voce on her cell phone, and as the elevator door closed, the Yorkie's mistress and I exchanged one of those awkward smiles New Yorkers do when they're trapped in a tight space with strangers. This polite silence was shattered after a few seconds by the Yorkie, who, with a shrill declaration of war, launched itself at Annie. The following dialogue ensued, pretty much simultaneously.

YORKIE OWNER: Lancelot, stop!
ME: Stay cool, Annie!
LANCELOT: (to Annie) I'm gonna tear you apart! I'm gonna shred you!
ANNIE: (to Lancelot) What are you, nuts? My head is bigger than your entire body.
LANCELOT: (to Annie) Bring it on, Big Stuff! (He pulls free of his leash, leaps at her chin, comes away with a mouthful of fur.)
ANNIE: (to Lancelot) Okay, now you're gonna die. (to me, as I grab her harness and pull her back) Come on, you gotta let me kill him. It'll be fast, I promise.

Meanwhile, the kid in the stroller had started to cry.

The nanny put away her cell phone, rammed a pacifier in her charge's mouth, and as the kid, Lancelot's owner, and I watched in fascination, she reached down, picked up the snarling Yorkie by the back of his neck, looked him in the eye, and began talking to him in Spanish. Whatever she said apparently convinced him to rethink his agenda, because he shut up instantly.

By the time Lancelot had chilled out enough to be handed back to his mistress, we'd reached the lobby, but the incident had acted as an icebreaker for us, so instead of taking off we hung around long enough to introduce ourselves. Lancelot's mommy—her word, not mine—was Abigail Barrow; she lived in the penthouse and was a partner at one of the biggest law firms in the city. The nanny's name was Gabriela.

"I don't know what gets into Lancie," Abigail said. "He's just started being so aggressive."

"You are using a new dog walker, yes?" said Gabriela.

"Canine Cuties, yes," said Abigail. "We just started with them."

"They take him out with the big dogs," Gabriela said.

"Oh, no, he gets an individual walk three times a day. I pay extra for that. A fortune."

"Maybe you pay, but I see him with the other dogs when I am in the park with the baby. The other dogs knock your dog over. I don't think it is to hurt him. Maybe they think he is a chew toy, you know?"

"Oh, God." Abigail moaned. "Canine Cuties came so highly recommended."

"Better find someone else," advised Gabriela, and with those comforting words she and the kid split.

"'Find someone else,'" Abigail repeated. "This is our third dog-walking service! The first one quit the business, the second one hired a kid who said it helped him bond with the dogs to urinate with them in the park, and now this! What am I going to do? I work twenty hours a day! I can't walk Lancie myself."

I thought about saying I'd do it for her. When I was writing I needed to take breaks, and Annie always stuck to her no-farther-than-the-curb-when-strolling policy. Walking Lancelot would be relaxing for me. But workaholics like Abigail make me feel like a slacker, and I knew I'd spend at least half an hour trying to explain why I had enough time to walk her dog, and then I'd start apologizing for my entire life. So I didn't make the offer.

After I'd settled Annie back in the apartment, I put on some lipstick in honor of my new status as a solvent person and headed off to Yorkville House.

"COFFEE? TEA?" CHICKY asked. "I can get you a bagel from the dining room. This joint buys really good bagels."

"Nothing, thank you," I said. I don't like to eat things that can stick in my throat when I'm nervous—and in a pinch a really chewy bagel can substitute for whatever that stuff is that expands to fill up the holes in plaster. What surprised me was, I was nervous. I hadn't expected that. I told myself I was being ridiculous. Chicky said she had the whole story in her head, so all I had to do was listen to her and take notes. It would be a couple of days before I actually had to confront my computer again. Not that I was afraid to confront it, I told myself.

Get real, said a voice inside my head. *You're scared to death of the damn thing. And given your last experience with it, who can blame you? Add to that the fact that you'll be writing a love story—*

"So, about our phone call last night," Chicky said, breaking into my thoughts. "What bugs you about writing a love story?"

I could have told her she was imagining things, but I don't think that fast when someone is reading my mind. "It's not an area of expertise for me."

Chicky sat on her daybed and gestured to me to take one of the chairs. "Tell me about that," she commanded.

"What do you want to know?"

"Why did your parents get a divorce?" She said it casually, but she seemed really interested.

"Excuse me, but what does this have to do with me writing your book?"

"I read *Love, Max*, remember? I don't think it was your dog who was angry when your folks split up." She grinned at me. "Doll Face, I'm a nosy old lady. I want to get to know you better."

I reminded myself once again that she was the boss. "Mostly, it was Betty Friedan's fault."

"The woman who wrote *The Feminine Mystique*?"

I nodded. "The book that launched the women's movement. My mother didn't get around to reading it until I was seven, but once she did she'd found her calling. See, Alexandra had always been a rebel. Maybe on some deep level she was pissed off at the world because her birth mother died. Or maybe it was because Grandma Karras indulged her too much trying to compensate."

"Your mother was willful?"

"When Alexandra was fourteen she wrote a term paper for history class, at her very conservative prep school, in which she attempted to prove that the United States government had railroaded the Rosenbergs to the electric chair without cause."

"I remember that case," Chicky said. "How'd she do on the paper?"

"How much do you know about pricey girls' schools in the late sixties?"

"She flunked."

"And she flunked again the next year when she wrote an essay saying that Charles Lindbergh was a Nazi, because Lucky Lindy was a big hero at Westwood Academy for Girls. Alexandra was also gung ho for the peace movement and civil rights. She was always trying to sneak out of the house to protest things in Washington—but she never could get out without waking her parents. Then she met Dad and lost interest in everything but him for a while."

"Until Betty Friedan and the women's libbers," Chicky supplied.

I nodded. "First she tried joining a consciousness-raising group. But she said they were nothing but a bunch of women grousing about the quality of their orgasms."

"Your mother talked to you about orgasms?"

"We were an open household."

"God love her."

"After the consciousness-raising didn't work out, my mother joined the National Organization for Women. Dad was afraid it would be bad for his business, because there were people who said the women in NOW were Commies. But Alexandra managed to smooth him down—in those days she still could—and then she went right back to her meetings. And marches. You name the cause—sex-segregated help-wanted ads, hiring practices that discriminated against women, the ERA, women's reproductive rights—my mother was there. She marched at the White House and at the Supreme Court. In her spare time, she went to college, where she graduated with honors and continued on to get her law degree."

"And what was your father doing?"

"He'd become the star salesman at his Cadillac showroom in Rockland County. Originally, he'd taken the job to piss off his family, but it turned out to be perfect for him. Dad loved cars, especially Caddies. His record for bringing in repeat business was legendary in northeastern automotive circles.

"Then one of his maiden aunts died in the mid-eighties and left him a small inheritance, and Dad bought a dealership of his own. He picked a location twenty minutes away from the town where he'd made his name and his customers not only followed him but brought him new buyers. He was really happy in those days; he made buckets of money, and he loved being his own boss."

I paused for a second and remembered my daddy back then. Sometimes after he'd closed up at night, he could be seen wandering around his showroom, lovingly stroking shiny fender fins and chrome grilles.

Chicky brought me back to the present. "Go on," she prompted. But suddenly it seemed kind of weird to be spilling so much personal family history. I'm usually more discreet. Chicky seemed to sense what I was thinking, because she added, "You tell a story so well, Doll Face. You got me hooked. No wonder you're such a terrific writer."

I'm sure anyone can imagine how these words sounded to a

woman who had just spent the last three years fighting a soul-sucking writer's block. I forgot about discretion fast.

"My mother didn't share my father's enthusiasm for his product," I went on. "If she found herself in a place where there was no public transportation, she preferred to drive the old Renault she and Dad had bought secondhand their first year together. It was an ugly little thing that had been scarred by years of being parked on New York City streets, and as soon as they could afford it Dad tried to persuade Mother to trade up, but she clung to it. Especially after we left the city—a move my brother and I agreed probably pounded the final nail into the coffin of our parents' marriage."

"I was wondering when we were going to get to that," Chicky said. "So far it sounds as if they were different, but they'd managed to adjust."

I thought about that one for a moment. "It probably was more of a strain than any of us realized, including them, but yeah, they did adjust. Even though Dad wasn't really comfortable with Alexandra's politics and she had real issues with big showy American cars.

"It was my mother's law practice that finally did Dad in. She worked on women's rights issues—sexual harassment, equal pay for women, child molestation, rape and domestic violence—and she annoyed some seriously hostile types. Our family started getting threatening phone calls at two in the morning. And Dad wanted her to quit."

"But she wouldn't, of course," said Chicky.

"He said she was endangering her kids. She said she was teaching us to stand up for our beliefs. Finally Dad said if she insisted on antagonizing thugs who enjoyed beating up women, he wanted us to move out of the rat trap where we lived to something safer. At that time, we were still in the building in Greenwich Village my parents had moved to after their wedding. It didn't have a doorman, and sometimes it didn't have a front door. If Mr. Stroika on the first floor had had one too many and forgotten his key when he came home at three in the morning, instead of waking his family, he just ripped the door off its hinges.

"But it wasn't just a safety issue for Dad. We had three bedrooms—well, two and a sleeping alcove for me—and the one bedroom with access to fresh air opened onto a fire escape, so the window was sealed and there were bars on it. It was okay in winter, but when the electric breakers shorted out in the summer and the air-conditioning went off, the place was an oven. The hot water was dicey because the furnace had been installed during the Hoover administration, and sometimes when the exterminator hadn't been around in a couple of months, calling the place a rat trap was the literal truth. Plus, back in the seventies, New York wasn't the well-heeled place it is today, and Dad was tired of the dirt, the noise, and the mayhem.

"To my mother, our Manhattan nest was a little slice of heaven. She loved the city, loved living on our street with the Chinese place on the corner that delivered our dinner most nights, and the greasy spoon on the other corner where she grabbed her breakfast coffee and roll on her way to work. She was even fond of Mr. Stroika, when he was sober. As far as she was concerned, all this far outweighed the lack of space and trivial annoyances like irregular heat and no fresh air. But she couldn't fight Dad about the safety problems. Our neighborhood was what was known as marginal, and the front-door thing was worrisome. She agreed to move out of the city.

"Dad bought us a big, beautiful Victorian in Rye, New York, where he installed a state-of-the-art security system and a big German shepherd—"

"Max," Chicky broke in.

"His name was Fierce, which turned out to be wishful thinking on Dad's part. Fierce was a lover, not a fighter; he greeted strangers with big slurpy kisses, and he cowered in our laps during thunderstorms. But as far as we knew, the security system was perfect. It was never tested."

"No crime in Rye?" Chicky said.

"Alexandra said the police carried briefcases instead of weapons. She didn't say it fondly. But Dad was in heaven. He'd already opened two more Cadillac dealerships in Westchester County, and he was glad to be moving closer to his work. He figured he'd seen the last of the Chinese takeout; he enrolled us in a country club, the most exclusive one in the area. It never occurred to him to find out if it had any minority members."

I watched Chicky process this information. "Your mother disapproved?"

"She said it was clear that the club was racist—just like the rest of the goddamn suburbs. Dad said, *Now who's being prejudiced?* She said, *When was the last time you saw a black person in Rye?*

"Alexandra never set foot inside Dad's club, not even after an African American lawyer and his family joined it. My mother just couldn't wrap her brain around the idea of grown-ups getting together to play sports and hang around a clubhouse for the fun of it—*fun* being a four-letter word in her dictionary. More important, she hated our new life. For the entire time we were in Rye, she and my brother, Pete, mourned for Manhattan."

I have to admit that as I was talking, I kept checking Chicky to make sure she still seemed enthralled. And every time I did, she did. That was what made me keep going, even though I was getting into more and more private stuff. I'm not proud of this, I'm just saying.

"I know now that Dad had dreams for us when he moved us to the burbs," I told my audience of one. "He saw himself playing tennis with Pete at the club on summery Saturday afternoons, and he hoped I'd become one of those cheery girls who swam in the club pool and collected a bunch of friends. Pete developed into a precocious math genius with lousy hand–eye coordination. I did my best to please Dad by signing up for swimming lessons, but I was seven pounds overweight by the time I was eleven, and I burst into tears every time I saw myself in a bathing suit.

"But Dad's biggest dream was about Alexandra. He didn't expect her to cook or clean or do laundry; he knew he'd have to provide a maid to do that. But now that she had such a gorgeous house, he hoped she'd take an interest in running it. He saw himself hosting friends at exquisitely served dinners for ten in a lovely home that ran like a well-oiled clock."

Chicky made a little clicking sound with her tongue. "Your father really thought that was going to happen?"

"Yeah. He should have known better. Mother continued going into the city to wage war against creeps with anger issues and large corporations with issues about equal pay for women. She worked as many hours as she ever had, but now she added a forty-five minute commute to her workday."

"No time for the well-oiled clock."

"Not much. When we lived in Greenwich Village the apartment was small enough that she could muck it out for an hour every couple of weeks, and if she missed a month or two, there was no direct sunlight so you never really saw the dirt. For dinner she had that trusty Chinese place. But the house in Rye was well-lit and showed every speck of dust. And you had to drive to the Chinese restaurant for your takeout—which, Pete liked to point out, wasn't authentic Chinese. Since Alexandra wasn't going to waste her precious time making beds and scrubbing bathrooms, the old Victorian quickly turned into a shambles."

"What about you kids? Didn't you do chores?"

"I don't think that ever occurred to Alexandra. She was more interested in our grades and what we were going to do to save the world. Dad begged her to hire whoever she needed to keep the house up—a cook, a maid, maybe a couple of maids. He told her money was no object.

"But my mother couldn't allow another woman to do the grunt work she was too liberated to do herself. When Dad got desperate and hired a housekeeper for us, the woman quit, because after a couple of months of talking to Alexandra she realized that she should aspire to a higher goal than cleaning up after other people. She did send us Christmas cards for years, though.

"My parents began to fight much more seriously than they had before. At first it was about housekeeping and work and lifestyle. But then it started to be about life. It got meaner and nastier. But I still thought—" I stalled out. This was the hard part, the part I still hate to think about.

"You still thought they could make it work," Chicky said softly.

"I thought *I* could make it work. I wished on first stars and birthday candles, and I prayed. I set up a little shrine in my closet, and I lit candles."

"In your closet where your clothes were hanging? You were lucky you didn't set the house on fire!"

"Actually, I had a couple of near misses. So I dumped the shrine. But whenever I had some spare change I bought *Ladies Home Journal*—they had an advice column for couples called 'Can This Marriage Be Saved?'—and I tried to pick up pointers for my parents."

"I bet that went over big with your mother. *Ladies Home Journal* wasn't exactly a women's liberation rag."

"I never told her where the advice was coming from. But I'd say something about pleasing your man, and she'd look at me like I had two heads."

"When did you give up?"

"On the marriage? Never. I didn't care how miserable we were, I wanted my family to stay together. Even if we hated one another."

Chicky studied me for a moment. "Remember when you told me all you've ever wanted was to be happy? I think I can see why that hasn't worked out so well for you."

"Well, it didn't matter what I wanted. My father found a woman who did please him, and he and my mother split up."

"And the message you got was, If you want to hang on to a man, you have to stroke him like a pet Pekinese."

"My dad wasn't like that!"

"I didn't say he was. I said that was what you thought. So when your husband didn't understand what you were going through with your new book, you thought it was *your* fault."

And right there she'd put her finger on the problem with being the kind of person who tries to learn life lessons. Sometimes you get one wrong. But I wasn't about to admit that.

"Jake wasn't all that bad."

"Of course not. But there are men who can actually help you when the going gets tough."

Before I could respond, there was a knock at the door and Show Biz poked his head in. "Hi, Francesca. Chicky, the van is downstairs."

"The hospital!" she said. "I forgot the Swinging Grandmas were performing today." She rushed over to her theater trunk, opened it, and pulled out a bunch of sheet music and a blue feather boa. "To be continued, Doll Face," she said, as she tossed the boa around her neck with a flourish.

"Wait," I said. "You were going to start talking me through the memoir."

She turned back. "I have something much more useful for you." She went back to the trunk and opened it again. "Let's face it, at my age, I'm not exactly a linear thinker anymore. I ramble." She rummaged around. "Aha, here we are." She fished out a plastic grocery bag and held it out to me. "This should get you started."

"What is it?"

"Some audiotapes I recorded for you. It's just the beginning of the story. I have more I'm working on. And I've got some pictures in the bag too."

"Chicky, we'll be late," Show Biz said.

"Right." She held the door open for me. "Those tapes should be easy to follow. If they're not, just give me a call."

"But this isn't the way I planned to work. I was going to listen to you and take notes and—"

"That's so last-century. It's all about technology now."

"I'm not sure I can work from tapes."

"Of course you can. I have total faith in you." And then she reached up on tiptoe and gave me a kiss on the cheek. "Working on this story is going to be good for you, Doll Face. You have no idea!"

I wanted to stop her, but she and Show Biz were already hustling down the hallway. There was nothing to do but follow with my plastic grocery bag. After all, she was the boss.

CHAPTER 12

I decided to walk back to my apartment. Reminiscing with Chicky had started the memories going, and I've found it's easier to stroll down Memory Lane when you're actually strolling, as opposed to fighting for a seat on the downtown bus. There may be a life lesson in that—but then again, I could be wrong.

I discovered the healing power of chocolate when I was fourteen. That was when Mother found out that when Dad said he was checking out the Cadillac dealership in Greenwich, Connecticut, he was actually in a motel in Rowayton with the twenty-two-year-old niece of one of his best friends at the club. The girl's name was Sheryl, and she was tall and blond, with legs that began somewhere under her armpits. She personified the word *cheery.* Her romance with Dad had started when she'd asked him for a few pointers on her tennis game.

"I guess that wasn't the only thing he gave her," Pete said.

I told him to shut up.

"Francesca, grow up," Pete said. "This family is history. Thank God."

When Dad started sleeping in the guest room, I told Pete it was a good thing. "They're giving each other space," I said. The night we heard Alexandra crying as she came up the stairs alone—the one and only time she did that, by the way—I took as a good sign too. "She's realizing how much she loves Dad," I said.

Then my mother and father had the Talk with us (there's the T word again). You know the one: where the parents call the kids into the living room and tell them they are not going to be part of a family anymore but they mustn't take it personally because these things happen, and it's nobody's fault, and the parents will still love the kids very much, just from different zip codes, and maybe different time zones, and definitely on alternate weekends. After this preliminary announcement was out of the way, Alexandra added an upbeat little speech in which she told us that even though she and Dad hadn't had a good marriage, they were going to have a great divorce; one that was low on drama and high on negotiation and compromise. Even after that, I still hoped my parents would work it out.

I finally believed the marriage was over when I saw Mother's to-do list. *Shop for groceries*, it read. *Take deposition for Sylwigger case*. And then, after several other entries, at the bottom of the page I saw *Divorce Nate*. Seeing the words written out in Mother's classy girls'-school handwriting finally drove home the truth.

Along with Pete, I refused the psychiatric counseling our parents offered us in case we had concerns we weren't comfortable discussing with them. I reassured them that I agreed with everyone else that this was for the best. But I was lying.

No matter how hard I try, I am not a fan of make-the-best-of-it thinking. Maybe it's true sometimes that when a door closes a window opens, but in my experience, most of the time you're just locked in the damn room. And while I get it that we have to make lemonade out of lemons, I'm a hell of a lot happier if we can all admit that the process usually isn't much fun, and when we're finished we'd probably rather be drinking champagne.

But it seemed I was the only one who felt that way about our family. My mother and father were so glad to be getting rid of each other that they were nicer than they'd been in years. Dad was on his way to California, where he was going to marry Sheryl and start a new life. His bride-to-be was a native of Pasadena—she'd been visiting the East Coast for the summer—and now she was homesick for perpetual sunshine and her family. And, to be honest, Dad wanted a fresh start. His affair with the niece of one of his now former best friends had caused something of a scandal in Westchester, and he didn't feel comfortable in his old haunts anymore. Plus, he'd gone to California to visit his future in-laws—Pete enjoyed pointing out that Sheryl's father was only a few years older than Dad—and he had loved the climate and the people and the business prospects. He was going to take a flyer on a new kind of dealership—selling fancy foreign cars to movie stars.

Dad had always loved the song "Everything's Coming Up Roses," and he sang it a lot during the weeks while we were packing up the only life I'd ever known. Sometimes Mother sang along with him. She was already checking the Manhattan real estate section of the *Times*. As for Pete, he was glad the fighting was over and he could concentrate on his schoolwork—at twelve he'd already set his heart on early admission to Harvard. Even our dog Fierce was going to benefit; he was moving with Dad and Sheryl to Pasadena, where it only rained twice a year—so no more scary thunderstorms for him. Everything was working out for the best for everyone. I hated how civilized it all was.

I didn't want Mother and Dad to be out for blood the way some of my friends' parents had been during their divorces, but it seemed indecent that no one was grieving just a little. I did my bit for the cause by discovering chocolate and putting on another fifteen pounds. I was a walking cliché.

The love fest moved forward. Alexandra asked for nothing in the divorce settlement; Dad graciously insisted on giving her the house. She agreed he must have visitation rights with us for the entire summer vacation; he wanted her to have all the big holidays because he wouldn't dream of taking us away from her. Dad did get a little teary before he left, when he took Pete and me for a fancy dinner at Ruby Foo's—my family just couldn't seem to shake the Chinese leitmotif—but he comforted all three of us with promises of his spring wedding and phone calls whenever we wanted to make them, and the fun we'd all have together during our California summers. By the end of the meal he was feeling quite perky again, I went to Ruby Foo's ladies' room and threw up.

Alexandra dumped the house in Rye and we moved back into the city. She bought a co-op in a prewar building on the Upper West Side, which, she said, was loaded with charm. But she never got around to furnishing it, so there really wasn't much difference between it and our original dump in Greenwich Village—except that it was in a better neighborhood. And she did let Dad pay for private schools for Pete and me—defending abused women didn't bring in the big bucks.

Pete was enrolled in the toughest prep school in Manhattan, where he quickly skipped two years and became the star of the mathematics department. Now he was in the same grade as I was. Ask me how much I loved *that* when I was fourteen. Especially since I was turned down at all the top-tier schools because I had developed what was diagnosed as a learning disability in math— and no, I don't want to dig into the probable psychological ramifications of that. I tested off the charts in language skills and the humanities, but my overall grade average wasn't all that hot. I finally wound up in that progressive school in Tribeca I've already described. The one for bright kids who need what the catalog referred to as a "special environment."

Every morning I woke up in my bedroom with the boxes that Mother still hadn't unpacked stacked in the corner, fought Pete for our one bathroom, and grabbed a stale French doughnut from the street vendor on my way to the subway to Tribeca. When we first moved back to the city, there were times when I missed Rye, but all I had to do was listen to one of Alexandra's stories about a kid she was trying to protect from a mother's abusive boyfriend or a molesting grandfather to know how lucky I was. I reminded myself of that every time I got on a packed subway train or stepped in dog poop on the sidewalk. I reminded myself that I lived in one of the greatest cities in the world, a city that was the rival of Rome, Paris, and London. And I *came* to believe it. By the time Pete and I were taking off for California and Dad's wedding day, I had really settled in.

PETE HADN'T WANTED to attend Dad's wedding. We were on spring vacation from our respective schools, and his physics teacher had offered to help him work on a project for some kind of statewide math-geek competition. But Alexandra had put her foot down.

"You're going to see your father get married," she'd informed Pete. "And you're going to make nice. It's good that someone's finally making the man happy. Just as long as I don't have to do it." It was great that she felt that way—unless you were wishing that she'd be just a little jealous over the man who was the father of her children.

Sheryl's three-ring circus of a wedding was everything my

mother had raised Pete and me to loathe. It featured two bands, a buffet for three hundred, and the bride looking gorgeous in a cream-puff dress, with the Girls as her attendants. As I said before, this collection of die-hard pals had been together since high school, and they would stick by one another through college, marriages, divorces, second marriages, finding God, therapy, illness, and, in one case, substance abuse. They also shared mani-pedi moments and the same trainer at their gym. They were an eye-opener for me; I had never met a group of women who shamelessly admitted that they never thought about world peace—or the plight of anyone they didn't know personally. On the other hand, they were very sweet, so I tried not to judge.

Actually, I tried not to judge anything in Dad's new life. Not his huge new house, that was almost an exact replica of the one in Rye but decorated in sherbet shades of chintz, or his new friends, who never seemed to notice when they were being sexist, or the fact that Sheryl insisted on referring to Alexandra as my Mommie even though by that point Pete and I had stopped calling her Mother and now referred to her as "Alexandra" because she felt it was more empowering for us. I didn't judge any of it. Pete, on the other hand, spent most of our time in Sheryl's cheery home rolling his eyes and making slips like, "When I get home to the United States . . . sorry, I mean New York—"

"I'll win him over," Sheryl said to me. "I'm good at that."

She did eventually. But it took years. And his resistance had nothing to do with Alexandra . . . at least, it didn't directly; it wasn't about Pete protecting her honor or any of that. Sheryl just wasn't the kind of woman Pete could appreciate when he was young. He'd grown up with a mother who was brilliant; a conversation with Alexandra could hopscotch from affirmative action, to gay rights, to the Supreme Court, to animal cruelty, to blood diamonds, without her breaking a sweat. By contrast, when Sheryl went to England with Dad she wore a full-length mink coat, and as far as we could tell she never thought about its origins. Ditto for the diamond earrings Dad gave her. As for the Supreme Court, I'm not sure Sheryl knew what it was.

The differences between Sheryl and Alexandra didn't end with political and global awareness. Alexandra's idea of entertaining at home was to boil up a pot of pasta, dump some bottled sauce on it, and tell her guests to grab a seat on the floor. These fetes were known in her social circles as Alexandra's Bad Spaghetti Nights. The ensuing discussions, fueled by some not-very-good wine, would become loud and impassioned and last until three in the morning. My mother would tell funny stories about the judges she argued in front of and the pols she worked with; her imitation of Mayor Giuliani was considered one of the best in the city. When Sheryl had a dinner party, a caterer cooked, a maid served, and finger bowls were involved. After the meal the sexes would separate to opposite sides of the living room to chat, which usually led to some comment from Pete about women binding their feet, which no one but Dad and I actually got.

I understood where Pete was coming from; there was no contest between our mother and the woman who had replaced her when it came to wit or worthy thoughts. And Alexandra was a good mother—she saw to it that Pete and I could use the Dewey decimal system the second we could spell the word *library*, and as soon as we were old enough to cross the street on our own we had memberships to the Metropolitan Museum, MOMA, the Museum of Natural History, and the New-York Historical Society. We saw Shakespeare in the Park every summer and *The Nutcracker* every Christmas. Alexandra also taught us both to play a mean game of poker.

But Sheryl had our father.

In addition to dressing badly and not allowing makeup to touch my face, I stayed faithful to my mother's ideals by refusing to learn any of Sheryl's homemaking skills—if I'm honest, that stuff really did bore the hell out of me—but I have to admit I was touched by the fresh flowers that showed up on the table next to my bed when I was in California. And I liked the embroidered hand towels in the bathrooms, and the special meals Sheryl made for me that were low calorie without tasting like it, so I always lost weight during the summer. I even enjoyed the spa days Sheryl planned. I liked the fancy robes they gave us, and the tiny lunch on the pretty china, and most of all I loved the idea that a dollop of avocado cream would make me into a raving beauty.

As far as Pete was concerned, Dad's domestic tranquillity could never outweigh Sheryl's deficiencies in the brains department. "What the hell can he find to *talk* about with her?" Pete would demand. "Doesn't he go out of his mind?"

There were times when you could see that Dad wished she read more than celebrity and fashion magazines. But it didn't really matter to him all that much. As I watched Sheryl smile her way through her orderly days, planning her pretty dinner parties and keeping her legs in shape, I knew she was a success at the one thing my mother had never mastered. I tried to learn a life lesson from that, but where the Sheryl model left me with my fabulous language skills, no discernible domestic ability, and not-so-taut inner thighs I had no idea. So I learned the wrong lesson. I didn't figure out that Sheryl was genuinely loving and caring and that was why she made my Dad happy. I thought the lesson was, You've got to pet your man like a Pekinese. *Thank you, Chicky, for pointing that out.*

I'D REACHED MY neighborhood. There was an electronics store on the corner where I was hoping to buy an old-fashioned tape recorder. Like most people, I'd gone digital in the last few years, but I was going to need a recorder in order to listen to Chicky's cassettes. The saleschild in the store was stunned to discover that her employers carried such an antique and listened in horrified admiration as I explained about the dark ages when I was a kid and we had to depend on video players and Walkmans for our instant entertainment. I left the store feeling very strong, like a survivor of a tougher, leaner age.

I continued feeling that way until I was in my apartment and heading down the hallway to my office. That was when I looked inside the grocery bag and realized that Chicky hadn't given me her check. Again. Now I wasn't sure what to do. According to all the ghostwriter websites I'd read, I shouldn't work until I had my first payment in hand. But I knew that my already shaky confidence would deflate like a defective pool toy if I had to wait to get started. Besides, Chicky had said she had faith in me.

I called Yorkville House, but of course, Chicky was off doing her thing with the Swinging Grandmas. I told myself it was understandable that she'd forgotten my money in the flurry of leaving her room. I left a message, asking her to put the check and the contract in the mail ASAP, and then I continued on my way to my office. Well, I *said* I'm a sucker for people who say they have faith in me. And I have that core of marshmallow fluff.

As soon as I walked into my home office, nasty flutters started in my stomach. The room itself was great; it was the brightest in the apartment and had a partial view of the park. But I'd spent too many miserable hours in there and had suffered too many defeats. "I can't work in here," I told Annie, who had accompanied me on the trek down the hall. Then I realized that I didn't have to.

Before I met Jake, I used to write on my laptop in bed. We'd set up my office because, during my desperate phase when I was trying to work through the nights, I kept Jake awake. But now the only beauty sleep I'd be disturbing was Annie's. She has slept through parades, fire alarms, and the time the former sitcom star who lived in our building tried to drive his Maserati through the lobby after a weekend of partying.

It took a couple of hours to move my bookcases and filing cabinets into the bedroom, but when I was finally on the bed, propped up with every pillow and cushion I owned, with my computer in my lap, the tape recorder plugged in, a huge glass of cold Diet Coke on my nightstand, and two chocolate bars at my side, I felt . . . not exactly brimming with confidence, but less fluttery.

"There are perks to living alone," I informed Annie.

(I know every newly single person discovers that, so it's not exactly a startling life lesson, but they don't all have to be eureka moments—do they?)

Annie seemed pleased to be in the bedroom with me. I don't think she'd ever liked my office, with the slick furniture our decorator and Jake loved; it was too slippery for canine napping. Annie had hung out in the office with me because the Good Dog Manual dictated that she stick to me like Velcro when I was in trouble, and whenever I opened the computer—the source of all evil, as far as she was concerned—she knew trouble was on the way. But the bedroom was much more to her liking. I'd persuaded the decorator to let me have a couple of cushy chairs in there, and a plush carpet, and Annie's bed was tucked away in the corner.

Annie's hackles went up briefly when she saw me take the Evil Laptop out of its case, and she did a little free-form growling at the tape recorder, just to let it know who was boss, but then she settled down next to me on the bed to keep her vigil.

It was time for me to get to work. There was an envelope in the grocery bag that had pictures in it. I put them on the bed next to me, said a quick prayer to whatever goddess handles female writers, unwrapped a chocolate bar, and turned on the tape recorder. Chicky's voice filled the room.

CHAPTER 13

"First, you're going to get a little history lesson, Doll Face," said Chicky, in her husky growl, "because you've got to understand what vaudeville *was*. I always think vaude, as they called it, was the real American show business. It hit big around the time when all the European immigrants were coming to this country—from around 1900 on. You had the Irish, the Italians, the Greeks, the Slovaks, the Germans, and the Jews from Russia and Poland. They all settled together in a big noisy mass in cities like New York and Chicago. It wasn't easy, but they were hopeful people with big dreams. That's why they came."

As Chicky talked, I pictured the areas of New York as I knew them today: Little Italy; Chinatown; the Lower East Side, where the Jewish families had settled at the turn of the last century; Hell's Kitchen, which had been mostly Irish; and Yorkville, where the Germans had lived. I tried to imagine those neighborhoods the way they must have been when they were teeming with people who came from different cultures and spoke different languages, all of them trying to make their way and give their kids a better life than they had had back home. What kind of courage or craziness did it take to stick it out in the American melting pot?

"Vaudeville was the immigrants' entertainment," Chicky went on. "You had Irish acts, Italian acts, 'Dutch' acts—performed in a German accent with German characters—and Jewish acts. There were African Americans working in vaudeville, starring in their own routines at a time when the best they could hope for on the legit stage was a bit part playing a servant. People learned about other nationalities in those vaudeville houses, even when the actors were making fun. You take a greenhorn from Amalfi, a kid who's only been in this country a couple of months and never met anyone who wasn't Italian. You bring him to the theater, and he sees an Irish act doing a clog waltz. A couple of minutes later, the Irish kid sitting next to him watches an Italian act doing the tarantella." Chicky laughed on the tape. "Hell, vaudevillians could have taught those bozos at the United Nations a thing or two."

I turned off the tape recorder. Once again, I could picture it: performers from all those different backgrounds, standing in the wings waiting to make their entrances. I could hear them murmur final instructions to one another: *Remember to wait for that laugh. Don't rush the last chorus of the song.* Then they'd say a quick prayer in Polish, or Yiddish, or whatever language they'd heard around the house when they were children. I thought about my mother, the self-proclaimed mutt. I thought of my own mixed bag of American forebears. And for the first time since I'd finished *Love, Max* I felt connected to the material I was going to write.

That's when writing is a joy. Please don't ask me to explain this, because I'm damned if I can. I turned the tape recorder back on.

"Good vaude had something for everyone," Chicky went on. "Animal acts, acrobats, dancers, singers, kid acts with a bunch of youngsters cutting up and doing stunts, and flash acts—those were the big numbers with chorus girls singing and dancing. There were novelty acts, like sideshows at the circus—Siamese twins and the double-jointed man, things like that. But the cream, the thing that really made vaudeville what it was, were the comedy acts: Burns and Allen, the Marx Brothers, Buster Keaton, Milton Berle. They all started out in vaudeville.

"Vaudeville was *family* entertainment—that was a big selling point. Before vaude you had variety shows that were aimed at a stag audience, and the material could get racy. But when women started wanting to have fun, vaude came in, and it was clean. There were warnings posted backstage at the theaters with lists of things performers couldn't say, like *slob* or *son of a gun*." Chicky's voice chuckled. "Can you imagine what those theater owners would have done if they could see cable television today?"

I started making notes as fast as I could.

"My pop started out as half of a double comedy act when he was just a kid; he worked with a boy named Benny George. Benny's real name was Benjamin Gerhardt; his folks were German and he'd been born and raised in the old German neighborhood on the Upper East Side. Benny and Pop came from very different kinds of backgrounds—and I'm not just talking about nationality or religion. Pop grew up in Little Italy, as the middle kid of five. His dad died when he was six, and his mother worked two shifts in the shirt factory, so the children pretty much raised themselves. Pop shined shoes, sold newspapers, and ran errands to bring in extra money. He stuck it out in school until he was thirteen, and then he hit the streets doing an act, telling funny stories and singing and dancing.

"As hard as Pop had it, Benny had it easy. His father died when Benny was young, same as Pop, but Benny was an only child, and his folks had their own business, a bakery that Mrs. Gerhardt continued to run as a widow. Benny's mother gave him all the advantages; he had his own bedroom, nice clothes, and music lessons, and she always saw to it that he had a little money in his pocket.

"She wanted Benny to be classy, so one summer she hired a student from Columbia University to teach him how to speak without a New York accent and which fork to use at a dinner party. Mrs. Gerhardt had high hopes for Benny. She wanted him to go to college and become a professional man, a doctor or a lawyer or a CPA. She was a tough bird who expected things to go the way she planned. But her Benny was even tougher, and he wanted to go into show business.

"Pop and Benny met when Pop was twelve and Benny was fourteen. They each had an act they'd put together—Benny was singing ballads and, like I said, Pop was dancing, singing, and telling jokes—and they ran into each other when they were both trying to work the same street corner outside the Metropolitan Opera House. It was a prime location because people lined up there a couple of hours before the performances to buy the cheap tickets, and if the weather was nice, the pickings were good for a decent street act. But not for two acts. Pop and Benny realized they could either fight or team up, and since neither one of them wanted to get their clothes bloody they went to a nearby soda fountain and worked out the details of their new partnership. They started an act called Masters and George, the Laughter Boys. Pop was Masters and Benny was George. Doll Face, you've got a picture of Benny and Pop when they were kids. Benny's the chubby one."

I looked at the pile of pictures she'd given me. All of them had been carefully numbered, with little notes telling me the order in which I was to view them. The first shot did indeed show two kids grinning into the camera for all they were worth. I recognized Joe Masters immediately; the face that didn't quite fit together had been even more memorable on him as a youngster. But Chicky had indulged in wild understatement when she'd said Benny was chubby; he was round. His head was a sphere that rested without a visible neck on the larger sphere that was his torso, and his legs, while long, were essentially an afterthought. His face would have been attractive if it were slimmer; his long nose and full mouth were handsome, and he had a mop of thick blond curly hair. But his eyes had an expression I knew only too well from my own mirror. It was that half-defiant, half-hangdog look worn by kids who spend most of their lives battling their weight and losing the fight. Since he had several inches on Joe, as well as his poundage, Benny dominated the picture—but not in a good way.

"Benny and Joe did okay in the streets for over a year," Chicky's voice informed me, "but they wanted to work in a real theater. They started putting together a new act. They rehearsed in Benny's mother's apartment; you can imagine how happy she was about that. Picture it, Doll Face, these two kids trying to come up with an act that was going to make them stars, while downstairs in the bakery, Mrs. Gerhardt was rolling out pie crust and glowering up at the ceiling."

I closed my eyes and pictured the boys I'd just seen, in a tiny turn-of-the century parlor. There would be wooden wainscoting halfway up the walls and some kind of dark wallpaper on the top half. A round rug on the floor that the boys would roll up so they could practice their dance routines. And below them, Mrs. Gerhardt's malevolent presence.

"My pop was in the apartment when Benny's mother found out

he had quit school to go into the business," Chicky's voice said. "Benny was sixteen and Pop was fourteen. Pop never forgot that day."

A description of the scene followed. I listened to all of it. Then, despite Annie's growled protests—she still harbored bad feelings about the Evil Laptop—I opened my computer, took a deep breath, and started typing.

CHAPTER 14

Upper East Side, New York City

1914

The bakery window was big, so it was way too easy for Mrs. Gerhardt to look out and see Joe Masters climbing up the steps that led to the family quarters above the shop. Benny's parents had purchased the building before Benny was born, and when his father had installed the bakery on the ground floor, he'd had a huge window cut into the front wall so he could display his cakes and pies. But his doughnuts were the bakery's biggest seller. Those small pillows of sweet dough were fried on the outside to crispy perfection, dusted heavily with powdered sugar, and stuffed with the fruit preserves Benny's mother made fresh every day. When Benny's father was alive, he woke up before dawn to heat the fryer, and the customers began lining up even before the aroma of the yeasty batter puffing up in the hot oil filled the street. After Mr. Gerhardt's death, Benny's mother took his place behind the fryer. She did a brisk business with commercial outlets too. There were at least half a dozen grocery stores that sold Gerhardt's doughnuts, and no self-respecting restaurant in the area would have dreamed of serving any others. Every morning, white bakery boxes with green trim containing one dozen doughnuts each would be stacked up in the window, waiting for the boy who would run around the neighborhood delivering them.

It was three in the afternoon now, and Joe was hoping Mrs. Gerhardt would be in the kitchen in the back of the shop. She spent her afternoons down there, whipping up batches of cookies and dinner rolls, emerging only when the front doorbell signaled that she had a customer. That was why Joe had timed his appearance at the house for this moment—so she wouldn't see him. Mrs. Gerhardt hated Joe. It wasn't anything personal, Joe knew that, she just didn't want her son to go into show business and Joe was Benny's partner in their act. If she caught sight of Joe climbing the steps to her front door, she'd stand in the huge window and glare at him as he rang the bell. Joe wasn't afraid of her, exactly, but he did try to avoid her as much as possible.

This afternoon he was in luck. According to a sign on the bakery door, Mrs. Gerhardt was running an errand and would be back in half an hour. Joe made his way up the stairs, waited for Benny to open the door, and followed his friend to the parlor, where Benny had pushed back the furniture and placed their sheet music—carefully annotated with their key and tempo changes—on the piano. Next to the sheet music was a sheaf of papers that was even more valuable; it was the only complete script Benny and Joe had of their entire act—patter, jokes, song introductions, stage business—all of it painstakingly written out by Joe.

"You got past Ma?" Benny asked.

"She's not in the shop," Joe assured him.

"Probably out buying sugar." Benny paused, then added grimly, "I've got to get out of this dump. Got to get a place of my own."

He said that every time Joe came over to rehearse. Joe, who had already moved out of his family's cramped apartment to make more room for his remaining siblings, thought Benny didn't know how good he had it, with his mother still providing his bed and board. But he kept his mouth shut. Benny got furious anytime anyone tried to say anything nice about Mrs. Gerhardt.

"We in the contest?" Joe changed the subject. A vaudeville theater on Coney Island held a talent contest for new acts three times a year, and the first one of the season was scheduled for the following weekend. The winning act would be awarded a spot on a tour that was playing a string of small theaters in upstate New York. It wasn't like booking the Palace, but for Masters and George it would be a big break. The challenge was getting into the contest; the list of entrants had been full for a couple of days by the time Benny heard about it. Benny was the one who stayed on top of theatrical opportunities for the act, but this time he'd been too late.

"I'm still trying to nab a spot," Benny said. When he wasn't keeping up on the latest show-business gossip, Benny hung around booking agents' offices, trying to make friends with anyone who could help their act. But none of his contacts had an in with the promoters of this contest. So for the past few days Benny had been schlepping out to Coney Island with a box of dougnuts for the stage manager who worked the vaudeville house. So far this freeloader hadn't agreed to put Masters and George on the list of contestants, but Joe had faith in Benny's ability to sweet-talk him into it eventually. You couldn't be as driven as Benny was and not succeed. And, according to Benny, the man was devoted to the doughnuts.

"Of course, he'd get us in right now, if I could . . . you know." Benny held his hand out and rubbed his fingers and thumb together in the universal gesture of paying a bribe. He brightened for a second. "You get paid tomorrow, don't you? We only need a few bucks."

Joe shook his head. He'd picked up a job working as an assistant for a house painter, but the money he was earning was already earmarked. "My rent is due. And my mother had to take my sister to the doctor," he said. "Don't you have any cash?"

"Just what Ma gives me." Benny never worked. Now he shrugged his meaty shoulders and grinned. "Don't worry, I'll think of something," he said. "Let's rehearse. Take it from the top."

And with that time-worn phrase, the boys began running through their material.

The basis of the act—which had been conceived and written by Joe—was that Benny was a bad piano player. And the truth was, he really wasn't very good, because Benny had never had the patience to practice. So the act opened with Benny, the pianist, accompanying Joe, the singer, and butchering the song. As Joe became more and more frustrated—with lots of mugging and comic takes—Benny hit more and more clinkers. Finally, he stopped playing and the zingers started to fly. The verbal fight turned physical—this was the knockabout comedy section of the act, carefully staged and timed to the second so neither performer got hurt. Mid-battle, the script called for them to realize they were fighting in front of the audience. More double takes and mugging followed and finally, in perfect harmony, they finished the song Benny had been destroying at the beginning of the act. They were practicing the harmonies when they heard a voice behind them.

"So," it said. The boys turned to see Mrs. Gerhardt standing in the doorway. She was wearing her second-best dress, a drab garment with a high collar and long sleeves that covered her arms down to the wrists. She only wore it for special events, and that—

added to the fact that her face was red and her bright blue eyes were shooting angry sparks—made it clear that something was up. But when she spoke her voice was low and calm. Too calm.

"So," she repeated quietly. "All my son's teachers tell me he's a smart boy. He could go to college, they tell me. He could be a doctor or a lawyer, he could do anything. That's what they tell me." Her face was getting redder. "But does my son listen to them? Does he stay in school and make something of himself?"

"Ma—" Benny began, but his mother rolled over him.

"No, my son the genius quits. He gets into a fight—like a hooligan. Like a bum. And when they tell him he's wrong he quits."

Joe watched Benny's face close down. "I didn't start it," he said stonily. The truth was, with his snooty way of talking, his fancy manners, and his weight, Benny was often the target of would-be bullies. These boys were surprised to find that Benny was not the easy victim they'd expected. In spite of his rarefied ways, he fought back. And Benny fought mean. "I was the only one the teacher put in detention," he told his mother. "It wasn't fair."

"It was your punishment! A man takes his punishment!"

"School is a waste of time. Joe has to work, so I'm the only one who can make the rounds of the booking agents' offices for the act. I was going to quit anyway."

"Without telling me? I have to find out from your principal? My son the genius makes a decision like this and doesn't even talk to me?"

"How could—?" Benny started to say, but once again she barreled over him.

"Sixteen years old!" she said. She stalked across the room and, as Joe watched, she grabbed the sheet music off the piano. "Sixteen and you're ruining your life. For this?"

"Don't!" Benny yelled, but she was already tearing up their sheet music.

"For this we came from Germany?" she demanded, as the confetti she'd just made fell to the floor at her feet. "For this your father worked himself to death? So you could quit school and be a bum?"

"I'm not going to be a bum. I'm going to—" But before Benny could finish, she had picked up the pile of papers on which Joe had written the final version of their act.

This time both boys yelled, "Don't!"

She ignored them, and the fragments of paper she was tearing floated to the floor. "You will go back to the school tomorrow," she told Benny calmly. "You will beg them to take you back."

"No!"

"You are going back to your classes—"

"No! And you can go to hell!"

The curse word stopped her. She slapped him hard across the mouth. Her fingers left red marks on Benny's big round cheeks, and his eyes filled with tears of pain. "Mr. Big Star!" she exploded in fury. "Mr. Al Jolson! I know why you want to do this stupid thing. You think you're going to start singing and dancing and all the girls are going to fall at your feet." She laughed. "They will fall down *laughing!* Like I am right now. They will *laugh* at the fat boy who thinks he's going to be Al Jolson." She leaned into her son's face and yelled, "All you have is what is up here!" She pointed to her own head. "Don't you understand? Look at yourself in a mirror."

As Joe knew very well, girls did laugh at Benny. In school he made himself into a clown for them and they screamed with laughter at his antics, but none of them had ever said yes when he asked them to walk in the park or to go have a soda pop. Not that

Benny had had the courage to ask very often. As for Benny looking at himself in a mirror, Joe knew Benny draped a towel over the one above the bathroom sink when he washed his face so he wouldn't have to see his double chin.

Mrs. Gerhardt seemed to think she'd made her point. "Tomorrow," she said briskly, "you will go back to school—"

"Never!"

"Then you can leave my house. Right now."

There was a silence in the room as mother and son faced each other. Joe knew the prospect of being on his own would be terrifying for Benny and waited for him to back down. Instead, Benny fought back his panic. "Fine," he said. "I'll get my things." He started for the stairway to the bedrooms, but his mother blocked his way.

"No," she said. "Everything you have is mine. You will not take anything with you." Joe watched Benny fight back his fear again. Then he nodded and walked to the door. "Don't come home until you are going to school again," his mother called after him.

Benny slept on the floor of Joe's room at the boardinghouse that night. "But we can't do it again, because my landlady will kick us both out if she knows," Joe warned. He needn't have worried. The next morning, Benny was gone before he woke up. When he walked into the parlor where the boarders' breakfast was served, he saw Benny in the doorway counting out a week's rent into his landlady's hand.

"What did you do?" he muttered under his breath, as they sat down to their coffee, toast, and fried eggs. "Where did you get the money?"

"I still have the key to the bakery. I delivered Ma's doughnuts for her this morning"—Benny's grin creased his face—"and I kept the money."

"You stole from your own mother?" Joe choked on his toast.

"She won't report it. I left her a note. She won't let the police take her little Benny to jail. She's too proud."

"But . . . she's your mother."

"She should be glad to help me. After all, she wants me to make something of myself." Benny slathered butter on his own slice of toast. "I'm going to see that stage manager who can get us into the talent contest today. Ma's doughnut money will grease his palm." He looked toward the landlady and smiled. "I had some money left over to give Mrs. O'Hara, so we can rehearse our act in the parlor every afternoon." He took a big bite of the toast. "Relax, Joey, everything's under control. All we have to do is win the contest." He swallowed and lifted the toast to his mouth again, but then he suddenly put it down and pushed his chair away from the table.

Still slightly dazed by everything that had happened, Joe asked, "Is something wrong with your food?"

"I think it's time I stopped being the fat boy," Benny said.

CHAPTER 15

I held my breath as I read through the scenes I'd just finished writing. Then I let the breath out in a long relieved sigh. It was still early to be sending up balloons, but . . .

"I think the kid is back," I whispered to Annie. "For someone who hasn't written a cogent sentence in three years, these pages are okay."

What happened next really pissed me off: I was so happy, tears started stinging my eyes.

"I hate this!" I yelled. "I don't want to be a work-obsessed, self-absorbed freak. I don't want my whole life to be about me and whatever I'm writing this week."

Well, get over it, said a voice inside my head. *This is who you are.*

I'd thrown out all my size fours, but I think that was the moment I really kissed the pink ruffles good-bye.

Life lesson: Sometimes getting to know yourself really sucks.

Still, you've got to get on with it. I'd upset Annie with my outburst, and she was eyeing the Evil Laptop anxiously. I tossed her a cookie. "Everything's cool," I said, and went back to work.

"POP AND BENNY won the contest," Chicky's voice told me when I turned on the tape recorder again. "And to give him his due, Benny tried to bury the hatchet with his mother. He paid her back most of what he'd stolen out of his part of the prize money, and when the act went on tour he sent her copies of all their reviews—which were pretty good, although they were in small local newspapers no one had ever heard of. Benny wrote little notes to his mother, like *Someday we'll be in* Variety *and the* New York Sun, to go with the clippings. But when their two-week tour was over, and he and Pop walked into their boardinghouse, all the envelopes were waiting for him, unopened. His mother had refused to accept his mail.

"Still, he kept on trying to reach her. When Masters and George landed a nice booking in Westchester, Benny saved all his money for three weeks and mailed her a train ticket so she could come and see them. He wrote her a letter saying he would take her out for a lobster and champagne supper after the show; she'd always told him they would go to Delmonico's for lobster and champagne when he graduated from college. Mrs. Gerhardt sent the train ticket back, along with the letter, which she hadn't opened.

"'She thinks I'm going to be a nothing,' Benny said angrily. 'She wants me to fail. I'm going to have all the things she wanted and didn't get. Well, I'm going to have a big fancy house, like she was always nagging my dad for. And a car. I'll have a family, and she'll never see her grandchildren!'

"But then word came that his mother had died. It had been two years since Benny had seen her, and she'd been sick for at least a year, but she hadn't let Benny know. Maybe she was trying to protect him or maybe she was still mad; Benny never knew. Mrs. Gerhardt didn't have any money at the end; she'd closed the bakery when she got sick and had been living off her savings. There was just enough left to bury her. Benny was on the road touring when it happened, and by the time her neighbors found him, he'd missed the funeral they'd had for her.

"After that, Pop said, he saw something harden in Benny. It was like he decided no one was ever going to hurt him again. Especially not a woman. And all of a sudden there were plenty of women in Benny's life. He'd lost a lot of weight by then, and he was a looker! Well, you can see for yourself, Doll Face. Look at the picture."

I pulled out a shot of Benny and Joe taken after Benny's weight loss. The two young men were standing next to each other and smiling broadly. Benny's fat-kid expression was gone. He was downright cocky now. And he *was* a looker—even in a picture taken a hundred years ago, when men decorated their upper lips with little mustaches, parted their hair in the middle, and loaded it with pomade. Benny's newly streamlined face was matinee-idol handsome, and his thick blond hair framed it to perfection. I couldn't help remembering my own days of peacocking around as the newly skinny wife of Jake. And if there was something a little shallow and surfacey about Benny's wide smile—well, I knew all about being shallow too.

Benny and Joe were wearing white straw hats—boaters, I think they were called—and white suits with vests, pleated pants, and jackets that were worn open. It was a good look for Benny's new physique, which featured broad shoulders and a tapering waist, but not so good for short, skinny Joe. But there was something about Joe, a sweetness and an intelligence in his eyes. For all of Benny's glitz, Joe was the one who got to me.

"Both Benny and Pop were smart." Chicky's voice brought me back to the task at hand. "But Pop was the artist. He'd work for hours to get a line or a piece of stage business right. Benny got bored easily; he liked to walk onstage not knowing what he was going to do and ad lib. But offstage, like I said before, Benny was the go-getter for the act. He was a first-class schmoozer, and in the early days, Masters and George got most of their jobs because Benny played up to the managers and the bookers. Don't get me wrong, Pop was as ambitious as Benny, but he didn't have Benny's gift of gab.

"So they had a good act—not great, but it was enough to get them work on the small-time. I bet you don't know what that means—the small-time."

"Nope," I said. "Hang on." I turned Chicky off, sharpened my pencil, and ate a chocolate bar. One of the advantages of working with a machine is that you can stop for snacks. I turned the tape recorder on again.

"Vaudeville theaters were organized into circuits, some of them covering whole areas of the country," Chicky's voice instructed me. "Performers were booked to go from theater to theater. The circuits were split into two classes: the big-time and the small-time. Some people said the small-time was actually split into small and small-small, but that's getting picky. Getting booked into the big-time meant a performer had made it. These theaters had marble lobbies, chandeliers, and velvet stage curtains. There'd be a first-rate orchestra in the pit, the dressing rooms were clean, the audiences sat in reserved seats, and they knew a good act when they saw it. Big-time theaters were usually in large cities with nice hotels and restaurants where performers could go after the show. And the work was easier. Big-time acts only had to do one or two shows a day, and they usually booked for a week or longer so they had a chance to settle in a town.

"The small-time was less predictable. On a bad circuit you'd do a one-night stand, and then grab a train for an overnight jump to the next town, and you could play six or seven shows a day. The theater might be a big room above a store with a platform for a stage and dressing rooms down in the basement with rats and no indoor plumbing. For an orchestra, the town barber might play the piano—if he showed up. The audience would be hicks and drunks who threw things. Performers called that kind of circuit a Death Trail.

"Or you could be booked into legit houses that were small but clean, and you'd do maybe two or three shows a day and you'd have half a day to catch your breath between jumps." The gruff little voice paused. "You got all that, Doll Face?"

"Yep," I said to the machine.

"Pop and Benny were playing a decent small-time circuit that covered Connecticut, New York State, and Massachusetts when they ran into my mother," Chicky went on. "She and her sisters had an act. Check out the pictures numbered three and four."

I paused the tape recorder and pulled out the next two pictures. The first was a formal shot of three girls in their late teens posed in a line with their right legs extended and their toes pointed. Their right hands held tambourines; their left arms were wrapped around the waist of the sister to the left. They wore matching plaid skirts, white blouses, dark tights, plaid sashes, and little tams pulled rakishly over the right eye. The outfits seemed childish for them and their pigtails tied with ribbons looked downright silly. I recognized the girl in the middle of the line as Chicky's mother. There was a caption under the picture that read, "The Dancing Doran Sisters and Little Ellie."

"Little?" I said to Annie. "She looks like she's at least five-seven."

The fourth picture featured Ellie alone. She was wearing a

white silk dress with a short, full skirt festooned with lace. White stockings and dance slippers with large roses on them completed the ensemble, which once again looked way too young for her. And what was up with that bow, perched on top of the beautiful hair tumbling over her shoulders?

I punched the button on the tape recorder. "Mom and Pop met in a theater in New Rochelle," Chicky's voice said. "Mom and her sisters had the second spot on the bill. To be honest with you, that was the slot the managers usually reserved for a weak act because the patrons would still be straggling in, so you've got to think that the Dancing Doran Sisters weren't all that good. Masters and George had a much better position; they were closing out the first half of the show, which meant the manager figured their act for a crowd-pleaser.

"Whenever Pop and Benny played a new theater Pop liked to go down to the stage early to get a feel for the house. So he was in the wings when Mom and her sisters were getting ready to go on."

I listened to the rest of Chicky's account of the scene; then I started writing again. This time there was no deep breath. I knew exactly what I wanted to say.

CHAPTER 16

New Rochelle, New York

1919

The backstage at the New Rochelle Opera House was narrow and dusty. As the orchestra out front began to play for the Dancing Doran Sisters, Joe Masters picked his way carefully through the darkness behind the backdrop, making sure he didn't brush up against anything. He and Benny wore white costumes because white caught the lights onstage, but it also showed every speck of dirt, and they only had enough in their budget to get their suits cleaned five times during this tour. New Rochelle was their first booking, and they had twenty weeks to go.

Joe kept on making his way to the side of the stage. Walking around during a show seemed to steady his nerves. Besides, he wanted to watch the rest of the bill he and Benny would be working with. Especially the tall strawberry blonde who was the lead in the Doran Sisters' act. He'd seen her back in New York when all the performers in the show got on the train at Grand Central

Terminal, and Lord, she was a beauty! He'd gladly look at her for the next twenty weeks if she and her sisters were going to be on the full tour. You never knew what was going to happen when you were on the road. Sometimes you worked with different acts in different theaters, and sometimes you worked with the same people for the whole time. An act could be canceled out of town if the booker heard from theater managers that it was no good, and a whole tour could be canceled somewhere out in the sticks because there weren't enough customers to fill the theater seats, leaving the actors with no way to get home. There were no guarantees in show business. But on a good small-time circuit like this one the managements were pretty decent, and he and Benny had a solid little act, so he figured they'd be safe. The strawberry blonde and her sisters were in the weak spot on the bill, so he was a little worried about her.

The Dancing Doran Sisters had just run onstage. Joe made his way to the left side of the stage, where the stage manager's box was, and, after nodding to the man, stood in the wings to watch. After a second he frowned. The girls were starting out with a little patter, after which, presumably, they would dance. There was nothing wrong with that setup—it was standard for an act of this kind—but the patter was all wrong. They were doing what was essentially a kid's act, and they weren't that young. The strawberry blonde—according to the program her name was Ellie—had to be sixteen if she was a day. At the train station she'd been a dreamboat in a stylish traveling suit. Now she looked overgrown and ridiculous in a kiddie costume, with her lovely hair scraped into pigtails. Someone had told her to deliver her lines with a lisp.

When the girls had started their act, the audience snickered a few times, waiting for a punch line that would explain why they were pretending to be children. But the punch line hadn't come so the audience was confused. That was bad, as Joe knew too well from his own past mistakes. You lost the audience fast if they didn't understand what you were doing. The beauty—Ellie—seemed to know it, because she was racing through the dialogue as quickly as she could. Unfortunately, her sisters weren't keeping up with her, so it only made things worse. The audience had started coughing—a fatal sign that its patience was at an end—but then, mercifully, Ellie gave the conductor the sign to strike up the orchestra and, as Joe heaved a sigh of relief, the girls went into their dance. The house could understand that.

The sisters weren't bad dancers, and Ellie Doran had a nice little air about her, so you could almost forget the silly costumes. But just as Joe was thinking she might even get a small hand when it was over, she took a pratfall, a hokey pratfall that came out of nowhere. It had to be a part of the act, because her sisters clustered around her and they all went back to doing baby talk again. The audience was completely turned off by now, and there was no way to get them back. Joe could tell that Ellie Doran knew they were dying; the flop sweat had started to come out on her. He almost couldn't watch. Suddenly, as if to back up what he'd been thinking, the girl looked offstage and he saw rage in her eyes.

A whiff of something familiar hit his nostrils, the sour-breath smell of someone who'd been at the whiskey bottle. It was early, but morning drinking wasn't uncommon in Joe's world. He turned to see who the boozer was. Standing next to him, weaving dangerously, was the man who had gotten on the train with the Doran Sisters. Joe remembered that one of the girls had referred to him as Pa. So this was Ellie's father. And when she'd thrown that look of fury offstage, she'd meant it for him.

The girls finished and bowed to a house that was sitting on its hands in disgust. The Doran Sisters had laid a big fat egg. If they hadn't been young and pretty they'd have been booed. They made their way offstage, with Ellie shooting fire out of her beautiful blue eyes. Joe backed up to see what would happen, and sure enough, she strode over to her inebriated parent as he swayed back and forth and fixed him with a blazing stare. "Are you happy, Pa?" she demanded in a whisper. "We flopped again. Are you happy now?"

What happened next was as quick as it was stunning. The drunk balanced himself and before Joe or the nearby stage manager could stop him, he hit the girl hard in the face with his open hand. "Bitch," he hissed. "I'll teach you to talk that way to your old man."

The fire went out of her eyes, and she put up her hands as her sisters tried to get between her and their father, who was winding up to swing again. Joe's fists clenched and without thinking he moved toward the man, but he felt himself being pulled back.

"No, you don't," the stage manager said in his ear. "You're not gonna start a fight back here while I got a show to run. Besides, you and your partner ain't gone on yet, and you got no time to be a hero." He signaled to a stagehand, who grabbed the drunk and threw him into the alley next to the theater. Meanwhile, Ellie had caught Joe's eye. Realizing that he must have seen her humiliation, she pushed her sisters away and ran to the back of the stage, where there was a staircase leading to the dressing rooms above. Her sisters huddled together for a few more seconds and then followed. Neither of them seemed shocked or even terribly upset by the fact that their father had just hit their sister broadside. That was bad.

The stage manager was motioning to the next act to get ready to make their entrance, and Joe backed off to the side to give them room. He was still thinking about what he'd just seen.

"It's just as well you kept your suit clean," the stage manager whispered as he gave the cue for the curtain to go up. "The owner here doesn't put up with bum acts. Those girls will be getting their pictures back by the end of the night."

All vaudevillians traveled with glossy photos of their act, which were hung in the lobby of the theater they were playing. When a management wanted to cancel you, they gave you your pictures back. Ellie and her sisters were going to be canned that night. Joe sighed; he couldn't blame the management, the girls' act was bad, but as he stood backstage watching the show and waiting to make his own entrance with Benny, he couldn't help thinking about the look in Ellie Doran's eyes.

MASTERS AND GEORGE did their turn and got their usual solid response from the house. After the curtain came down, Joe made his way to the dressing room he and Benny shared. Benny was off somewhere, probably flirting with the chorus girls who danced in the big flash act that opened the second half of the bill. In the five years since he'd left home, Benny had changed. The cynical fat boy with a chip on his shoulder was now a handsome man who seemed to need to make every girl he met fall in love with him. And the girls usually did. Benny had learned to hide his cynicism behind a façade of sweetness and boyish enthusiasm that females found very appealing. Also, they sensed a sadness in him— a sadness Joe knew to be real. The girls were convinced that there was some mystery behind Benny's sorrow and they all wanted to be the one who took it away. But, as Joe knew, they were all doomed to fail. Benny's pain came from the death of a mother who had never forgiven him or said good-bye. None of the girls who fell so hard for Benny had ever mattered enough to him to make that hurt go away. He just needed them to prove to himself that he was no longer fat Benny Gerhardt.

But Joe did have to admit that Benny was a cut above the other vaudevillians. He had never bothered to try to cover his boundless ambition, and with his refined air and the classy way of speaking his mother had insisted on, Benny always seemed like a man destined for great things, even when he didn't have two dimes to rub together.

There were several hooks on the dressing room wall where performers could hang their costumes. Joe took a piece of white linen out of his traveling trunk, stretched it between the hooks, took off his white suit, and hung it up so the linen protected it from the dirty wall. He put on his street clothes, checked his face in the mirror, and saw that the greasepaint was holding. If he didn't go out to eat between shows he probably wouldn't have to redo it. Finally, after all his backstage rituals were completed, he sat down and began to run through the performance he and Benny had just finished. He wasn't very happy about it.

The applause they'd gotten was respectable—nothing like the stony silence that had greeted the Doran Sisters—but it wasn't the kind of response he and Benny had dreamed of when they won the contest in Coney Island that launched them in the business. It certainly wasn't the roaring approval that elevated an act to the big-time and to an eventual shot at that vaudevillian holiest of holies, the Palace Theater in New York City. Masters and George were stuck in the small-time.

The problem was their material. It wasn't bad, it just wasn't good enough. They should start over, but it was hard breaking in a new act, and Joe was afraid Benny wouldn't want to put in the work. However, Benny also knew they weren't getting ahead and he was frustrated about it. That was a big worry. Benny had never been one to put up with something that wasn't going his way. If he were to walk, Joe would be without a partner, and Joe wasn't sure he could do a single. Not that he hadn't thought about it. When Benny skipped a rehearsal or *dried* while they were onstage—the performer's term for forgetting your lines in front of an audience—being on his own would seem real good to Joe.

If he were to try going solo, it would be as a monologuist—a man who stood on an empty stage all alone and held the audience by telling stories and jokes. A good monologuist needed an ear for comic voices and an ability to slip in and out of a variety of characters, as well as having the ability to come up with one-liners. These were all talents Joe knew he had. But the move would be risky.

He leaned back in his chair and closed his eyes. This was a debate he'd been having with himself more and more lately. Benny was exasperating, it was true, but he knew how to make friends in the right places. When they were between jobs, back in New York, Benny was the one who hung around the joints where the booking agents had lunch and sold Masters and George to them over a hot pastrami or a corned beef on rye. It was Benny's charm that got them many of their gigs, and Joe wasn't sure he wanted to find out what would happen to him without it. Besides, they had an act that worked—even if it wasn't great enough to play the Palace. The history of vaudeville was littered with tales of partners who broke up a decent act and went out on their own, only to bomb horribly.

Joe opened his eyes. He wasn't going to rock the boat, no matter how tempting the idea. The real question was, what was Benny going to do? Because Joe knew his partner would leave him high and dry in an instant if he thought it was in his own best interest.

Joe sat up and shook his head to clear it. There was no need to think about any of this now. For the next twenty weeks he and Benny were committed to the tour, and Benny wasn't the kind to welsh on a contract. Their act had gone well enough today, and the management had to be pleased with them, No one was talking about handing them their pictures.

That thought brought up a vision of the lovely Ellie Doran and the way she'd looked at Joe when she realized he'd seen her father hit her. She'd been angry and humiliated and she'd run upstairs to hide. Joe looked up at the ceiling. He'd already checked, and he knew her dressing room was on the floor above his. Ellie Doran was probably up there right now. Her father's hand had caught her near the eye, so it was probably turning black and blue—her whole face had to be hurting. Joe looked at his watch. There was a restaurant across the street from the theater and he didn't have to be onstage again until the final curtain call, which was at least an hour from now. He picked up his hat and hurried out of the dressing room.

WHEN HE CAME back from the restaurant, Joe raced up the stairs to the Dorans' dressing room. He started to knock on the door, and then he stopped. What if Ellie wasn't there? What if her sisters were in the room with her? Somehow he'd just assumed that she'd be alone, but if she wasn't . . . He looked down at the parcel in his hand. He didn't want to embarrass her more than he already had. He'd seen how proud she was. He stood outside the door, not sure what to do. The chorus girls who had been onstage were coming back up the stairs, laughing and chatting, which meant the second half of the show was under way. He didn't have time to waste; it was now or never. He knocked.

His luck was in. She opened the door. He stole a quick look over her shoulder and saw she was alone. And she definitely wasn't pleased to see him.

"Can I come in?" he asked fast, before she had a chance to close the door in his face. She studied him for a second, shrugged, and walked back inside the room. He decided that meant yes. Being careful to leave the door open so she wouldn't think he'd gotten any ideas, he followed her. The little room was furnished with one rickety chair, a mirror that was in need of resilvering, and a makeup table that would have been small for one person, let alone the three girls using it. It was the kind of bad dressing room that managements assigned to the lesser acts on the bill.

Ellie Doran sat in the chair and looked up at him warily. The fire had gone out of her; her whole body seemed to sag with weariness now, and the bruises around her eye had already started to bloom. Joe opened his mouth and realized he didn't know what to say. This was a new and unwelcome sensation. He wasn't in the same class as Benny when it came to smooth-talking women—few men in the world were as gifted as Benny was in that area—but Joe had always been able to hold his own with the opposite sex. He was in show business, for God's sake! He wasn't some tongue-tied rube from the sticks; he'd been around beautiful girls most of his adult life. But now, when it was so important to say the right thing . . . just call him Johnny Hayseed.

"Well?" she said.

"I saw what happened downstairs," he blurted out idiotically.

"I know." She turned to stare at the wall. "It was my fault. I know better than to fly at Pa when he's been drinking."

"No one should do that to you," he blurted out again. There didn't seem to be any way to stop himself.

"It wasn't as bad as it looked."

"You're going to have one hell of a shiner."

She shrugged again. "Nothing a little greasepaint won't cover. I've done it before."

She looked defeated sitting there, when she should have been smiling and happy. She was born for smiles and happiness. Joe looked again at his package, wrapped in butcher's paper and tied with a white string. He held it out to her. "Here," he said.

She hesitated for a long moment, then she took the package and opened it. "What the . . . ? You're giving me a chunk of raw meat?" For a moment he thought she was angry, but then—oh, thank you, God—she grinned. "This is a gift? You couldn't even have it cooked?"

"It's for your eye. It'll help." He was grinning now too.

"Where did you get it?"

"Across the street. At the restaurant. They thought I was crazy."

"Aren't you?"

Maybe about you. "They understood when I told them I was in show business. You know how that is—civilians always think we're cuckoo."

It was the wrong thing to say. Her grin faded. "Yeah, I know civilians," she said bitterly. She turned away from him. "Thanks for the steak." He was being dismissed.

"Well, take care of that eye," he said, back to being idiotic again.

He started for the door, but before he could reach it she said softly, "I know about civilians because I'm going to be one soon." He came back. "Our act . . . we're going to be canceled."

The stage manager had said she and her sisters would get their pictures back after the second show. That was the way it was usually done; an act was canceled *after* they'd finished performing. It would be mean to do it when they still had to go on a second time. "Who told you?" he demanded.

"When you've been canned as often as we have, you don't need anyone to say it."

There was resignation in her voice. She'd faced the truth, and as much as he wished it wasn't so, it would be unkind to give her false hope. "There are other tours," he said gently. "Other managements."

"Not for us. Not anymore." Her eyes started to fill with tears—she wiped them away fast. "Our act is dead."

"I wouldn't say *dead* exactly. Your patter . . . and the movements . . . may be a little young for you and your sisters. . . . I don't know if you've ever thought about changing—"

"You think I don't know what we look like onstage?" She cut him off angrily. "You think I don't know I'm making a fool of myself when I go out there?"

"No, no," he said hastily. "I'm sure you know how bad . . . I mean . . ." He trailed off miserably.

"Yes. I know how bad we are."

"Then why do you do it?" he heard himself ask.

"Pa." The one syllable came out as a sigh. "He put the act together when I was six. In the beginning, we were pretty good." She smiled at the memory. Then she frowned, and it looked like she was going to clam up again.

"I bet you were," Joe said, to encourage her and keep her talking.

"That was ten years ago." She closed her eyes. "We've grown up since then."

"You mean your father hasn't changed the act since you were children?" She shook her head. "But that's—" He couldn't find the word for how stupid and wasteful and . . . downright criminal that was. It was one thing to have an act that wasn't working and not know why. But to go onstage the way she did, knowing what was wrong and not being able to do anything about it—that went against every instinct he had as a performer. "You have to tell him you won't do it anymore! You can't!"

"You saw what happened backstage. You think that's the only time I've been hit? He wants us to keep on being babies. And when he's been drinking . . ." She sighed again. "He didn't drink like that when Ma was alive. Not that I remember, anyway."

She was looking far off now. He stood very still so he wouldn't interrupt her thoughts. Anything to keep her talking.

"Pa was in the profession," she said. "He started in the music halls in England with a single act—a couple of songs and a buck dance—but it was the singing that put him across. Pa had a beautiful voice. He came to this country, and everyone who heard him said it was just a matter of time before he broke into the big-time.

"He met my ma and they got married and she had us kids, and Pa was doing great. He had a booking in New York City; all the important scouts and agents were coming to catch his act. The night before he went on, Ma got sick—the influenza. She got bad real fast. Pa was torn up about leaving her in the hotel room, but this was the chance he'd been waiting for." Her eyes were sparkling with tears she was holding back. Joe had a feeling she was one of those rare girls who got prettier when they cried. "Pa went onstage and his throat closed up. He tried to sing anyway, he pushed so hard he ruptured something in there—that's what the doctor said. His voice was gone after that. And Ma never did get better. After two months, she died. I was six, Florrie was eight, and Dot was ten.

"Pa was in a bad way for a while—that was when the drinking really started. But one day he told us we were going into show business. He put the act together for us, and we've been touring with it ever since. Ten years."

"You and your sisters need to stand up to him. Tell him you want a new routine, new costumes—"

"It's too late for that."

"If the three of you stand together—"

"We won't. Florrie and Dot are quitting the act. Florrie's getting married next July, and Dot found herself a job in a milliner's shop in Manhattan and she's moving there. And I"—her mouth trembled—"I'm going back home to Brooklyn to live with Pa. But now there won't be any act for him to think about. Nothing for him to look forward to." She couldn't hold back the tears any longer. They started to fall; without thinking, Joe moved toward her. "Living with Pa is going to be hell!"

Joe believed her. He could imagine how bad it was going to be. And it shouldn't be allowed. *No*, he wanted to shout. *You can't go back and live with that old drunk!*

All of sudden, she seemed to realize she'd been spilling her family secrets to a total stranger, and she was embarrassed about it. She turned her back to him. "Thank you for the steak," she murmured.

He was being dismissed again. But he couldn't leave. *Let me fix this for you*, he wanted to say. *Just tell me what to do*. But she never would; he knew that about her already. And then it came to him in a flash: Maybe there *was* something he could do to help her. It would take a little work and he'd have to convince Benny to go along, but it might be just the ticket for all of them.

There was a roar of applause from the stage, a hand big enough to carry up three flights of stairs. The headliner act had just finished, and clearly they had killed. The second half of the show was coming to an end. He had to get downstairs fast and start working on Benny. "I gotta go," he told the beautiful girl. "I gotta find my partner."

She turned to him and held out her hand, and he'd been right, she was even prettier when she cried. "I'm Ellie." She smiled through her tears. "Ellen Doran."

He didn't tell her that he already knew her name. "Joe Masters," he said.

Then he ran out of her dressing room and down the stairs.

CHAPTER 17

Joe found Benny in their dressing room, leaning back precariously in a chair with his feet propped up on the makeup table, his eyes closed. Benny hadn't taken off his dashing white suit, and he hadn't even put a towel on the chair to protect it. Benny's mother had spoiled him for so long that now, even though she was gone, he still acted as if he had someone doing his laundry for him. At this rate, his suit was going to need cleaning before they left New Rochelle, which would make a dent in their carefully calculated budget. Joe was the one who had done the calculating, and normally he would have yelled at Benny for being a careless jerk, but Joe was about to propose something that was going to make a much bigger hole in their finances. So he didn't scold his feckless partner—not even for resting his dirty shoes on their makeup table.

Instead, he put on his own suit for the curtain call, doing it fast, while, in his head, he ran over the idea he was about to propose. Then he sat in the chair next to Benny and plunged in. "I been thinking," he began.

Benny sat up. "Me too," he said. "We're getting nowhere in this business, kiddo."

It was the same complaint he'd been making, but this time it seemed to Joe that there was something more urgent about it. Momentarily dropping the speech he'd been about to make, he said, "It's our material. When we finish this tour, we need to rewrite it. That's all, Benny. We're a good team onstage. Our timing is great, and the way we look and sound—all that works."

For a second Joe thought Benny was going to argue, but he seemed to think better of it. He began patting powder on his nose. "If you say so," he said.

But that didn't mean he agreed. And the tricky thing about Benny was, if he ever did quit the act, he'd give his partner the news in his own sweet time, if he bothered to do it at all. Benny hated any kind of unpleasantness. When he was finished with something he just walked away—as dozens of girls around the country had learned the hard way. His favorite method of telling a lady the romance was off was to send her a good-bye note and a red rose to remember him by. That was his signature—one red rose. He gave them to his girls at the beginning of a courtship— and at the end. And whenever he could manage it, the final rose and the accompanying note were delivered after he was safely out of town.

Joe studied Benny out of the corner of his eye. Given his mood, this was the wrong time to make the suggestion Joe had in mind. But if he didn't say something now, Ellie and her sisters would be packing their trunk and heading back to New York City. "I've been thinking maybe we should add something to the act—until we can rework it," Joe said.

"You got a miracle?" Benny asked. He contemplated himself in the mirror; sometimes Joe thought it was as if he still couldn't believe how good-looking he'd become and had to reassure himself periodically.

"We need a new finish, something big," Joe said. "Right now, it's just me yelling and trying to strangle you—which the audience has been watching me do for ten minutes."

"Tell me something I don't know." But Benny had turned away from the mirror and was looking at Joe. He was interested.

"What if we have a girl—a real doll—walk across the stage in front of us?" Eagerly, Joe jumped up and started acting out his idea. "She's snobby, see? Isn't going to give a couple of dopes like us the time of day." He sashayed across the dressing room. "She passes by and we stop dead." He mimed himself and Benny forgetting their stage battle, their eyes bugging out when the girl came into view. He began improvising lines for the snooty girl and himself and Benny, and as he did it, he found himself getting genuinely excited about the possibilities. He'd come up with this new ending because Ellen Doran was beautiful and sad and he wanted to rescue her. But now he was thinking that adding her to the act might actually help put it over. A little, anyway.

"It's like we're hypnotized," he said eagerly to Benny. "I'm so stunned, I drop you. You hit your head on the piano." He acted out Benny's head hitting the keyboard. "Then I slam it a couple of times because I'm too busy watching the girl to pay attention to what I'm doing." He demonstrated the business with plenty of mugging. "We follow the girl offstage with our tongues hanging out," he finished breathlessly. Benny gave him a knowing smile.

"I bet you have a girl in mind, right, Joey?"

There was no point in beating around the bush. "You know the Dancing Doran Sisters? In the number-two slot? They're getting their pictures back tonight, and the act is breaking up. The youngest one doesn't want to go home—I think there are some troubles there. But she doesn't have any other choice."

"The youngest one? That's the blonde?"

Joe nodded. "I don't know how good she is as an actress, but it's not like she's got to be Sarah Bernhardt to walk across a stage and be snooty. If we put her in the right clothes, and fix her hair—"

Benny's smile widened. "Yeah. She *is* a doll." So he'd seen her on the train platform too. He leaned back again and smiled.

"You like the idea?" Joe held his breath.

Benny shrugged. "What can it hurt?" he said.

Joe couldn't believe it had been this easy. For a second he thought about bringing up the subject of Ellie Doran's salary and how they were going to pay it, but he decided to quit while he was ahead. Benny spent lavishly on himself, but he watched his pennies when it came to anyone else; there were several restaurants on Forty-second Street where his reputation as a lousy tipper was well known. Mentioning money might give him second thoughts. Besides, Joe had been thinking that he'd like to take care of Ellie out of his own half. It would make his finances tight, but he wasn't a big spender like Benny. And he could picture the day when she found out about his generosity. Not that he'd tell her—certainly not right away—but these things did have a way of coming out.

"Well, this is great, just great!" he said heartily. "I'll go upstairs right now and give the poor kid the good news!"

"I have a better idea. Let's wait until after the second show and tell her together. We can take her out to supper to celebrate."

"Fine. Whatever you want." And if Joe felt let down because he'd have preferred to tell Ellie by himself, without Benny, he told himself this wasn't the time to quibble with his partner about anything.

• • •

THEY ONLY HAD a couple of hours between performances, but when Benny disappeared after the curtain came down, Joe didn't think anything of it. Benny often liked to get out of the theater and walk around between shows. Meanwhile, Joe was planning the celebration supper for Ellie. He decided they'd take her to the restaurant where he'd bought the raw steak—it was the best one in the neighborhood. He wanted their celebration to make her feel like a queen.

Once, when Joe was a kid—maybe six or seven—he'd earned a dime running some errands for one of the guys in the neighborhood, and he'd bought a Christmas present for his mother. It was a pin in the shape of a butterfly with big yellow stones on it. When he looked back, he realized what a foolish gift it was because where would she ever wear such a showy thing? But when he was seven, he'd only thought that it was beautiful, and he couldn't wait until the twenty-fifth of December to see her open the box. He was feeling the same kind of childish anticipation now as he thought about telling Ellie that he and Benny were offering her a job. His mother had cried when she'd seen her present all those years ago, and told him he was her son from heaven, and remembering that made him even more eager to give Ellie the good news today. But he had to wait until he and Benny could do it together. He had promised.

Somehow he managed to get through the second show—their act went over better than usual—and the last curtain call. It wasn't until he was onstage taking the company bow that he realized Benny wasn't there. In fact, the last time he'd seen Benny was on-stage when they finished their act. It wasn't important, he told himself. Benny had missed the final curtain call before, usually because he'd gotten tied up flirting with some girl. But as soon as the heavy velvet curtain had hit the stage floor for the last time, Joe pushed his way through the crowd of performers milling around and rushed up the stairs to their dressing room. Benny wasn't there. But his white costume had been tossed over a chair, which meant he'd changed into his street clothes. Joe wiped the stage makeup off his face, changed into his own street clothes, and went up to Ellie's dressing room. He found Florrie and Dot packing their trunk. They'd been canceled, they told him. Their pa was already at the railroad station, and they were taking the last train back to New York that night so they wouldn't have to spend their money on a hotel room. But Ellie wasn't going with them.

"She went out for supper with someone," said Florrie—or was it Dot?

"She's not coming with us to New York," said Dot—or Florrie. "She's got a new gig, and she's staying with the tour. She's welcome to it. Thank God I'm getting out of this rotten business."

Suddenly all the pieces fit together. He knew where Benny was—and who he was with. Joe ran downstairs, out of the theater, across the street, and into the restaurant where he'd bought the steak.

Benny and Ellie were sitting at a table near the window. He'd ordered root beers for both of them. Benny saw Joe first. For a moment, Joe thought he wouldn't look him in the eye. But then Benny gave him the big care-for-nothing grin that Joe knew only too well. It was the grin Benny used when he was going after what he wanted, and to hell with anyone else.

Ellie spotted him and called out, "Joe!" He made himself walk over to the table. Ellie was bubbling over. "Joe!" she cried, "Benny had the most wonderful idea, and you've got to say yes. He says you will, if I ask you, so please, please, *please*, Joe!"

So she begged him to let her have the job he'd created for her—the job he and Benny were supposed to offer her together. "Benny says it won't cost you a thing," Elllie went on, bubbling. "He'll pay my salary out of his half. I told him I don't need much—"

Joe couldn't listen to any more. "We'll both pay you, Ellie." He cut her off. "It'll be a three-way split."

He stood there as she heaped thanks on him. After which she hopped out of her seat to throw her arms around him. But it wasn't the embrace he'd anticipated, because she wasn't hugging the man who'd rescued her—that role had gone to Benny. Joe had been cast as the sidekick who was going along for the ride.

And throughout it all, Benny was watching him and enjoying it, because he knew there was nothing Joe could do. If Joe tried to tell Ellie that putting her in the act had been his idea, she'd think he was trying to steal Benny's thunder. Or that he was jealous. If Joe confronted Benny with his betrayal later on, Benny would say, "I was just trying to make a little time with her, Joey. I didn't know you had a yen for her." But of course he *had* known.

Benny liked competing with other men for the attentions of women. Every time he won—and he usually *did* win—Joe knew it helped erase memories of the time when he had to beg girls to have a soda pop with him. And there was a special reason why Benny would try to make time with a girl Joe liked. It had taken Joe a few years to realize that his partner envied him. On the surface that idea seemed ridiculous; Benny had it all over Joe in the looks-and-charm department. But Benny could never forgive Joe for having a mother who had adored him without question when he was a kid. Joe's mother had died several years ago, but Benny still begrudged him that.

Now, as Joe stood at the table and looked at Ellie, he wondered once again why the hell he put up with Benny—even though he knew all the reasons. Then his heart sank. Because not only was Ellie gazing at Benny as if he were every hero in every storybook she'd ever read, but she was holding the red rose Benny had run out to buy for her between shows. And Joe knew from experience that she was a goner. But then as he watched Benny lean across the table toward Ellie, Joe thought there could be one more reason why Benny had gone after her. Maybe she was the one girl who could actually matter to him. Because even at her young age, there was something about her, something more than her extraordinary beauty. Ellie Doran had class. And Benny had always said that when he finally settled down, the girl would have to be a lady.

Joe sighed quietly. It would take a lifetime to try to untangle the reasons why Benny did the things he did, but right now, there was work to do, because they had to have a new ending for the act written and rehearsed by tomorrow evening.

He sat down at the table. "Welcome to the act, Ellie," he said, to the girl who should have been gazing at him like *he* was her hero. "I guess now we call it Masters, George, and Doran."

CHAPTER 18

It took me a week to finish writing the first two chapters of Chicky's memoir. When I came to the end of the tapes she'd made for me, I felt like someone had cut off my supply of chocolate.

"I know it's just a vanity project," I told my mother on the phone. "I know I said I wasn't going to get emotionally involved, but—"

"Not getting emotionally involved is a load of crap," Alexandra broke in. "Of course you are—it's your *work*, for God's sake!"

"It sounds like vaudeville was like *American Idol*!" Sheryl said, when I called her in Pasadena. "I bet a publisher would see that right away."

"I'm not even thinking about a publisher—and I've warned Chicky not to. This job is about paying the bills," I said. But after

I hung up, I couldn't shake the thought that maybe there could be a chance. . . .

"I feel the way I did when I wrote *Love, Max*," I said to Pete, when he checked in from Tanzania.

"So what's the problem?"

"I didn't say there was a problem."

"Francesca, I've known you all my life."

"I'd hate it if something happened and I couldn't finish the book."

"What might happen?"

"Nothing. Not anything."

But that wasn't exactly true. And Annie picked up on my tone of voice. After Pete and I finished talking, she went into Lassie Urging Timmy to Speak Mode. This is when she fixes me with an unwavering stare and waits for me to spill. "Chicky hasn't paid me yet," I confessed. "And I don't know what to do. I don't want to nag her."

Nag, said Annie's stare. *My kibble costs fifteen bucks a bag.*

I called Chicky.

"Doll Face!" said the husky voice that was so familiar to me now. "How are you doing?"

"Not too bad. Look, Chicky—"

"You get started writing yet?"

"Yes. And—"

"You really did? So soon? You're a treasure."

"Well, I don't know about that—"

"Take it from me. Talented, smart, and a hard worker. That's a winning combination, Doll Face. I knew I was right to put my faith in you."

"About that, I . . ." But I couldn't bring up money after what she'd said. Not on the phone; it would be way too cold. "I'd love to show you what I've written so far," I said.

"Come today," she said. "I'll make us tea."

"Stop looking at me like that," I said to Annie, after I'd hung up. "I know I wimped out."

CHICKY MADE A very good cup of tea. And the cookies she served had chocolate in the middle. After I'd handed over the pages of my manuscript, I had to resist the urge to open the cookies and lick the filling. I was a little . . . very . . . nervous. I was terrified that she wouldn't like my writing. Well, what do you want from me? She was the first reader I'd had in three years—and I've already said I have no dignity when it comes to applause.

Chicky started reading and I started pacing. No way I could stay still. Finally she looked up and addressed me. "Doll Face, on a good day I have vertigo. You keep walking around in a circle like that, and I'm going to pass out in front of you. Sit down and let me finish."

I had polished off all the cookies by the time she looked up again. When she did, there were tears shining in her eyes. "It's good," she said softly. "You understand who those people were."

I nodded.

"I knew you would."

Since I seemed to do well with the recorded tapes, we decided I should continue working with them. Chicky handed me two more plastic grocery bags, and told me she hadn't finished recording, but the last tapes would come to me excitingly soon. Then we chitchatted for a while, about vaudeville and show business and everything—except my money. Finally, I couldn't avoid the subject any longer. Not if I was going to keep Annie in kibble. "Wow!" I said, as I hefted the bulging bags. "This is heavy. I'll probably have to get a cab—and speaking of cabs . . . and the money to pay for one . . ." I stopped myself. Even I knew that was one of the clunkiest segues anyone had ever tried. "Okay, Chicky, here's the thing," I said. "I haven't gotten your check yet. You said you were going to send it to me, and I don't think it's a problem with the mail, because I've been getting all my bills."

For a second she was still. Then she laughed. "Doll Face, I'm sorry. I'd forget my head if wasn't on my shoulders."

"It was a mistake!" It was stupid how happy that made me.

Chicky took a battered checkbook out of her nightstand, wrote out a check with a flourish, and handed it to me. "Here you go," she said.

"Thank you," I said, and then I hugged her. After a second she hugged me back. Then she pulled away to look at me.

"You really are enjoying yourself, aren't you?" she asked. "You like this story?"

"Yes."

"Good."

"It makes it easier to write," I started to say, but she wasn't paying attention. She was looking at the picture on the wall. Then she turned back to me. "It's the little gifts you don't expect, Doll Face. You don't know where they're going to come from, but when they show up they make it all worthwhile. It took me too long to learn that."

I thought about this job I hadn't wanted to take because it was beneath me. "I'll try to remember that," I said.

She turned to the picture again. "There's always a second chance—that's one of the things I love most about life."

I DEPOSITED CHICKY'S check on the way home. I bought some fancy dog biscuits for Annie and some more chocolate bars for me, and I raced from the store to my apartment building. For the next two days, I listened to Chicky's tapes. When I'd heard the last one, I opened the laptop and started the first tape over again. "My mother joined the act, and Masters, George, and Doran toured together for the next twenty weeks," said Chicky's voice. "Then all hell broke loose."

I turned off the tape recorder and started to write.

CHAPTER 19

New Palton, New York

1919

The Mansion House was like dozens of other hotels in dozens of small towns all over the country. The elevators were slow, the hallways were lit with five-watt bulbs, fish was served four nights a week, and the clerk was never happy to see performers walk in because his preacher and his mother said they weren't respectable—even though he should have been used to them because his hotel was two doors down from the theater. Ellie had been staying in places like the Mansion House, and places that were much worse, since she was six years old, so she'd never expected life to be easy. She'd blistered her hands carrying the theater trunk off the train in Pittsfield when Pa didn't have enough money to hire a porter, she'd gotten frostbite walking to the theater when the temperature in Minnesota was thirty below, and she'd sprained her ankle when the rotten stage floor had given way under her in Kingston, New York. But no matter how bad things had gotten, Ellie had never been as miserable as she was right now, sitting on the bed in her dark little room at the Mansion House. Sitting and praying that three o'clock this afternoon would never come.

If anyone had said three months ago, back in New Rochelle, that she'd be in this mess, she would have told them to go to hell. Or she would have laughed.

New Rochelle was where it had all started. Joe Masters had shown up at her dressing room door with his raw steak for her eye, where Pa had hit her, and because Joe seemed nice she'd let her guard down. Then, after the last show, Benny had knocked on the same door with a red rose. And his smile. And the plan he was proposing.

"You're Ellie," he'd said. She'd nodded. "I'm Joe Masters' partner."

She'd nodded again, because all of a sudden she was tongue-tied. She'd seen Benny George from a distance, and she'd known he was handsome. Every woman in the show knew that. But now he was standing in front of her. Now she could see the rogue strand of thick blond hair, curling over his forehead, and the fullness of his mouth. She could feel the warmth of his blue eyes. Somehow she'd never thought blue eyes could be warm, but his proved her wrong. He was looking down at her, and the warmth was all around her like a lovely hot bath. Yet there was something a little sad about him. She wanted to know more about that . . . maybe someday. . . . She came out of her trance fast. She remembered that she and Florrie and Dot were packing their trunk because they'd been canned one more time. And she'd been crying, so she looked a mess.

"May I talk to you for a moment?" Benny had asked.

They had to catch the train to the city and they were running late. She should send him on his way. But those blue eyes were still gazing at her. And he was acting as if he didn't see the mascara that had run down her face or the black eye that was starting to show under her stage makeup. So she'd said, "Why not?" And she'd stepped out into the hallway.

He'd hesitated as if he didn't know how to start. Then he'd handed her the flower. "This is for our new partnership," he said. "If you're willing."

"I don't know what you're talking about."

He gave her another smile—did anyone else in the world have a smile that was as confident and reassuring as his? It could make you believe in angels and miracles. "I could try to pretend I didn't know what happened to your act, but you're too smart for that," he'd said, and she'd felt her face turn scarlet with embarrassment.

"Your partner talks a lot," she'd said.

"He can," Benny had said. "But this time, I'm glad he did. He told me you have to quit the business." He'd paused, as if he was a little hesitant about paying her a compliment. "I can't let that happen to the prettiest girl I've ever seen," he'd finally said.

A part of her thought it was probably a line, but she decided she didn't care. He was being kind to her after one of the worst days of her life. He'd given her a rose. And he was so handsome.

"What do you have in mind?" she'd asked.

He'd told her about his dissatisfaction with his act—especially the finish. He'd decided they needed a girl to spice it up, and he'd seen her onstage and knew she had the goods. "And that's not malarkey or me feeling sorry for you," he'd said. "I've got a feeling about you."

When he'd said that, she'd thought he wasn't handing her a line—not totally. Young as she was, she'd had plenty of men promise her things because of her looks, but Benny had cared enough to watch her work onstage. She wasn't sure she agreed with him about her talent; she'd never been sure she was a good performer.

But he was offering her an escape from Brooklyn. And Pa. And who knew? Maybe she really did have the goods. "Where do I sign up?" she'd asked.

Benny's eyes had lit up. "You mean it? You'll do it?"

She couldn't remember the last time she'd made anyone this happy. She couldn't remember when she'd been so happy herself. "Are you kidding? You're giving me the best break of my life."

"And you're giving me . . ." He trailed off. "Well, I just hope you never find out what you're giving me."

"Why?"

"Because I wouldn't want anyone to have that much of a hold on me." There was no wink, no knowing smile when he said it. Normally the men she'd known didn't make themselves vulnerable like that.

"Do you mean that?" she heard herself ask. And she could have bitten her tongue because it sounded like she was accusing him of something. But he suddenly looked thoughtful.

"Yes," he said finally. "I think I do mean it." And she could tell he hadn't expected to feel that way, and she suspected it had surprised him. But in the next moment he had thrown it off. "There's just one thing," he went on. "I haven't told Joe about this yet."

"He wouldn't stop you from giving me the job, would he? Could he do that?"

"I won't let him say no."

"If he doesn't want me—"

"It's my act too."

"But—"

"I'm promising you it will be all right," he said. And once again, he was looking at her with those warm eyes. "Trust me, Ellie?" he asked quietly.

She nodded.

His face seemed to explode with happiness. "I want to take you out to supper right now to celebrate! Let me see that smile again. The world is a better place when you smile, Ellie Doran."

So she had smiled. And she had gone to supper with him. He had ordered root beer and chili and he had told her they were going to pretend it was champagne and lobster. And even after his partner showed up, looking sour-faced, Benny had made the night light and happy. She was probably in love with him even back then.

Over the next three months she'd learned about him—and herself. She discovered that she loved Benny's self-confidence. The years of defeat with Pa, of being the worst act on the bill and running around the country playing dives and living in dumps, had almost killed her self-esteem. But Benny believed in himself. "I'm going to make it big," he told her, after she'd been his girl for a couple of months. "I'm not going to be broke forever. I'm going to have the best of everything, clothes and a car and a big penthouse on Park Avenue, and everyone in New York will know my name. And someday I'm going to settle down, and—" He'd stopped short. "But that's not something I talk about," he said, and he looked at Ellie. "You're turning me into a blabbermouth."

"I do my best," she said sweetly. But she could tell he was surprised at himself again. "Why shouldn't you talk about what you hope for?"

"It's a long way off. I have a lot to do before it all happens. There's no point in talking about it now."

Ellie had nodded. But he'd said the words *settle down*. And even though he hadn't meant to talk about it, he had. *To me*, she'd thought. *I'm the one he told!*

Ellie wasn't clear about how Benny's big success was going to happen, because he wasn't even a little enthusiastic about working on the act. But she'd believed in him. With his classy way of talking and his confident air, he already stood out from the other vaudevillians. He had a way of walking into a room like he was a prince. And when she was with him, Ellie was his princess.

Ellie got up and went into the bathroom to pat some cold water on her face. Most of the rooms at the Mansion House shared common bathrooms—usually one to a floor—but she had her own. Joe was the one who insisted on that luxury for her wherever they stayed.

Joe was a hard one for Ellie to read. When she and Benny had first popped the idea of her joining the act to Joe, she'd thought he was going to have a fit, he'd looked so mad. But he'd said yes, and the next day he'd started coming up with lines for her. Sometimes, in the beginning, it had seemed to Ellie as if Joe was doing more to work her into the act than Benny was, even though the idea had been Benny's. Joe was willing to rehearse with her until she felt absolutely secure, and when they were onstage he set up her one punch line so that she always got her laugh. Benny, on the other hand, hated to rehearse. He preferred to wing it onstage, which terrified Ellie. And even though she owed him everything, she had to admit that Benny never set up anyone to get a laugh, only himself. She felt safer acting with Joe. But when they were offstage she didn't know what to think about him. One minute he'd act as if he resented her being around, then a minute later he'd be insisting that she have a private bathroom.

"Don't think about it," Benny advised her once when she brought it up. "Joe's an odd duck, I don't understand him myself."

Benny was never moody. He gave her a rose every day. He sat next to her on the train during their long jumps, and he listened to her stories about the early days when she trooped with Pa and Florrie and Dot. Sometimes he catnapped with his head resting cozily on her shoulder.

Joe made her laugh. On their train rides, he would read stories from the newspaper out loud and make up monologues about them that had her—and the rest of the train car—in stitches. But then, all of a sudden, he'd be back in one of his bad moods again, so she figured you couldn't count on Joe.

Benny took her to supper every night after the show—they would always pretend it was lobster and champagne—and he held her hand when they walked back to the hotel. He could make her forget every worry she had. Even when she'd gotten more bad news about Pa from her sister Florrie.

Pa had moved in with Florrie and her husband, but he hadn't stopped drinking. If anything, he had gotten worse. Sometimes it seemed to Ellie as if there was a letter from Florrie in every town she played. And each letter was the same: Pa had gotten into a fight or a jam of some kind, and Florrie needed money to get him out of it. And Ellie, who felt guilty because she'd skipped out on them, sent whatever she had.

"What the hell are you helping him for?" Joe would demand, when she asked for another advance on her pay. "He was bad to you."

"Leave her alone," Benny would say. "He's her father. You don't want to walk away from a parent. Never." And that would always silence Joe.

Benny seemed to understand that even if you didn't want to live with your pa and take care of him, that didn't mean you didn't love him. Or that you'd forgotten the days when he was a good father, before all the trouble had started. After a letter came from Florrie, if Ellie was upset, Benny would take her to a park, so she could feed the birds with the crusts she'd saved from her lunch, or he'd buy her a hot fudge sundae because he'd discovered that was her favorite treat. He would sip seltzer water—he never ate sweets— and he would tell her his dreams, and the time would pass until she was feeling better and they had to go to the theater.

But then a day came when Florrie's letter wasn't about paying for the mirror in the bar that had been smashed or the beer mugs that had been broken. *We didn't know how sick Pa was*, Florrie had written.

The doctor says he's been eaten up with cancer for months. Pa has known it, but I guess he didn't want to tell us. I'm sorry this won't reach you before the funeral, but maybe it's just as well. You couldn't have made it back in time anyway, so you just would have fretted the way you do. The service was nice, and the preacher said Pa's in a better place. But I say if he thinks that, he didn't know Pa.

Good-bye for now, from your loving sister,
Florrie

Ellie had cried in Benny's arms that night until she fell asleep, and in the morning, when she woke up, he kissed her. A real man-and-woman kiss. So when he told her he loved her, it wasn't a surprise, it was just something that had to be true because it felt so right. And when he stayed all night in her room, that really wasn't a surprise either. And what they did together didn't seem wrong.

"How could it be," he'd whispered in her ear, "when I love you so much?"

She could have said that she'd been taught differently. But the mother who had taught her about right and wrong was dead, and so was her father. And her sisters had their own busy lives. There was no one in the world to love her now but Benny. So she didn't tell him to stop.

The truth was, she didn't want him to stop. Not when it was nighttime, and he came into her room after everyone else was asleep. Benny's long, hard body gave her more pleasure than she'd ever dreamed was possible. She felt herself floating through the days on the memories of that pleasure, and she couldn't wait for night to come. During the days Benny gave her roses, and hot fudge sundaes, and he made her smile, and all she needed was the touch of his hand to make her forget the hard knocks that had come before she met him. But she wasn't a fool. She'd heard about Benny's way with girls, and even though she was young and in love for the first time, she'd screwed up her courage and asked Joe about it.

"I know Benny has had other girls," she stammered. "And I need to know . . . am I different from the others? Does he care for me? Really care?"

But suddenly Joe seemed to be in one of his bad moods. "Ask him yourself," he'd said.

"If I'm not different, do you think he'll admit that?" Joe had looked at her hard. "Please, you know him better than anyone," she'd said. "And this is my whole life."

After a moment, she'd seen the hard look melt from his face and something sad replace it. "God, you're just a kid," he'd said softly. Then he'd drawn in a deep breath. "Benny had a bad time when we were young . . . there were things that happened, that . . . closed down something inside him. I don't know if he *could* care the way you're talking about. Even if he wanted to."

That was when Ellie realized she wasn't as brave as she'd thought she was. This was hurting too much and she didn't want to hear any more.

Joe must have seen that in her eyes, because he had added, "But he hasn't had anyone else since he met you. And I've never seen him do that before. Certainly not for this long."

When he'd said that, Ellie had felt fearless again. So fearless that later on, when she and Benny were alone, she'd asked him about the rumors she'd heard.

"Yes," he'd said. "I've played around," he'd said. "But this is different."

"How many other girls have heard that from you?" she'd asked.

He'd had the grace to redden when he grinned. "Lots." Then

he'd gotten serious. "But you—" He'd stopped, and she'd known he was picking his words carefully because he was trying to be honest. It seemed like he was trying to figure out his feelings for himself. "You're good for me, Ellie," he'd said finally.

Her heart had started to beat harder, but she couldn't let him know that. "Thanks," she'd said.

"Don't laugh. You've got me thinking about things."

The beating was so loud, now, there was no way he couldn't hear it. " 'Things'? Like what?"

Instead of answering he'd kissed her, and after that there was no more talking. But she couldn't forget the tantalizing words: *You've got me thinking about things.* She'd wanted to hear more about that.

Meanwhile, Joe was worrying about the future of the act. "Benny's restless," he said to Ellie. "I used to think it was because we weren't headlining at the Palace, but it's not that."

It's because of me, Ellie thought. *He's thinking about settling down.* And for days she felt like she was flying high above the world. But she had to be sure she was right about that, so one night, after she and Benny had made love, when they were lying next to each other and it was still hard to catch their breath, the question came out.

"You said I make you think about things—what did you mean?"

"I think about"—he paused, and then he went on slowly—"do I want to keep on running around the country playing the small-time for the rest of my life. Because that's the only future for Masters and George, no matter what Joe says."

That wasn't what she had wanted to hear, and she felt like someone had burst her lovely hot-air balloon. She sat up and pulled the sheet around her.

"We'd do better if you'd work on new material with Joe and me," she said tartly. "We need a new act. . . ."

He sat up and covered himself too. "You think I don't know

that? You bet that's what we need—from the bottom up. But I've been through that before. I know how it'll go." He held up his fingers and ticked them off one by one. "First, we take a couple of weeks to lay off, with no money coming in, while we write all this new material. Second, we rehearse—still with nothing coming in—until we're ready to try it out; that'll take another three weeks at least. Then we get ourselves booked on the small small-time, playing tank towns for almost nothing, to break the act in and see how it goes over; say another three or four months. If we flop, we're out of money, and it's back to the old act until we can start over again. If the new act does work, we keep on booking on the small-time while we polish it. Say another three months."

"You have to be patient."

"That's not me. It never was, and now"—he looked at her, and her heart started pounding again—"now I think it's time for me to get serious."

She waited for him to add the magic phrase *About you, Ellie*.

"I'm not a kid," he went on. "Joe is nineteen, but I'm two years older. I'm tired of living in boardinghouses and two-bit hotels. I'm done with putting makeup on my collar when I'm between jobs so everyone will think I'm working, and I'm done with waiting for that one shot at the big-time." He fixed his face in a silly smirk and made his voice go high and stupid. *"We killed them in this little hick town, next stop is the Palace,"* he said, in a mockery of every hopeful vaudevillian. "I don't want that anymore."

He still hadn't said anything about her—or them—but he hadn't taken his eyes off her either. "What do you want?" she asked breathlessly.

"Money. Respect. I want to be my own man."

So I can be with you, forever. That was what he should have said next. But he didn't.

"We're on the wrong end of the business, Ellie. It's the theater owners and the booking agents back in New York who have the right idea. We work like dogs and they have all the power. We're dumb."

He didn't notice how hurt and mad she was becoming.

"Think about it," he said. "The theater owners hire the bookers, and the bookers decide where we're going to tour and how much we get paid. We don't have anything to say about it because they all work together."

It was a gripe Ellie had heard a million times. Vaudeville was dominated by two organizations: Keith's and the Orpheum. Each had its own circuit of theaters and a staff of booking agents who hired the acts that played them. There were a few small independent circuits, but they didn't really count for much. Keith's and the Orpheum had a stranglehold on the industry. They dictated pay and working conditions for all but the biggest stars, and any performer who went against them could be blackballed and never work again. It was unfair, but it was nothing new, and Ellie couldn't believe Benny was bringing it up now, when they should have been talking about themselves.

"Yes," she said, disappointment making her voice harsh, "Keith's and the Orpheum have a monopoly. So what?"

"So I'm thinking if a smart fellow had a chance to be a booker for Keith's because he had some good friends in the organization who liked him and wanted to help him out, that might not be a bad thing."

"You want to give up the act and work for management?"

He smiled that confident smile that made everything in the world seem possible. "You think I couldn't make my way up the ladder? With my gift of gab?"

"But what about Joe?" *What about me?*

"We still have a couple of months left on the tour, and I'm not saying anything to Joe until it's over. Don't you say anything to him either. Because it isn't set yet."

Because you don't want to face him. You'll just walk away, she thought. And for a second she knew that, even though she loved Benny, she didn't trust him. That thought made her heart break.

Benny pulled her close. "Don't look so sad. I told you, I've been thinking about all this because of you." He paused for a second. "You're different from the other girls I've known, Ellie." At that, her heart had mended.

During the weeks that followed, Ellie felt badly about keeping Benny's secret from Joe, but she had to stay loyal to Benny. Besides, Joe's moods were getting even more sour as the end of their tour came nearer, so perhaps he knew what was up. She'd discovered that Joe was often more sensitive to the people around him than her beautiful Benny. So even though it didn't feel quite honest, she kept her mouth shut. And then the time came when she had a lot more to worry about than being honest with Joe. Because now she had a secret of her own. A terrible secret.

CHAPTER 20

Ellie checked her watch: she had three more hours before she had to be downstairs in the lobby. That gave her time to lie down. Maybe she'd try to read. She'd been doing a lot of reading lately; it helped pass the time when she was alone.

There had been a time when she wouldn't have been alone in her room on a pretty spring day. In the beginning, when she and Benny were newly in love, he would have been knocking on her door, calling out that this town had the best ice cream parlor—or candy shop, or lunch wagon—on the entire eastern seaboard, and he had to take her for a sundae or a hot dog right this minute, and he wouldn't take no for an answer. She would giggle as she rammed on her hat and went out the door and into his arms. And he would scandalize anyone who happened to be in the hallway by kissing her like he never wanted to stop. Sometimes, instead of going out, they would rush back into her room and shut the door until it was time to go to the theater. Other times they would run out of the hotel, giddy and laughing. But now Benny was avoiding her. He had been for two weeks.

Ellie put down her book and lay down on the bed. She'd rest for a while, she decided; maybe she'd even go to sleep. She was tired all the time now. But that would end this afternoon. And by tomorrow the morning sickness would end too. At least, she thought it would. She wasn't sure what happened when you were carrying a child and you "got rid of it." That was the way Benny had said it. "You've got to get rid of it, Ellie."

But that was after they knew. First, he'd found a doctor for her to see and he'd gone with her. He'd said gentle, calming things to her on the bus trip to the doctor's office, so she'd convinced herself that everything was going to be all right. She'd kept on telling herself that after the doctor gave them the news, even though Benny couldn't meet her eyes. And he hadn't looked at her once on the ride back to the hotel. She'd told herself she understood; it was only natural that he'd be upset, because having a baby wasn't part of his plans. But he'd do the right thing. He'd take care of her.

Actually, he had said something close to that. "I'll take care of the arrangements," he'd told her, as he paced back and forth in her hotel room. She could see he was thinking fast, and the pacing reminded her of an animal trying to get out of its cage. "There's a woman I know about in Poughkeepsie," he'd continued. "It's the next town over, and we can go on our day off. She's a midwife, so she knows what she's doing, and she's clean and careful. You'll be fine." And then, his problem solved, he'd smiled at her. That was something he hadn't done since she'd first told him what she suspected. But now, he did. And he'd taken her in his arms. "Poor kid," he'd said gently. "You must be scared out of your mind. There's nothing to it, you'll see." And she'd been too sick and shocked to ask how he knew that. In fact, she hadn't said anything at all. So he'd made the *arrangements*. And now, this afternoon, they were going to Poughkeepsie, where the clean, careful midwife who knew what she was doing would get rid of Ellie's problem.

Ellie turned on her side and tried to stop her racing thoughts. But they came anyway. *What will the woman do to me? How will she . . . but Benny says I mustn't think about that. Benny will be there with me. Think about Benny. He says this is what I have to do. And he knows. Because Benny loves me, and . . . and he wants me to get rid of it . . . it . . . my baby. . . .* She sat up. *It's not an it, it's my baby!* It was as if a mist had been lifted, and for the first time in days she could see clearly. *I can't do it.* The thought was so simple. *I won't do it.*

The nausea was gone. She got up from the bed, and ran out of the room and down the hallway to the room Benny shared with Joe. Benny was going to be upset when she told him she couldn't do what he wanted. She was prepared for that. He thought he'd solved their problem, and he wasn't going to like hearing that he hadn't. But she'd tell him how she felt, and when he understood, he wouldn't want her to go through with it. Not her Benny, who smiled at her with his warm blue eyes and bought her hot fudge sundaes and made love to her. He'd said she was different from all the other girls he'd ever known. He'd said she was good for him, and he'd stayed faithful to her all these months. Benny loved her. And he wouldn't do this to her. Not when he understood. She knocked on the hotel room door and said a quick little thank-you to heaven when Benny opened it and there was no sign of Joe. She and Benny could talk in private. She drew in a breath and began.

"WHAT DO YOU mean, you can't go through with it?" Benny demanded. His face had gone as white as the sheets on the bed behind him. "You have to go to the midwife," he said. "There isn't any other way."

"Yes, there is! I love you. And you—" But his eyes were dark and big with panic, so she couldn't finish her thought. She couldn't say, *And you love me.*

She was starting to shiver; she had to clasp her hands together to keep them from shaking. She'd been so sure she could explain this to him, so sure she could convince him, but now, as she looked at his stricken face, she was shivering. "There is another way, Benny," she said. She waited for him to answer but he stayed silent. Finally she repeated, "There is another way."

"I can't do that." She could barely hear him.

"Can't do what?" He turned away from her. "What can't you do?" she asked, and suddenly she stopped shaking. Her voice was low and calm. That was the way she reacted when the worst was about to happen.

"You know. I don't want to hurt you, so don't make me say it."

But that was exactly what she was going to do. "What can't you do, Benny?"

He started pacing—he seemed to be doing that every time he was with her. "I locked in the job with Keith's, just a couple of days ago. When this tour is over I'm going to work in New York as an assistant booker."

"And I'm going to have a baby."

"I'm just getting started. Don't you see? I'm finally on my way! I'm going to make it!"

"And you're going to be a father."

"Ellie, when we started out . . . in the beginning . . . I thought it was just for fun. But you're the kind of girl—you're everything I want. You're beautiful, and you're smart, and you're classy. . . . And you make me happy."

I think the same thing about you. Or I used to.

"I thought we'd wait and see . . . and in two years . . . or even a year—" He was stumbling now. Benny never stumbled. He had the gift of gab. "We never talked about the future, Ellie! We never promised anything. You know we didn't."

And that was when she realized that he was right. A lot of words had been said, but none of them were about the future. And no promises had been made.

"Things have changed," she said.

"They don't have to!" He was pleading now. "I know how it must feel to you right now, sweetheart. You're scared of . . . what's going to happen today. But you're not the first girl to go through this. It happens more often than you think. And it'll be over in a few minutes. Afterward, you'll know you've done the right thing."

"I won't."

"Ellie, for God's sake. I'm not going to be making a dime. I can't afford a wife and a kid. Not now!"

"Other people manage."

"I'm not *other people*, damn it! I thought you knew that."

Of course she did. She'd loved him for it. But now she had to live with it. "I guess you finally said it," she heard herself say. "You won't marry me."

"I can't do it now."

"And I can't go to the midwife in Poughkeepsie." She started for the door, but he stopped her.

"What are you going to do?"

She had no idea.

"You can't have a baby on your own."

"That's none of your business anymore," she said, and she walked out.

She went back to her room and lay down on her bed. She had all the time in the world now. She didn't have to catch a bus. She didn't have to be in Poughkeepsie for a three o'clock appointment. She could stay here for the rest of the day and night, if that was what she wanted.

ELLIE HAD NO idea how long she'd been sleeping—she must have dozed off—when she was awakened by someone knocking on the door. She sat up fast. "Benny?" she said joyfully. She flew to the door and opened it and the joy died. Because it wasn't Benny standing in front of her, it was Joe. And his expression was grim.

Joe looked at Ellie's face and saw the traces of tears. She'd been crying again. She'd been doing that a lot lately. And of course he knew where to lay the blame. Every girl who fell for Benny wound up crying sooner or later. There had been times in the past weeks when he'd thought it served Ellie right for being a fool. Then he'd tell himself she was just a kid—not even seventeen—so he should try to understand. But then he'd get mad at her all over again. She should be smarter than that. Damn it, she *was* smarter than that.

He knew how quick and smart she was, because when he started telling his jokes about things he'd read in the newspaper she got the punch lines faster than anyone else. And once she'd even suggested some dialogue for him and Benny to say in the act, and they'd put it in and it always got a big laugh.

So why was a smart girl like that throwing herself away on Benny? Benny couldn't love anyone but himself. It was because Mrs. Gerhardt died while she was still mad at him, and all the girls laughed at Benny when he was a kid—and there were probably other reasons Joe didn't even know about. But why couldn't Ellie see what a phony he was? Even if he did decide he was in love with her, Benny would never take care of her. Sometimes Joe would see her smiling at Benny with her beautiful eyes shining and he'd want to shake her.

And he had to admit that he was angry at Ellie for not realizing that he was the one who did take care of her. He saw to it that she had the bottom bunk on the train on the overnight jumps, and he made sure she had the best hotel rooms. He took care of her onstage too. He upstaged himself to make sure she got her one laugh, and he was always trying to come up with new bits for her that weren't too difficult, so she would look good.

And what had she done? She'd started sleeping with Benny. After he'd found out, Joe told himself he was through looking out for her. When they'd checked into their new hotel, he had let the clerk book her into the worst room—he'd figured what the hell, Benny was spending his nights there, let him complain about the ceiling that was falling on her head. And Joe had let Ellie fend for herself onstage when Benny went up on his lines and didn't feed her the right cue.

But then she had tried to act tough, like she didn't care that she was sleeping in a dump, and she tried to pretend she didn't care that she hadn't gotten her laugh and instead she'd just looked young and hurt. And so beautiful. So Joe had made the desk clerk change her room, and he'd been real careful to set up her punch line the next night so she'd get a roar from the house. And she'd gone off to dinner with Benny after the show. And that night, after everything was quiet, Benny had made his way down the hall to her new room.

But then a couple of weeks ago, Ellie had started crying all the time, so Joe figured Benny had finally gotten tired of her. Joe told himself he wasn't going to try to comfort her—she'd had a longer run than most girls did—and he had waited for the dust to settle. But it hadn't. Instead, it looked like whatever had gone on between the lovebirds had caused a catastrophe. And now, Joe was standing in Ellie's doorway, preparing to deliver some very bad news.

"Benny's gone," he said. "He packed up all his clothes and left. The desk clerk in the lobby says he checked out of the hotel. Do you know where he went?"

"New York City." She started to cry some more, in big gulping sobs. And even though he'd promised himself he wouldn't try to help her this time, that this time she'd have to face the consequences of her stupid romance on her own, he couldn't do it. He walked into her room and made her sit down until she had finally sobbed herself dry. And then he made her tell him the whole sad, miserable story.

CHAPTER 21

Ellie was sitting on the edge of her bed. Joe was in a chair opposite her. It was funny, she thought. This was the second time she'd sat in this same spot and told a man she was going to have a baby. But this man wasn't pacing back and forth and avoiding her eyes. This man was facing her. And after she'd told him about the midwife in Poughkeepsie he'd asked very calmly, "Are you sure that's not what you want to do?"

And because he was so calm she was able to answer firmly. "Yes. I'm sure."

He took a moment; then he said, "Benny won't change his mind about marrying you."

He could, said her heart. *He could walk in the door and say he'd made a mistake. God could let him do that.*

"I know," she told Joe.

"What are you going to do?"

"I thought . . . maybe one of my sisters . . ." But Dot lived in a room in a boardinghouse, and her landlady wouldn't welcome a pregnant sister who had no husband. As for Florrie, her husband was so straitlaced, even if he did take Ellie in he would be ashamed of her and would lecture her about the disgrace she'd brought on his family. "I don't know," she said. She made herself smile. "I'm not the first girl to get into this pickle. What do the rest of them do?"

That seemed to make Joe angry. He jumped up out of his chair. "Stop that!" he said. "Stop trying to be a wiseguy!"

"Well, what do you want me to do? Cry? I've done that and it doesn't help. Anyway, this isn't your problem, so you better go."

"Right," he said and headed for the door. Then he turned back. "You can't have a baby on your own."

"Looks like I'm going to."

"It won't have a last name."

"I think what you're trying to say is, it'll be a bastard."

"I told you not to try to be tough."

"You don't get to tell me anything."

"Yeah, I do."

"How do you figure that?"

"Because . . . Look, Ellie, you're in a jam, and I . . . can help."

And suddenly, she knew what he was going to say. And she saw in his eyes that he knew she knew. "No. I can't let you—"

"What else are you going to do? We'll get married." And for a quick second she thought she saw something else in his brown eyes, something she couldn't understand. Then she thought how desperately she had wanted to hear those words from another man just a few hours ago.

"Why?" she asked.

She watched him decide not to answer. "That doesn't matter now."

"It does to me." Then she added brutally, "I don't love you, Joe."

"I never said anything about love."

"Then why?"

"Stop asking so many questions. You're going to have a baby. It's going to need a father's name on the birth certificate. I can give you that. Take it. For the baby."

"And what happens to you and me after the baby is born?"

"We stay together until you're on your feet. Eventually one of us is going to want to get out. We'll split up."

"Get a divorce." Pa would have said divorce was a disgrace. She didn't even want to think about what her mother might have said.

Joe was reading her mind. "It's better than the alternative." Then his face got red. "And . . . if . . ." Now he was stumbling around. "If you're worried about . . . I don't expect . . ."

"I know," she said quickly. Joe would never ask a girl who didn't love him to sleep with him.

"So it's settled?"

It was wrong to let him do this for her. For a moment she wondered if, in spite of what he'd said, he might be a little in love with her—which would make it even worse. But she couldn't believe that. Joe had never been the least bit romantic with her; half the time she thought he didn't even like her. There had to be some reason why he was willing to do this for her, but clearly he didn't want to tell her. And no matter what his reason was, she couldn't turn him down. He'd said there was no other way for the baby, and he was right. She told herself not to remember the time, just a few short weeks ago, when she'd thought that the day she got married would be the happiest of her life. "When?" she asked.

"As soon as we can."

"I still wish I knew what you are getting out of this."

It was his turn to try to make it light. "A new partner for my act. Now that Benny's gone—"

"The act! Oh, my God, what will we do about the act?"

"I guess we'll have to come up with a new one."

"By tomorrow?" Because that was how fast they'd have to do it. Today had been a rare day off, but tomorrow night the show would be back on. And at the moment, Masters, George, and Doran was missing one third of its cast.

"No," Joe said. "We can't do that." She watched him draw in a deep breath. She knew he'd never walked out on a performance before. It went against the core of everything he believed. It was blasphemy.

"I've never been a no-show in my life." Ellie put his thoughts into words. "Not since Pa put me onstage when I was six."

They looked at each other. "We'll have to cancel," Joe said.

CHAPTER 22

It was noon when I turned off the tape recorder. I'd been writing every day for a week without taking a break, and I was beat. Plus, I'd run out of chocolate bars. So even though a part of me wanted to keep on going, I decided that Benny's exit was a natural place to stop. And it was definitely time for me to have a little human contact. I picked up the phone.

I'm really working hard, was what I reported to Alexandra. *But it's very fulfilling. I'll email you the part of the manuscript I've written.*

I'm having a ball, was what I told Sheryl during our phone call. *It almost doesn't seem like work. I'll email you the chapters I've finished so you can tell me what you think.*

"I know, I know," I said to Annie. "Sending them my pages is pathetic. What do you want from me? I'm an applause junkie. I'm looking for a twelve-step program. But in the meantime, I'm sending out those pages so I can get my fix." The truth was, I knew I was going to get applause, I was that sure of this story. "It's as if I've always wanted to write about these people," I told Annie. She yawned, and threw a meaningful glance at her empty food bowl. Life lesson: Dogs keep you from getting too artsy.

Annie was out of kibble, so a trip to the store was in order. I e-mailed the chapters to Alexandra and Sheryl and headed out. The elevator seemed to be stuck on the penthouse floor. When it finally did move, the sound of shrill barking preceded it. It was coming from inside the elevator cab and you could hear it echoing up and down the shaft. The doors opened, and I heard a familiar voice say, "Lancie, be quiet! Mommy is already upset. She had to come all the way home on her lunch hour to take you out for potty time!"

I stepped inside and saw the lawyer from the penthouse with her Yorkie. Abigail something.

"You haven't got a dog-walking service yet?" I asked.

"I thought I was on the trail of one, but they don't have an opening until one of their schnauzers goes to the Hamptons for the summer. That's almost six months from now. I'll probably be certifiable by then."

The day before yesterday, I would have mentally rolled my eyes and dismissed this as a spoiled-rich-person problem. But now that I had Chicky's five thousand bucks in the bank, I clucked sympathetically.

In the lobby I detoured to check my mailbox. I'd been working so hard it had been a couple of days since I'd picked up my magazines and the bills that I could now pay. When I opened the box, the first thing I saw was a long, ominous-looking envelope from my bank. I ripped it open. Then I yelled a phrase that wasn't very ladylike. "Is everything okay, Francesca?" Abigail asked.

"I may need a lawyer," I said darkly.

"Are you in trouble?"

"I will be. I'm going to kill someone." And I raced out of the building.

"I NEED TO talk to you right now, Chicky!" I yelled. I'd barged past the woman sitting at the front desk of Yorkville House and raced to Chicky's room, where I'd begun banging on the door. I figured she'd probably seen who I was through the peephole and was hiding, but I was prepared to stay there all day if I had to.

Chicky opened the door when I was midway through my second onslaught. She seemed thrilled to see me. For a second I'd thought maybe I'd misunderstood the missive from the bank. But there was no mistaking the phrase *insufficient funds*.

"Doll Face, what a pleasant surprise," Chicky said. "Come on in. Tea? Cookies?"

Her sweet-old-lady face was so innocent. So shiny with welcome. No way she could have deliberately tried to screw me. Now I felt guilty for all the ugly thoughts I'd had on the bus ride over. The poor little thing probably made a mistake in her checkbook, I told myself. I still haven't learned to balance mine, and I'm years younger than she is. Thank God I hadn't accused her of anything. "Chicky," I said gently. "I'm afraid there's a problem. The check you gave me, it—"

"It bounced like a rubber ball?"

"I'm afraid so," I said, still with the gentle tone. Because it was clear that she hadn't grasped the gravity of the situation.

She nodded. "That'll happen when you don't have any money in the account."

So she *had* grasped the frigging gravity! Innocent little old lady be damned. *"You knew?"*

"Oh, I know to the penny how much I have. I'm very good with figures. I kept the books for my family business for years."

"You don't have any money?"

"I have enough to cover my expenses here. See, I bought an annuity." She paused to chuckle. "Those poor dopes thought they were getting a bargain with someone my age, but I plan to live forever. I love being alive. Every time you turn around there's something new and fantastic happening. Or you get a second chance at something fantastic you thought you'd lost—"

"You don't have the money." I broke into her happy riff.

"I'm not broke, but I don't have enough for extras. I'm awfully old, you know, and I do live on a fixed income."

"But you said you could pay fifteen thousand dollars."

"Yes, about that. When I read your advertisement on your website, you know—when you said you were looking for work—I got the feeling that making money was very important to you."

"It's the reason I'm doing this!"

"Exactly. If I had said, 'I can't pay you now, but I'll give you a piece of the action when we sell the book,' you probably would have turned me down."

"Not *probably*. Definitely."

"So you understand the problem. I had to promise you something. And fifteen thousand dollars is a nice round sum."

"Which you do not have. And the contract we both signed?" She shrugged. "So you gave me a check that was no good."

"There wasn't any other way to get you started."

"That's fraud."

"Probably."

"I could have you arrested!"

At that, her sweet smile vanished. She looked down at her gnarled little hands and began twisting them nervously. When she looked up after a couple of seconds, there was a tear streaming down either cheek. She looked tiny and vulnerable and frail. I felt like the love child of Hitler and Cruella De Vil. "I would never do that, Chicky," I said.

Instantly her face was wreathed in smiles. "I know, Doll Face." She patted my hand. "I was just giving myself a little test run. Crying on cue is my only real theatrical gift. I'm rusty, but I've still got it." She patted my hand. "And I wanted to be sure you're as nice as I thought you were."

I wanted to throttle her. But nice people don't hurt octogenarians. "I can't believe you've done this to me!" I cried.

For the first time she looked concerned. "Doll Face, it's doing you a world of good, working on this story. For one thing, there's no pressure when you're writing a vanity memoir for a little old lady in a nursing home."

She was right about that. "That's not the point."

"Sure it is. You needed to get your confidence back. You choked for a while there, but now you're writing again."

"Because I was suckered into it."

A hand waved dismissal. "Potato, pot*ah*to. You say *suckered*, I say *persuaded*. I knew this story would be right up your alley."

That was the hard part—because it was. Really and truly. And I had to drop it. "I have to earn a living. I'm sorry, but I can't write for free." I started for the door, but Chicky's voice stopped me.

"You've never really had it hard, have you, Doll Face?"

It was the last straw. I whirled around. "You don't know anything about me!" I shouted. "You don't know what my life was like!" But even as I was shouting I was thinking, *How hard was it— really? Yes, my parents got a divorce and, yes, my husband dumped me, but sixteen-year-old Ellie Doran was pregnant with nowhere to go. She had to marry a man she didn't love or have an abortion back in the days when that could kill you.*

But I'd been so used to feeling sorry for myself. "I've had it plenty hard!" I yelled. And I stormed out of Chicky's room.

In the lobby, I ran into Show Biz. Literally.

"You might want to slow down a little," he said, as he massaged the shoulder I'd plowed into. "Balance—as in staying on one's feet—is an issue in a residence for older folks. It doesn't take much to tip some of them over."

"Did you know?" I demanded. "When you answered my ad for Chicky, did you know she never had any intention of paying?"

There was a pause. "Not exactly. I did wonder about the money . . . but she wanted you to write that book so much—"

"Why me?"

"Damned if I know. But when you two hit it off the way you did, I just hoped it would all work out."

"We hit it off because she conned me!"

But that wasn't the reason. I liked Chicky. And I liked her book . . . which I wasn't going to be writing. Suddenly I was crying—right in the middle of the Yorkville House lobby—which really pissed me off, but I couldn't make myself stop. I rushed out the front door, going at warp speed. Show Biz had to run to keep up with me.

"What are you going to do now?" he panted.

"I'm going to go home, pack up the rest of those damn tapes, and send them back."

"Do you have to, Francesca? All Chicky wanted was—"

"Don't say that name, okay?"

"But maybe there's a way—"

"She lied to me! Now I have to start all over again and try to find a real job."

And whatever that job is, I won't be writing about Joe and Ellie.

At my side, Show Biz was now running and limping. I slowed down. "You don't have to keep me company," I said.

"I'll come with you to your apartment and pick up Chicky's . . .
uh . . . the tapes."

"You don't have to do that."

"I want to."

WE REACHED MY building just as the sun was going down. The
park was bathed in pink. Show Biz stopped dead in his tracks.
"Wow!" he whispered. "You get those sunsets every evening? Talk
about a view!"

The awe in his voice dragged me out of my self-pity. I looked
up and saw the scene through his eyes. "Yeah, it's great. You should
catch it from the roof garden. You can see the whole city."

"You own or rent?" The longing in his voice was like something
you could touch.

"Own," I said. "For the moment. As long as I can afford the
maintenance."

"Right." He forced himself to stop staring at the park and the
glowing sun and went inside the building with me. I gave him a
quick tour of my apartment—more cause for awe on his part—and
then I started putting the tapes back in Chicky's plastic grocery
bags.

"I wish you could reconsider," Show Biz said.

"Remember that maintenance I mentioned? The condo gets
real nasty with delinquents."

He nodded. I looked at the grocery bags in my hand. When
Show Biz left, the whole Chicky episode of my life would end for
good. I guess he was thinking something similar, because he
started searching around in his pockets. After a second he produced a scrap of paper and wrote his phone number and email ad-
dress on it. "If you ever feel like having a cup of coffee," he said, as
he handed the paper to me.

"Thanks. We'll have to do that." But of course I knew we wouldn't, because this was New York and you always made empty promises like that. Which was too bad, because he was one of those people you think you'd probably like a lot if you really got to know them. But I handed over the bags, he took them, and he was gone.

And it was over. No more Chicky. No more Joe and Ellie. No more book—the one I knew I could actually write.

"I'm fine," I said to Alexandra on the phone. "I'm moving on."

But the apartment was so damn quiet.

OVER THE NEXT few days it got worse. I'd gotten used to Chicky's taped voice talking to me throughout the day. Now I felt like I was getting divorced again—only without the husband-cheating-on-me part. And I had to find a job. All over again. I looked at my bed and thought about how much I wanted to get into it and pull the covers over my head.

"Why shouldn't I?" I said to Annie "Nothing ever works, no matter how much I try."

You've never really had it hard, have you, Doll Face? Chicky had asked.

"It isn't fair."

You've never really had it hard, said Chicky's voice inside my head.

"I don't deserve this."

Please! said a new voice inside my head that I recognized as my own. *You never really had it that hard!*

I washed my face, opened my laptop, and typed out my résumé. And here's the thing I want to say right now about life lessons: Sometimes they come to you from the damnedest places.

I pitched for jobs on the Internet for three days. I didn't give up and I didn't feel sorry for myself—well, not a lot. On the fourth evening, just after I'd packed it in and was turning on the TV for a *CSI* rerun, I heard someone turning the key in my door. Only two people besides me have ever had the key to the apartment, Alexandra and Jake, and Jake handed his over when I bought him out. Annie wasn't barking her warnings against intruders; instead she was jumping against the door in a display of canine welcome. So it wasn't a surprise when Alexandra waltzed in. The fact that Sheryl was with her . . . well, that was a shock. Alexandra was holding a sheaf of papers. So was Sheryl.

CHAPTER 23

Alexandra bent down to pet Annie, who had rolled over on her back in adoration. Annie has never forgotten who rescued her, I don't care what people say about dogs having no memory. Besides, Alexandra had named Annie for her mother, and these things create a bond.

"This is very well written." Alexandra held up the pages.

"I finished it in the airport before I got on the plane," Sheryl added.

"I called Sheryl and asked her to come out East so we could talk to you together."

"Like an intervention. This is my second. The first was one we all did for Gracie Mamaront, when we found out she was drinking grape-tinis at seven in the morning."

"We think you should keep on with this." Alexandra waved the pages at me.

"This book is better than *Love, Max*. Your heart's in it more," said Sheryl.

"Do you want to write it, Francesca?"

"That doesn't matter," I said. "The woman who hired me can't pay me. I have dog food to buy."

"But if you could, would you want to write it?"

They were both looking at me, faces a little worried, maybe, but encouraging too. They loved me and each of them, in her own way, had always been there for me. Even though most of the time I hadn't been very grateful for it.

Ellie didn't have a mother, and her father beat her. That was a weird thing to be thinking about at that moment, but unfortunately that's how my head works.

"Yes," I said, to my mother and Sheryl. "I would like to finish writing the book. But I'd have to do it on spec, and I'd have to support myself while I did it."

"Lenny and I don't have a lot of money," my mother said. "But there *is* a second bedroom in our apartment. If you need a place to live . . ."

My mother's second bedroom was the size of a large closet. Her favorite form of entertaining was still a Bad Spaghetti Night that lasted until 3 A.M. Also, Lenny had two sons who sometimes came to visit him, and whenever Pete and his family were in the country they stayed with Alexandra and Lenny. I could see Annie and me crammed into the closet while I tried to follow my creative muse.

"Or," said Sheryl, "I can give you whatever you need. I have a check right here . . ."

And what would I do when the money ran out? Would I take more from Sheryl? And then, if I didn't find a publisher for my masterpiece, keep on taking more? For how long? I looked at my mother and my stepmother and realized that neither of them had ever been very practical. They hadn't had to be—because of the man who had left Sheryl a wealthy widow and had seen to it that Alexandra was a comfortable divorcée. The man who had married against his family's wishes in a big romantic gesture but then made sure he earned a hell of a good living.

Just to prove that sometimes mothers do read their daughters' minds, Alexandra chose that moment to say to Sheryl, "You know who Joe in Francesca's story reminds me of?"

"Nathaniel," Sheryl said. "I saw the likeness immediately. No wonder she wants to write the book."

"Joe wasn't anything like Dad," I said.

"Of course he was," my mother said, "in the ways that matter."

"You could always count on Nathaniel," Sheryl said.

"Actually, I couldn't," my mother said thoughtfully. "But then, he couldn't count on me."

Sheryl turned to me. "You could, Francesca. That's why you like this story so much."

Alexandra handed me her copy of the pages I'd sent to her. "You're a good writer—and this is good work. You really should read what you've written. It would be a shame for you to give up just because you're facing a few challenges."

And before I could point out that "a few challenges" didn't exactly cover the situation, Alexandra and Sheryl headed for the door.

"Where are you—"

"Your mother and I are going to give you some time to think this over," Sheryl said.

"We're going out to pick up dinner," my mother said. "There's a place in this neighborhood that has the best Kung Pao chicken."

"Do they use canola oil or peanut?" Sheryl was asking as my front door closed behind them.

I read over the pages I'd written. And I thought it over—as directed—because I do take orders well. I thought about the whole writing thing, and how I'd gotten into it, and how it had been the only thing I'd ever loved doing. And I thought about my dad, and how he was really the one who first got me started writing. Remembering that, and the way Daddy stood by me throughout my teenage and college years, still makes me want to smile. And cry.

PETE AND I had continued our yearly visitations to California until he was a sophomore in high school. That was when he won an award for doing something esoteric with numbers, and suddenly he was in demand for a whole laundry list of Budding Genius programs. They were so impressive that even Alexandra had to agree it was time to let him skip his annual two-month sulk next to Dad's pool so he could follow his geek bliss. Pete spent the next three summers in garden spots like Irvine, California, Washington, D.C., and, for some reason that escapes me, Reykjavik.

Since, unlike Pete's, my vacations weren't devoted to mindbendingly difficult academic work, I probably could have continued spending two months in Pasadena. But somehow by the time summer rolled around each year I had lined up a job. I think I've already mentioned that I usually worked for my mother's friends, most of whom were operating day-care centers in poverty-stricken churches, helping illegal immigrants stay in the country, or trying to force landlords to provide the services mandated by law for their tenants. All these organizations worked on a shoe-string, so my salary—if I earned anything at all—was always tiny. I tried to tell myself that I did this work because I had a burning need to make a difference. But my dad knew different.

He and Sheryl were driving me back to LAX after I'd taken a fast trip to California to see them. I was rushing back to New York to continue assisting with a literacy program at a halfway house for recently paroled female convicts. To a woman, our clients began each reading lesson by first intoning, "I thank God I'm straight and sober one more day."

"But you could stay here and have some fun," Sheryl protested.

A part of me wanted to. The halfway house was old, and when the drains backed up it got a little ripe. And, to be honest, a couple of the inmates scared me. But I couldn't quit my job. And I couldn't explain why.

"It's okay, honey." Dad came to my rescue. "We understand. Your brother's in Iceland, and you don't want to be the sibling with free time on your hands."

And, pathetic as it was, that was my motivation. Several times in the past few years, people had introduced me as Pete Sewell's older sister, and it had seemed to me that the phrase *who doesn't do much* was implied. And while I might have my girly moments, I had not been raised to be the family airhead. I was Woman, and my mother expected to hear me roar.

Dad had picked up on my thoughts. "Lotta pressure, honey. Don't let it get to you."

But it did. Alexandra never understood why I felt I was in a footrace with Pete. Or with anyone, for that matter. "The only person you have to compete with is yourself," she told me one time. "It's not about Pete." There was no point in trying to explain to her that it *was* about him, not only because he was a freaking genius but also because he had developed into the spitting image of our beautiful daddy, while I had a long nose—actually it was Alexandra's nose—and those sturdy hips and thighs.

But I plunged onward in my adolescence, trying without any success to figure out the mixed signals I was getting from the two female role models in my life. I was too girly to be my incredible mother, and I was too intellectual—and chubby—to approach being Sheryl.

Each of them tried in her own way to help me.

"Just be yourself!" Alexandra advised.

"Francesca, stop thinking so much!" said Sheryl.

I couldn't do either.

I did fall in love a lot. As I think I mentioned earlier, the boys were what was euphemistically labeled *troubled*. Because I wasn't totally self-destructive, just hormone-crazed, I knew the junior sociopaths who caught my fancy were unacceptable. But that didn't mean my heart wasn't constantly being broken.

Dad was the only one who really knew how unhappy I was, and he knew there was no way I could talk about it. Instead, he had a friend from his Westchester days deliver a jazzy Corvette convertible to our apartment building for me. And I'm sorry to be a materialist, but it helped. I spent many a dateless weekend riding around the outlying suburbs of Manhattan in my car with the top down and the sound system blasting. I became one hell of a driver, and to this day I can change a tire on any vehicle that doesn't qualify as heavy equipment.

Meanwhile, Pete was sailing through his teenage years unscathed. He was in one of the few schools in the United States where being smart and career-oriented was not the kiss of death socially. Unlike me, Pete had friends and dates—lots of them. In his junior year, he settled on a girl who played the cello with the New York Philharmonic and had a grade point average almost as high as his. The boy I was in love with at the time was going to be facing charges for possession unless his father could pull some strings.

Of course, Pete had already made early admission to Harvard. I'd finished high school too and was headed to a liberal arts college that had a history of progressive thought in the Hudson River valley; with my arithmetic phobia the Ivies weren't going to happen for me. But I had also settled on a career. I was going to be a lawyer.

"Wonderful!" Alexandra enthused. "We'll start a family dynasty."

"Are you sure, honey?" Dad asked. "The law is awfully . . . demanding."

But having made my pick I was determined to stick to it. I polished off my required courses in my first two years at college and began on my career path.

I made it through Criminal Justice and Juvenile Criminology— barely. But the New York State Penal Code? Don't ask. The good news was, I was studying so hard that I didn't have time to fall in love anymore. The bad news was, I gained eighteen pounds. And then there was the night when I was talking to Dad on the phone and I started to cry and couldn't stop for two weeks.

Sheryl wanted to send me to the Golden Door. Alexandra wanted to send me to a shrink. Dad sent me a red Porsche. Actually, he bought it from his Westchester buddy and then he flew east and drove it up to my campus to give it to me personally. Alexandra joined him, Pete came down from Harvard, and we all went out to the lousy Chinese restaurant near my campus. Dad held my hand while I wept into my moo shu pork. "There's no disgrace in changing your mind, honey," he soothed.

"You're smart and strong, Francesca," my mother said staunchly. "You'll get a grip on this."

But I knew I wouldn't. Dad said, "If being a lawyer is wrong for you, drop it, honey."

Alexandra intervened. "I wouldn't say you should give up because you're finding the work difficult, that's never a good reason—"

"It is, if you're miserable," Dad broke in. "Were there any subjects you liked in school, honey?"

I quit sobbing. "There was one class . . ." I started to say, but I stopped. Because the class I'd enjoyed was going to sound totally fluffy to my overachieving brother and mother.

"What was it?" Dad urged. The three of them stared expectantly at me.

"A creative writing workshop," I said, as Pete and my mother tried not to roll their eyes. "I had to submit a short story to get in," I hurried on. No need to tell them that I'd whipped up a tale about a divorce as told from the viewpoint of the family dog. "It was really quite competitive. I never thought I'd make it." In fact, everyone who had tried out for that workshop had been accepted. Of the seven who were not me, five were the kind of girls you know had problems at home, and two were guys trolling for dates. "The work wasn't easy," I said. That was actually true. But compared to beating my brains out over the penal code, it had been a walk in the park. "The instructor said I had a real flair."

Alexandra and Pete picked up on that right away. "Instructor?" Pete repeated.

"He wasn't a full professor?" my mother demanded.

"Didn't you listen, damn it?" Dad said. "She liked doing it! And the teacher said she was good at it."

"I suppose, if you wanted to major in English, you could switch over," my mother said dubiously. She had always been opposed to what she called "amorphous liberal arts degrees for girls that don't prepare them to do anything in the real world."

"She could teach," said my brother.

"Do you think you'd enjoy that?" Dad asked me.

But I was damned if I was going to get an airhead English degree. Or become a teacher. Not when my brother had just signed on as architect for a prestigious not-for-profit group. And there was a rumor that he might be presenting a paper at the UN.

"We just want you to be fulfilled in your work," said my mother.

"To hell with that," said Dad. "I just want you to stop crying!" And, amazingly, *his* usually stiff WASP upper lip twitched, and *his* eyes welled up.

"It's okay, Daddy," I reassured him. "I'm going to ace the rest of this year. And I'm going to ace the LSATs."

I pulled myself together enough to graduate, but as for the acing part? I got the damn diploma, okay? As for the LSATs, you know that sad story.

I soon discovered that my degree in political science was about as much use as one in English would have been in the job market, so I went back to work for one of Alexandra's friends. I continued living in her apartment on the Upper West Side. I continued falling in love with idiots. I did that until my father died.

Dad died quickly. People told me it was a blessing, because he'd had a massive stroke and if he'd lived he probably couldn't have walked again. He would have spent the rest of his life in a wheelchair, and everyone agreed he would have hated that. So it was better this way. For his sake. Personally, I thought it would have been better if he hadn't had the goddamn stroke. He was only in his fifties, he exercised regularly, didn't smoke or drink more than a couple of glasses of wine with his dinner, and he was as slim as he'd been the day he met my mother. He was in great shape. Except for one tiny son-of-a-bitching piece of plaque that no one even knew was there, which broke loose, clogged an artery, and killed him.

But my father was gone—unexpectedly and too young. Alexandra hunted down Pete—he was in a desert somewhere in Africa—and he and I flew to Los Angeles for the funeral, which I've already described and which I did my best to tune out. When I came home, there was a box waiting for me at the apartment. Dad had sent it the week before he died. Inside was a pile of brochures from every college and university in the New York City area that had a writing class. My father had picked out one he thought would be good for me and put it on top of the heap. The class was called Write Your Bestseller! He'd inked in a big star next to the name. *Bet you'd like this one*, he'd scrawled in the margin. *No tests, no pressure.* (I learned later that he'd called and found out.)

I put the box in the back of my closet. I wasn't ready to try the writing thing yet—and his note had done me in. I didn't take the box out again until Sheryl started dating. Then I found out that the class my dad had picked for me was still in existence. I signed up for it, and I wrote *Love, Max*. I've already told the rest of that story. But what I've never told anyone is: I saved the brochure he sent me.

I walked into the bedroom, opened the bureau drawer where I keep my sweaters, and pulled that little pamphlet out from under the bottom of the pile.

There was something else Dad had written in the margin. *I'm so proud of you I could bust.*

By the time Alexandra and Sheryl came back with dinner, I knew I was going to finish Chicky's book. And I realized I was more my father's daughter than I had ever known. Because if I was going to do something that impractical, I wanted to be sure I could take care of myself first. And I knew exactly how I was going to make that happen.

"I have a Plan B," I told Alexandra and Sheryl. "The interior decorator from the Dark Side was telling the truth when she talked Jake and me into buying all our furniture. I've been online searching a couple of websites dedicated to hideous household goods, and it looks like those two big sofas and the chairs and tables will bring in about two thirds of what Jake and I paid for them."

"Francesca, you don't have to get rid of your furniture," Alexandra began, but Sheryl broke in fast.

"Yes, she does!" she said, as she looked around with a little shudder. "What about that clock?"

"It's history."

"Thank God," said my stepmother.

"After I sell this crap I can replace whatever I need from a thrift shop—there are a couple of great ones on York Avenue—and I'll still have money left over," I went on. "And I have a Plan C."

Alexandra and Sheryl were staring at me. I think they were a little thrown by this new resourceful Francesca. I know I was.

"Tomorrow morning, first thing, I have to see a woman about a dog," I said.

Sheryl and Alexandra shot each other looks of concern. I could see where they were heading: Maybe the new resourceful Francesca was starting to crack. God knows, she'd done it before.

"It's a Yorkie with anger issues," I explained.

There were more looks exchanged.

"Stop worrying. I'm not getting ready to take another dip in the nut-job pool. I'm not going to cry for three weeks, or hole up with an industrial-sized drum of chocolate Häagen-Dazs. I'm simply going to have a job. Now can we eat our kung pao chicken?"

CHAPTER 24

When I told Abigail Barrow the next day that I was willing to hire myself out as Lancelot's dog walker, her reaction was downright embarrassing.

"I'll pay you anything!" she said, as her eyes welled up. "My firstborn if I ever have one. If you ever need a fresh kidney, I'm your girl!"

"How about three half-hour walks a day, five days a week?" I countered. "I'll charge whatever a regular service gets."

"Make it seven days a week, and I'll pay you time and a half on weekends. I need to catch up at the office."

"WITH THE OVERTIME, that's even more money than I thought it would be," I told Annie when I was back in the apartment. "I figured someone who never gets out of the office until

after dark would at least take weekends off." I grabbed my calcula-
tor. "With the Lancelot pay and whatever I get for the furniture,
we can carry everything except our maintenance. And I've got a
Plan D for that." I was so excited I couldn't stay in the apartment
another second. I ran to the closet for Annie's leash. "You're going
to have to suck it up, babe," I told her. "You and I are going for a
walk. It'll get me in training for my new gig with Lancelot."

And maybe it was my imagination, but I think Annie heard
something new in my voice, because she began dancing around me
the way she hadn't since she was a pup, and when I snapped on her
leash she actually pulled me to the front door. If you're in a funk
that lasts, say, five years and counting, can you depress your dog
too?

"I'm sorry I've been such a jerk, Annie," I said, as I tickled her
chin. "I'm going to do better. Try to think of me as a work in
progress."

When Annie and I came back from our walk, it was time to put
the remaining piece of my survival strategy—that little Plan D I'd
mentioned—into place.

"I have to make a phone call," I said to my dog, as she collapsed
on the sofa.

SHOW BIZ ANSWERED on the second ring. "You caught me just
as I was heading out the door," he said.

"But your shift at the center doesn't start for another two hours."

"I have to give myself extra time. I don't know whether it's all
those new budget cuts or what, but it seems like I wait forever for
the train these days."

"Funny you should mention your commute," I said. "Can we
have that cup of coffee today?"

"I get off work at three."

• • •

"YOU WANT ME to be your roommate?" Show Biz said, a few hours later.

"I have a big room with park views I never use, and I need someone to share expenses with me. You're already paying rent out in Rockland County. Pay me instead, and you can stop making the trip from hell every day. Sounds like a win-win situation for everyone to me. Unless you hate dogs or watch reality TV."

"No way, and I wouldn't be caught dead. You're offering me a chance to rent that fabulous room at the end of your hall that overlooks the park?"

"Say the word and it's yours."

He said the word—along with the amount of rent he was paying, which was enough to cover the maintenance on the condo. We closed the deal. Then Show Biz leaned back in his booth. "Have you ever had a roommate, Francesca?" he asked.

"Do my mother and my husband count?"

"Not really."

"Then . . . no."

"Sharing space has been a lifestyle for me. So let me outline the potential problem areas. There are three. The first two, the kitchen and the bathroom, can be handled with rigid scheduling."

"I don't cook. Unless you consider nuking cooking."

"Never. So this means you won't be trying to borrow my wok. You may be the roommate I've been looking for all my life."

"You cook Chinese?"

"I've been told my dim sum is the best in the city outside of Chinatown."

"I love Chinese. And I promise to do all the cleaning up."

We smiled happily at each other. "What's the third problem area?" I finally asked.

"Dating. And that one we just have to wing. You never know who a roommate is going to fall in love with."

"No one—in my case. I won't be dating." He gave me a that's-what-they-all-say look. "I am not a cute twenty-two-year-old. I am an overweight neurotic who is no fun—and believe me, when I was married, I tried hard to be."

"Which kind of goes against the whole spirit—"

"Whatever. I'm a workaholic. I didn't mean to be, but that's how I turned out. When things aren't going well for my work I forget to stroke the guy's ego. Sometimes I forget he's alive. I also forget to wash my face and brush my hair. Any man who wants me has serious problems."

"I think there's probably a straight guy out there who can handle that."

"No dating for Francesca. Not without a prefrontal lobotomy."

He shrugged. "If you say so."

We ordered Diet Cokes to celebrate our new living arrangement, and then I grabbed a bus for York Avenue.

"I'm GOING TO write the book," I told Chicky. "And then I'm going to sell it, and I'll split whatever I get with you."

"I thought you said there wouldn't be a market for it."

"That's negative thinking. We're into positive now."

"I see."

"Success is our only option."

"Whatever you say, Doll Face," Chicky said demurely. Way too demurely.

"You knew I'd find a way to make this all work, didn't you?"

She looked down at her hands. "I hoped you would," she murmured.

"No, you knew it. How? Because this isn't like me."

"You sure?"

"Chicky, I'm a wuss. Everyone who loves me knows it."

"Maybe they don't know the real you. I have faith in you, Doll Face."

"Why? I really want to know what you saw in me that no one else ever has."

She paused. "Actually, I think about three thousand people saw what I saw in you, Doll Face. I caught your star turn on YouTube. The one where you dumped water on that skinny woman with the great dye job."

"Oh—my—God. You saw that?"

"I said to Show Biz, *She's a slugger*. That's what sold me on you." Chicky leaned over and patted my cheek. "See? Isn't life grand? You do something off the top of your head, never thinking about the consequences, and bingo! Look where it leads. To me and my book—the best thing that ever happened to you!"

She was grinning at me like a pint-sized buccaneer, daring me to disagree. I took a deep breath—followed by a huge swig of Chicky Kool Aid—and I said, "You're right. This is my lucky day. Now can I have the tapes back?"

"I'm still working on the last one," she said. She handed me the plastic grocery bags I'd given to Show Biz a couple of days earlier.

"You never unpacked this. You *were* sure."

"I'm never sure about anything. I just try to believe."

IT SEEMED LIKe old times later that afternoon when I finally settled down on my bed with my chocolate bars and diet soda. Lancelot had been a prince on both walks with me, and I had three hours of uninterrupted time before I had to take him out again. I had already listened to the tapes to reorient myself. I opened my laptop.

"After Joe proposed to Ellie and she accepted, they sat in the hotel room in New Palton for a long time without speaking," I wrote. "Benny was gone. Ellie was carrying his child, and Joe was going to give it a last name. There didn't seem to be anything else to say."

CHAPTER 25

New Palton, New York

1919

No matter how hard she tried, Ellie couldn't keep her eyes off the clock on the wall. It had been exactly an hour and eight minutes since Joe had knocked on her door to tell her Benny was gone. At first she'd been sure that there would be another knock on the door and she'd open it to find Benny standing there. Her brain knew what had happened; she'd refused to do what Benny wanted, and he'd walked. But her heart hadn't believed it. He was the first man she'd loved. He'd given her roses and brought bright colors into a life that had been so gray. They had been a beautiful couple; people saw them and said they were made for each other. There was no way, argued her heart, that he would throw all that away. He'd come back.

But he hadn't. She and Joe had been sitting in the hotel room for an hour and—she checked the clock—nine and a half minutes now, and there'd been no knock on the door. Ellie's heart felt like it had started to bleed.

"We'll have to find time to get married while we're on the road." Joe broke the silence in his matter-of-fact way. "I don't think we should wait until we finish the tour, because by then it'll be too close to the baby's birth." He was being practical, making plans. And that was good. You couldn't feel your heart bleeding—not as much anyway—when you were making plans. "We're playing split weeks on the next two jumps," Joe went on, "so there won't be time to get a license. But we have a full week in New Haven. I think it would be best if we did it there." He paused. "If that's all right. I mean, if you're sure this is what you want."

No, this is not what I want. I'm too young to give up on love, I'm only sixteen!

But there had been no knock on the door—and no Benny.

"Yes," she said. "I think we should get married in New Haven."

"Good," Joe said. He started to leave.

"Where are you going?"

"I have to go over to the theater."

Then she remembered. "We have to cancel the act." He nodded. "Isn't there something else we can do? Could we find a replacement for Benny?"

"Even if we could find someone way out here to stand in, Benny and I did a lot of physical gags. Timing is everything when you're doing knockaround. It would take days to rehearse a new guy, and we don't have them."

"Could we cut all the knockaround?"

"And fill with what? The management is expecting a fifteen-minute routine."

"So . . ." She trailed off, and they both looked away. This was going to be a big blow for them. Big-time acts could get away with canceling; sometimes a headliner would walk because he'd gotten a better offer or because he didn't like his dressing room. But a small-time act like Masters, George, and Doran—which was now just Masters, with Ellie doing a walkover—was expected to be reliable. A small-timer played through high fevers and exhaustion; he went onstage and gave his all when his child was deathly ill or a family member was being buried. That was the code of the small-time: They worked harder and longer and more gratefully than the stars. And a small-time performer who canceled in the middle of a run, leaving the management scrambling to fill his slot, would earn himself a big black mark. News of his default would spread across the show-business grapevine, and people would be reluctant to book him because he couldn't be trusted.

"Joe, I'm so sorry," Ellie said. "It's my fault. If I hadn't—"

"It's Benny's fault, all of it," he snapped. He headed for the door. "I'm going to tell the stage manager right now. Get it over with."

It wasn't fair. She and Benny had made this mess and now Joe was the person everyone in the business would remember as the no-show.

"I'll come with you," she said.

He shook his head. "If I bring you with me, I'll look like I'm too scared to face the music by myself."

"Why don't you wait until tomorrow? The theater is dark tonight, and the stage manager might not even be there."

"The house manager, or someone else, will be. I have to give them as much advance notice as I can, so they can find a disappointment act to replace us."

After he was gone, she prowled around the room. Finally, to distract herself, she picked up a newspaper and sat in a chair to read it.

And then it hit her. She ran out into the hallway with the newspaper in her hands. "Joe!" she called out. But of course he was gone. The elevator was on the ground floor, so she took the stairs down to the lobby two at a time. Joe wasn't in the lobby.

"You missed him. He left about ten minutes ago," said the desk clerk. So she raced out of the hotel.

IN THE BASEMENT of the theater, Joe prepared to knock on the door of the tiny cubbyhole that served as the stage manager's office. He'd never had to explain himself to a theater management before; he'd never been fined for lateness, or for using racy blue jokes in his act, or for breaking any of the rules that governed backstage conduct. Joe was used to being on good terms with the people who paid his weekly salary; that had always been a big source of pride to him. Until now. Damn Benny! But there was nothing to be done.

"Joe!"

He heard Ellie's voice behind him and whirled around. She was out of breath, and clearly she had been running to find him. She'd probably come to back him up—even though he'd said he didn't want her to. He let out an exasperated sigh. He'd meant it when he told her he didn't blame her for what had happened. But he had wanted her to let him do what had to be done without getting in the way.

"Ellie, I asked you to stay in the room."

But she waved a newspaper in his face and gasped out, "You're going to do a single!"

CHAPTER 26

"Have you lost your mind?" Joe demanded. But she was just trying to help, so he made himself add, more patiently, "I know you mean well, but—"

"You ad-lib monologues all the time," she broke in. "Every time you read the newspaper, you find something to make jokes about. And it's not just me who thinks you're funny. Everyone says so."

She wasn't thinking straight. It must be the guilt. "Ellie, you know better than this. There's a big difference between fooling around for the heck of it, to get a couple of laughs, and performing in a theater."

"Why?"

"It takes months to come up with a good monologue. You have to write it and then work out the kinks. Get the timing and delivery just right."

"I'm not talking about a *regular* monologue. This is a whole new kind of act. Every day we'll get the local newspaper wherever we are and you'll find the stories that you think are funny. Then you'll write a routine around them, and you'll perform it that night onstage."

"You want me to write a new act every day? And rehearse it? That's impossible."

"People won't expect perfect delivery and timing. Your monologue will go over because it's about their town and what's happening in it that day. And you have a way about you onstage. You're not showy like—" She barely stopped herself from saying Benny's name. "You're different from most performers. You're the fellow who lives down the block, an ordinary Joe. I think if you just walk out onstage and start talking about everyday things, it'll go over."

He'd thought about doing a single for so long, and he'd been afraid of it. To be out onstage alone without a partner to fall back on—without even a prop to play with or some music to fill in the silence if your jokes died—that was the toughest kind of act there was.

That's why the good monologuists, like Jack Benny, are stars, said a mad voice in the back of his head. *If you could do it, you'd be one too.*

But what Ellie was suggesting—a totally new act every night— that was suicide. No one could carry it off.

But what if you could? whispered the mad voice.

"Just try it!" Ellie was pleading. "It's better than canceling. What do you have to lose?"

My pride. I've never bombed before. But she thinks I can do it.

"I'll write the material with you," Ellie said. "It'll be easier if there are two of us." He thought about the lines of dialogue she'd added to their act, and how they always got a laugh. But that was a far cry from filling fifteen or twenty minutes every single day. It was crazy even to consider it.

But her lines are funny.

"How am I going to remember that much new material? It's too much memorizing for anyone."

"It doesn't have to be word perfect. It's only you up there, so you're not feeding a partner cues. And I'll sit out in the house every night and be your stooge. If you start to go dry, just look to where I'm sitting and I'll heckle you and ask you questions that will get you back on track." She paused. "And the good thing about that is, I won't be onstage. If I'm sitting in the house like a member of the audience, it won't matter when the baby starts to show."

That was the first time she'd mentioned her pregnancy since she'd told him about it. The prospect of working on this crazy idea had made her forget how unhappy she was. That was good.

And there was always the chance that he could make it work. If he could, it would be a whole new kind of act—with humor that was local and fresh each night. He didn't know anyone else who was doing that. Plus, if he didn't have a new act by tomorrow he'd be crawling away from his contract with his tail between his legs. Wouldn't it be better to fail by trying something bold and daring? He pulled himself up tall. "How many newspapers do they have here in New Palton?" he asked.

The town boasted two, morning and afternoon. Joe and Ellie worked for the rest of the day, combing through every article for funny tidbits, and by evening he had his first monologue. He stood in the middle of the room and read the material through. When he had finished, one look at Ellie's face told him all he needed to know.

"I'll go to the stage manager in the morning and cancel," he said.

"No. It's going to work. Just make it sound like you just thought of it. You're working too hard to make it perfect."

When Joe went to bed that night he didn't sleep. Throughout his professional life he'd believed in careful preparation followed by thorough rehearsal that left nothing to chance. But now he was getting ready to go on the stage with a monologue he'd thrown together in a few hours, and no one but a sixteen-year-old girl in the house to bail him out if he went dry. As he ran his words over and over in his head he wondered if anyone had actually ever died of flop sweat. But the next morning Ellie greeted him with a smile.

"You're going to knock them dead," she told him.

He was never really sure how he got to the theater that day; he assumed he had walked there with Ellie, but he couldn't remember checking in or climbing the stairs to the dressing room. Ellie seemed to be all over the place, giving the stage crew orders about the new lighting they wanted and ordering Joe to tone down his makeup and leave his flashy white suit on the hook. "Work in the sweater and pants you're wearing," she told him. "Remember, you're not an entertainer, you're the neighbor next door. Just another ordinary Joe. Wear your street clothes."

Finally they heard the orchestra in the pit start playing. "I'm going to go sit in the house," she said. "I'll be in the third row, second seat from the aisle if you need me." Then she grabbed his hands. "You'll be fine," she said. And he realized that her hands were as icy as his own. She was scared too.

JOE ONLY LOOKED at Ellie twice during the act. And it wasn't because he needed prompting. Some internal comic clock had told him the audience needed to hear another voice, so he turned to her for heckling. That same clock paced him as surely through his material as if he'd been doing a single all his life. Being onstage by himself felt as comfortable as wearing a favorite pair of old shoes. He knew the house was sensing his enjoyment and they liked him for it.

Meanwhile, a part of his brain was keeping track of what material was working and what wasn't. *They don't like jokes about working people*, he noted. *They laugh when I poke fun at anyone who is rich or in charge. They want to hear me take on the bigwigs.*

Ellie had come to the same conclusion. After the curtain had come down—and he'd gotten a respectable hand—he found her in the dressing room writing notes on a piece of paper.

"No more gags about waiters or shoeshine boys," she said.

"Ellie, they liked the material."

"But we're keeping the jokes about the mayor—"

"They liked me! I think I can do this!" He shouted out loud because it was so hard to believe. She stopped making notes.

"Yes. You can."

The dressing room door opened, and the stage manager stuck in his head. "What were you doing out on that stage?" he demanded. "Do you call that an act?"

"I cooked it up fast. My partner had to go home—family business, really urgent—and I didn't want to leave you in the lurch."

Ellie stepped in. "The audience laughed, didn't they?" she said.

"Because the mayor is in the news today. By tomorrow those jokes will be old hat."

"By tomorrow Joe will telling new jokes—in a new monologue."

"A new monologue?" The stage manager looked bewildered.

"Joe will do a new one every day. We get the material from the newspapers," Ellie said proudly.

The stage manager turned to Joe in disbelief. "Some performers, you know they're nuts. I always had you pegged as one of the sane ones. Goes to show how wrong a man can be!" He walked out.

Ellie went back to her notes. "Don't mind him, he's an idiot," she said. "I think we should call this act Ordinary Joe. Do you like it?"

Joe was still trying to take in what had happened. "I'm just an ordinary Joe," he said softly.

"Exactly," Ellie said. "It's perfect for you."

"Right," Joe said. He was happy—of course—but he felt a little sad too. They'd had a modest success, and bigger things could come. They hadn't had to cancel—that was the happy part. But it made him sad that she thought he was ordinary.

CHAPTER 27

There were sounds of final party preparations coming from the kitchen when I stopped typing. I would have liked to have continued working, but since the shindig was taking place in my house, that would have been rude. I had to get ready.

"Joe Masters was like Jay Leno or David Letterman, only better," I told Annie, as I ran a brush through my hair and put on my gray velour sweatsuit. It wasn't exactly a festive outfit, but I hadn't had time to do my laundry. The sweats were clean—and hey, they *were* velour. "Those guys do a new monologue about current events every night. But they have a staff of writers. Joe had one teenaged girl helping him research his stuff and write it. Can you say amazing?"

Annie gave me her paw to shake. She hadn't done the paw shake since my life had gone to hell with Second Book Syndrome. I tossed her one of her doggie biscuits as a reward. She gave it a disdainful little sniff, picked it up, and buried it under the bed. Then I remembered—my dog did not lower herself to eat store-bought treats anymore. Not since her Uncle Show Biz started baking homemade dog cookies for her.

Yes, my friends, there was food being cooked in our little home; well-balanced meals appeared regularly. Of course Show Biz had told me he liked to cook, but I hadn't expected it to happen three times a day. The whole thing started when he found me forking congealed kung pao chicken out of a cardboard container one morning. He'd only been in residence about a week.

"Do you really like eating that?" he'd demanded.

"It's breakfast," I told him.

"No," he said firmly. "It's not."

The next morning a high-fiber muffin made with blueberries and flaxseed oil showed up. It was fantastic. Talk about little gifts that come to you from out of nowhere. After that, we had new kitchen rules. I was allowed to wash up, microwave, and chop certain items under supervision, but the actual measuring, mixing, frying, and baking would be done by Show Biz. It worked out beautifully. For instance, he'd taken care of the food prep for the party we were throwing, and I was going to be the cleanup crew. And when I saw *we* were throwing this wingding, technically that was true, but it had been his idea. Show Biz was billing it as a celebration of his return to Manhattan. Or, as he liked to put it, God's Country.

"You sure you want to do this?" I'd asked, when he proposed it. Images of Alexandra's Bad Spaghetti Nights clashed with Sheryl's finger bowls in my head, and I started gulping air. Entertaining at home has always been way too fraught for me. But Show Biz wasn't even slightly overwhelmed. He invited all of his nearest and dearest, including the staff of Yorkville House and the Swinging Grandmas. Then, early that morning, he'd picked up Chicky and installed her in the kitchen. "Chicky knows how to cook for a crowd," he informed me. And for the next few hours the two of them rustled around the various appliances, producing amazing aromas.

Halfway through the afternoon, when I couldn't resist the smells anymore, I took a break and went in. They had whipped up quantities of meat loaf, gravy, mashed potatoes, green beans, macaroni and cheese, and several lemon meringue pies that had to be eight inches high.

"The food of my childhood," Chicky said, as she wiped her hands on her apron. Then she paused. "Didn't your mother ever cook comfort food for you?" she asked.

"My mother once said that the kitchen was the last bastion of slave labor for women," I told her.

SHOW BIZ'S PARTY was a big success. The apartment, now decorated in Thrift Shop Chic, was warm and comfortable. The food was amazing, and the wine flowed nicely. And to my dismay, Chicky was telling everyone about her book.

"Wait until you read it," I heard her crowing at one point. "Doll Face is doing such a great job. Somewhere my folks are smiling."

And even though I'd said so confidently that I was sure the book would sell, when I saw how her little face glowed, I started to panic. Because you never do know. And the thought of disappointing Chicky was suddenly more than I could handle.

I was sitting in the kitchen, worrying, when I heard someone behind me. "Why aren't you out there soaking it in?" Chicky demanded.

"Excuse me?"

"This night. It's one of the good times, Doll Face. You've got the place running over with friends and good food, and in a couple of minutes Emmy's going to have another glass of wine and start doing eye-high kicks. It doesn't get better than this. You've got to soak it up while you can."

"I have a couple of things on my mind."

"Sure, so does everyone. But it's a sin to let a good time go by without paying attention. And soaking. Didn't anyone ever teach you that?"

I thought about my mother, who was always so busy. And I thought about all the times in California before my father died when I'd been too self-conscious to go swimming with him. And I thought about Jake begging me to take a vacation with him. "No," I said softly. "I never learned that."

"There's no time like the present to start," she said, and held out her hand. I started to go into the living room with her, but then I stopped.

"Hang on," I said, and I raced into my bedroom.

All my pretty size fours were long gone, of course, but I did have one box of accessories left over from my Sheryl days. I pulled out a heavily ruffled pink chiffon scarf and wrapped it around my neck. Since I was wearing a gray sweat suit, the resulting fashion statement was just this side of Bag Lady Chic—but the scarf was so long it fluttered partway down my back in a way I found enchanting. And it was *very* pink. "Ready!" I sang out to Chicky. We made it back into the living room in time to see Emmy do the first of her Rockette kicks, and after a few more glasses of wine, I capped off the evening by joining the Swinging Grandmas in an a cappella rendition of "Shine On, Harvest Moon."

THE NEXT MORNING, before I was out of bed, my phone rang. "Hey, Doll Face," said a familiar little growl. "Now you can go back to worrying about the book and not disappointing me. Have a great day."

So I swallowed the pomegranate smoothie Show Biz had left in the blender, walked Lancelot and Annie—separately, since Lancie still had his big dog paranoia going on—and hurried back to my room to work. And to worry about not disappointing Chicky. I think I've already mentioned how well I follow orders.

I opened my laptop and picked up the story where I'd left off. "Ordinary Joe and his monologues were a hit," I wrote. "But he and Ellie had to take time off when the baby was born, so by the early twenties he was still playing the small-time circuits."

CHAPTER 28

Shell Point Amusement Park, Connecticut

1921

Ellie pushed the carriage over to the steps leading up to the boardwalk; then she stopped and peeked inside to make sure Baby was still sleeping. Baby—that was what she and Joe called her daughter. Ellie wasn't sure why the nickname had stuck, but the child was almost a year old and it still seemed to suit her.

Ellie turned and began pulling the carriage up the steps. It bumped against the railings, and for a moment Baby seemed to waken; then she closed her eyes again. Ellie was determined to walk on the boardwalk. She had always loved the beach, but she and Joe didn't have many opportunities to go there. It wasn't as though they could take a Saturday off to lie on the sand and eat cotton candy like other people. Vaudevillians worked on weekends as well as weekdays—except when they were between engagements, and then they stayed home to save money. But Joe had

landed a booking at a theater in a shorefront park, and Ellie was
going to enjoy it.

Shell Point Amusement Park was not only one of the biggest
and best amusement parks in New England, it was located on one
of the prettiest stretches of the Connecticut coastline. The three
beaches at Shell Point were famously rock-free, and the boardwalk
was deep and long, lined with candy and picture-postcard stands,
food stalls, games, and rides. There were piers that branched off
from the boardwalk, featuring fancy restaurants with big windows
overlooking the sound. At the tip of one pier was the park's heart-
stopping roller coaster. Ellie had never ridden it, but she'd heard
that when you were going around the hairpin turns it felt as if you
were going to plunge into the water below. She didn't think she'd
like that. There was enough danger in her life with opening
nights, reviewers who could kill an act with a couple of sentences,
and bookers who could cancel your tour on a whim, leaving you
high and dry with a child to feed.

At the opposite end of the boardwalk, away from the screams of
the roller-coaster riders, there were two vaudeville houses. Joe was
playing the bigger of the two, the Grand. He'd been booked there
for a split week. Ellie drew in a deep breath of fresh air, happy that
they would be staying in one place for three days. She pushed the
carriage to a bench and sat in the sunshine.

Joe was sleeping back in their room at the hotel. Ellie tried to
get out with Baby before he woke up in the mornings. He needed
all the rest he could get when he was performing, and they shared
their room with the child, who could get fussy. But now, lulled by
the sea air, she was sleeping too. Ellie leaned back, closed her eyes,
and let her mind wander.

The Grand was a good theater—not big-time but very close—
and booking it was a step up for Joe. He'd corrected her when she
said that. "No, Ellie, it's a step up for *us*."

"I'm not out on that stage every night," she'd said.

"But we're a team, all the same. We're partners." He always insisted that he was her partner.

Her partner—and her husband. That's what it said on the all-important marriage license they'd signed two years ago. That's what it said on her daughter's birth certificate. They were husband and wife, a respectable couple, with a child who had a respectable last name. And what else were they? Ellie opened her eyes and sighed. She'd been with Joe for two years and she still didn't know.

They had gotten married in New Haven, one morning before Joe's matinee. At his suggestion, they'd had breakfast together in the coffee shop around the corner from their hotel before going to the courthouse in the center of the town. The restaurant breakfast was more expensive than the one they could have gotten at the hotel and she'd been moved, thinking he was trying to make this day special. But then he'd pulled out a newspaper.

"We need to start on the monologue for tonight," he'd said. "I'll do yesterday's material at the matinee, since we're busy this morning."

She'd wanted to reach across the table and slap him. She'd wanted to tell him she was sorry if being "busy" marrying her was getting in the way of his damn work. She wanted to break down and cry because this was not the way it should be for a girl on her wedding day.

But it wasn't a real wedding day. She and Joe were simply taking care of a problem. And he was doing her a big, big favor. She had no right to be angry. So she'd grabbed half the newspaper, said brightly, "The show must go on," and started skimming the front page. By the time they had to leave for the courthouse, they'd written half the monologue.

The justice of the peace who pronounced them man and wife had cut himself when he'd shaved that morning. Their witnesses were two strangers the town clerk rounded up for them because they hadn't known they'd need any. After they'd muttered their I do's, she and Joe had kissed like a brother and sister being forced to be affectionate at a family party. She didn't have a bouquet, and there wasn't anyone playing music. They were back out on the street in twenty minutes. That was how long her wedding had lasted from start to finish—twenty minutes. Then she and Joe had stood in front of the courthouse and stared at each other.

All she could think about was Benny. If she'd been marrying Benny, he would have found a way to make it a happy day. He would have laughed because the justice of the peace had a bandage on his chin. He would have given her a red rose. In spite of the nasty little ceremony, he would have found a way to make her heart sing.

"I'm not hungry yet, are you?" Joe's voice had broken into her thoughts.

"No, we just finished breakfast," she'd said.

Benny would have arranged for a grand lunch of lobster and champagne. At the very least, he would have grabbed her hand and run with her to the ice cream shop across the New Haven green to buy her a hot fudge sundae.

But Joe had seemed relieved that she didn't want him to make a fuss. "If we go back to the hotel and get to work right now, maybe I can still do the new monologue at the matinee," he'd said. She had looked at her husband—the kind, matter-of-fact man who had been so very good to her—and thought, *He'll never make my heart sing.*

But that night, after the show was over, she found she was grateful for Joe's matter-of-fact personality. Because they had to start living in the same room. This was something they had agreed on.

"We don't have to make any big announcements about getting

married," Joe had said. "That way no one can really trace back the date, if . . ."

"If anyone counts the months before the baby is born." Ellie had finished his thought.

"You'll just start using my name and we'll share a room and people will figure it out."

That was the way he'd said it—casually, as if it was going to be the easiest thing in the world for them to sleep in the same small room. But he was right. If they wanted to make the marriage look right, they had to live together.

So on the night after the hurry-up ceremony at the courthouse in New Haven, she had taken her suitcase into Joe's room. And she had tried not to look at the single bed that sat in the middle of it, because she was afraid her teeth would start chattering if she did.

Joe had said calmly, "I can take the bed apart, and one of us can have the mattress and one can have the pillows and the rest of the bedding, if you like—but I don't think it'll be comfortable, and we'll have to put it back together in the morning before the maid comes in. Or we can share the bed and stay on our own sides. I'm pretty good at that. I had three brothers, and there was only one bed for all of us when I was growing up."

"Florrie, Dot, and I slept together too," she'd said, and somehow discussing it made her feel less cold and shaky.

"Then we're old hands at this." And he'd picked up his night clothes and started for the door. "I'll change in the bathroom down the hall," he'd said. "I'll be back in ten minutes. Will that be long enough for you?"

"Yes," she'd said. "That will be fine."

And it had been. She'd gone to sleep and hadn't bumped into Joe once all night.

The next morning she'd been relieved, and it wasn't just because sleeping in the same bed with Joe had not turned out to be too much of a problem. Ever since Joe had offered to marry her, she'd lain awake nights, worrying that, in spite of everything he'd said and the unromantic way he behaved, he did have feelings for her. She'd told herself she wasn't going to think about it, but she couldn't stop. Because if Joe did have feelings for her, and she didn't have any for him, marrying him would be the cruelest kind of selfishness. But if she didn't marry him, what about her baby? Round and round her mind had gone, night after night. And in her heart she was still hoping—and praying—that the baby's real father would come back, and that would solve everything.

But after that terrible little ceremony, she could stop hoping and doubting. She had to trust Joe when he said that this was what he wanted, and she had to stop torturing herself with questions, because there was no turning back. They were married; it was done. She was grateful for the finality. She'd felt bruised in those days, as if her spirit had been in some kind of violent accident and was trying to recover. Through the pain she'd been aware of only two things—she was going to have a baby, and in spite of everything she was still in love with the baby's father.

Ellie closed her eyes again and let the sunshine play on her face. She'd let Joe sleep a little longer before she started back toward the hotel.

AT THE HOTEL, Joe woke up and looked around. Once again, Ellie had taken Baby outside so he could get his rest. He leaned back on the pillows. It touched him that Ellie watched out for him like that. He'd never been sure how she felt about him; he still wasn't. She was grateful to him for getting her out of a bind, that much he knew, but was there anything more? In the beginning he'd known there wasn't. He remembered the way she'd stood there in front of the courthouse in New Haven after their sad little wedding conducted by the justice of the peace who was hung over. Joe had wanted to tell her then that she deserved better than this. He'd wanted to buy her a bouquet of flowers to hold, and he'd wanted to take her someplace nice for a big lunch. But he'd known this wasn't a happy day for her. She wasn't a joyful bride marrying the man she loved, and it seemed to him that he'd be rubbing salt in her wounds if he tried to pretend otherwise. Besides, to do it under the circumstances would make him feel foolish. So they'd gone back to the hotel to work. Because work was something they could always share.

But that night when Ellie had come into his room, he'd almost called off the whole marriage. She'd walked in carrying her suitcase and she'd put it down on the floor and stared at him with eyes full of fear. This beautiful girl with the strawberry-blond hair was looking at him as if he were some kind of monster. And he'd wanted to yell at her, *I bet you didn't look like this when you were getting into Benny's bed. I bet you were smiling then!* But then he remembered the way she'd looked the first night he'd seen her, when her drunken father hit her, and he remembered how she'd looked when she realized Benny had walked out because she wouldn't abort her baby. At sixteen she'd known very little kindness in her life, and now she was all alone in a bedroom with a man who was in many ways a stranger. And, stupid as it was, she still loved the man who had deserted her. Joe had wanted to put his arms around her and tell her she would be all right. But that would only scare her more. So instead he'd talked some nonsense about sleeping arrangements and asked her how long she'd like him to stay out of the room while she changed into her night clothes. And then he'd spent the whole night wide awake and hanging on to his side of the mattress so he wouldn't roll over and touch her by accident.

Joe shook his head and leaned back on his pillow. He'd wanted to take care of Ellie that night because she was afraid, and at the same time he'd wanted to shake her for being such a little fool about Benny—and he'd wanted to kiss her. If he lived to be a million years old, he would never understand why he felt the way he did about Ellie.

THE SUNSHINE ON the boardwalk was getting too warm. There was a grove of trees in the park across from the beach where Ellie was sitting with Baby. She stood up and began pushing the carriage. The little girl was still sleeping, which was a blessing. She was tiny, but Ellie could see changes in her already. She was growing up fast—too fast. Sometimes Ellie wished she could turn back the clock to the day the child was born and make it stop there.

ELLIE'S DAUGHTER HAD been born in a small town called Millertown. It sat on the Hudson River, near the railroad line from New York City to Albany, and Joe had seen it for the first time when he and Benny were traveling to a booking upstate. There was an apartment building with a view of the river that had caught his eye from the train window, so the next time Masters and George were between gigs, he'd gone to Millertown to rest for a few days. He'd discovered a first-class diner across the street from the train station, a pretty park, and friendly people, and later he'd remembered the town when he and Ellie were making plans. On top of all its other good points, Millertown had a small but well-equipped hospital where she could have her child.

Ellie had been afraid that Joe might say she should stay with her sister Florrie and her horrid husband and have the child in New York while he continued working on the road. And she couldn't have done that. Because New York was rapidly becoming Benny George's town. He was making a name for himself as a booking agent and people were already saying he was going to be one of the men who could make or break a careёr. Given the incestuous nature of their business, Ellie would have run into him sooner or later, and she knew she couldn't have taken it—not while she was carrying the child he'd wanted her to get rid of.

But the subject of New York never came up when she and Joe were making their plans. Joe said he couldn't do the act without her to help him, so they'd both lay off until the child was born. They settled in Millertown, in an apartment in the pretty building overlooking the Hudson River, and Joe had stayed with Ellie as they waited for the birth together.

It had been a strange time, Ellie thought, when she looked back on it; in some ways it had been like a vacation. Their days had taken on a peaceful pattern that she had never before known. They had made friends with the elderly couple who owned the diner and eaten there every Sunday. Ellie had discovered a library in the center of town, and for the first time in her life she had the leisure to read books. It wasn't a life she could imagine living forever; eventually she knew she'd want to get back to the hustle and bustle of the road and show business, but for a while there was something soothing about it. She got to know Joe better during those long lazy days. She learned that, in spite of his fast mind, there was a part of him that was delighted by simple things. He liked the local band that played—badly out of tune—in the park gazebo on Saturday nights. He could watch the river for hours on end and always see something new.

During that time, Ellie was almost able to forget that she and Joe weren't an ordinary married couple—and that the child she was carrying wasn't his. And if every once in a while she did remember, and wondered once again if Joe was in love with her, she pushed those thoughts aside. Joe seemed content with this bargain he'd made; making herself miserable with doubts and guilt would be a terrible way to thank him. Instead, she'd tried to find little ways to show him how grateful she was—like making his coffee exactly the way he liked it and taking it to him in the morning. And not asking questions. And being content herself.

Then her daughter was born. The nurse put her in Ellie's arms, and for a second Ellie felt her heart stop, because the infant was so clearly Benny's. Even her tiny head was covered with a soft yellow down that was going to turn into his golden mop. Without meaning to, Ellie tensed when Joe was brought in to see "his" child. She watched the nurse hand her to him—because of all those brothers and sisters he was far more expert at holding an infant than Ellie had been—and braced herself as he looked at the child's telltale hair. She told herself she'd understand if Joe turned away or handed her back. She reminded herself that Joe had agreed to give Benny's child a name, but loving her had never been a part of the arrangement. Ellie told herself she didn't expect that of him.

Joe had looked into the tiny face, then he'd stroked the little head covered with the golden fuzz that was going to be just like Benny's. "Like a little bird," he'd murmured. He'd turned to Ellie. "We can name her Eleanor, after you, or we could name her Joanna, after me."

Ellie had not cried since the pains had started the night before, because she'd been determined to be strong through this ordeal she'd brought on herself. But that was when she started to sob.

ELLIE HAD REACHED the steps. Pulling the stroller up them had been hard, but getting it back down was going to be even harder. It was too heavy to roll down, and too big to lift. She looked at her watch; the time had flown. Joe would be waking now, and they needed to get to work as soon as he'd had his morning coffee.

•   •   •

JOE GOT OUT of bed and turned to look at the corner of the room where Baby slept. He liked to see her there when he woke up, and he missed her when she was gone. From the beginning he'd been her willing slave . . . well, almost from the beginning. There had been one bad moment the first time he'd held her and really looked at her. Even then, tiny as she was, she was unmistakably Benny's child. Joe had thought about the years ahead when she'd grow to look more and more like his former partner, and he'd wondered how that would feel.

But then he'd seen that Ellie was watching him. She'd turned away fast and tried to look tough, like she didn't care, which was what she always did when she was afraid of being hurt. At the same moment, the infant in his arms had shifted. She was so small and defenseless. And it was because of him that her mother had been able to keep her. So even if he wasn't her father, she was his. Somehow Ellie had read his mind, because the tough look had faded from her eyes. It wasn't until he started suggesting names that she had started to cry.

The next day Ellie had gone back to being tough again. "We're going back on the road as soon as the doctor says Baby can travel," she told Joe. He'd tried to argue that there was no hurry and they could wait a little while longer to let Ellie rest. But she wouldn't hear of it. "This layover cost you, Joe," she'd said. "You were just starting to get noticed when we stopped working." She was right about that; by the end of their last tour, Joe's act had been the one that was regularly singled out, both in reviews by the local newspapers and in the weekly reports that theater managers sent back to the bookers in Manhattan. "You know how the business is," she said to Joe. "You should have been building on those reviews."

"We had something else to do," he'd said.

"You need to get back in front of the public right away."

So the sixteen-year-old kid he'd married had started trouping with an infant that was still only a few weeks old. She'd worked right along with Joe, reading the newspapers and writing the monologues, and at night when Baby cried, Ellie stumbled out of bed quickly to quiet her. "Go back to sleep, you need your rest," she'd say to Joe. "You're the one going onstage."

That first tour after the layoff hadn't been a picnic. They booked a small circuit out in the sticks so Joe could get his timing back. It had been three months of one-night stands, five shows a day, and hotels that were clean but that was all you could say for them. When they finally managed to book Shell Point, he was beat. He could only imagine how Ellie felt. But she never complained. Not the tough girl who was his partner.

Joe got out of bed and put on his robe. Ellie and Baby would be back soon. It was time to start the day.

ELLIE HAD MANAGED to maneuver the carriage down the steps by clamping on the brakes and dragging it behind her. Baby was crying now. Ellie reached into the carriage and picked up the child and then as she straightened up she saw it: an automobile parked by the curb at the far end of the park. It was probably a Stutz Bearcat, or maybe it was a Duesenberg—Ellie didn't know much about cars—but whatever the make it was a dashing vehicle and very expensive-looking. It was painted white, and the man behind the wheel was dressed in white too. He was so far away that Ellie couldn't make out his features, but she didn't need to. She hadn't seen Benny in two years, but she would have known the shape of his head, and the way he held himself, anywhere. The boardwalk behind her and the beach and the bright sunny sky started to spin. She put her crying daughter back in the carriage and watched her own hands cling to the wicker-covered handle for support. It was as if she had no connection to those hands, or the carriage handle, or the sky, or the trees at the end of the park where Benny's car stood. She wondered if she was going to be sick.

The last time I saw him, I was sick too. But then it was morning sickness. That thought steadied her. She looked up. Even from this far away she could see his bright blond hair gleaming in the sunshine. For a brief, crazy moment she thought about holding up his child so he could see the head of golden curls that were exactly like his. The baby's eyes were his shade of blue—although he wouldn't be able to see them from this distance. As these insane thoughts raced through her brain, he must have realized that she'd seen him, because across the park the sleek car roared into life and pulled away from the curb. She thought maybe he was going to drive to her side of the park and stop in front of her, and her heart raced painfully in her chest. But the car turned in the narrow street and went off in the opposite direction. The sound it made lingered in the air after it was out of sight. Then everything was still again—so still it was as if nothing had happened. It was as if the car and the man had been a figment of Ellie's imagination. As if she'd been daydreaming. Maybe she had. Maybe the whole incident was nothing more than wishful thinking on her part. But she knew better.

He wanted to see us. He wanted to see me. But he left. Again.

Her heart stopped pounding. She leaned over to soothe her crying child. And she felt the tears on her own cheeks. She began pushing the carriage—fast now. She had to get back to the hotel. She would pick up the morning newspaper in the lobby and take it upstairs to Joe so they could work on the day's monologue. She'd be safe, working with Joe.

● ● ●

ELLIE NEVER TOLD anyone about that day in Shell Point when the sporty roadster appeared across the park. There wouldn't have been any point in telling Joe—at least that was what she told herself. Besides, there were times when she thought she really had imagined the whole thing. Certainly, Benny never did it again. At least, not as far as she knew.

And while it would be a lie to say she didn't know what Benny was doing—he was rising so fast in the Keith organization that the trade papers were full of stories about him—she and Joe had begun a two-year odyssey of their own. With Baby, they endured milk-train jumps from small town to small town, as they made their way from New York to Canada to Oregon, Colorado, and Illinois. And in every town and in every theater, their one topic of conversation and their one goal was improving the act. It took all of their energy and left time for nothing else. They kept at it for two long years, until Joe finally got his shot at the Big Time.

CHAPTER 29

Pastor's Boardinghouse, New York

1923

Ellie ran out the front door of Pastor's Boardinghouse and headed east. The boardinghouse was on Forty-fifth Street and Broadway and her destination was St. Patrick's Cathedral. She was going to ask God to help Joe when he opened his act the following week. Because after two years of touring the small-time she and Joe were in New York City, and Joe was booked—for a whole week—in a theater called the Jefferson. All the New York scouts and booking agents went to see the new acts that played the Jefferson, and if Joe went over, he'd work the big-time circuits for the rest of his career. Being a hit at the Jefferson could lead to an engagement at the Palace.

Ellie turned toward Fifth Avenue, moving quickly. When she'd left their rooms at the boardinghouse, Joe was just beginning to wake up. He'd wait until Baby was awake, then he'd dress her and take her downstairs for breakfast. He loved doing things with

her—there was a connection between them that Ellie found confusing. Sometimes she thought life in general was confusing.

She still had memories—golden little scraps of them—of
Benny smiling his dazzling smile or ordering a hot fudge sundae
for her. There were memories of nights with him in her hotel
room after everyone was asleep. And there was a newer memory,
of a white automobile gleaming in the sunshine at the edge of a
park. There was the vision of that automobile driving away—and
the tears on her cheeks as she'd watched it go. The confusing part
was, even now she wasn't sure what she would do if someone were
to tell her she could have those lovely little scraps back, that she
could have the nights again, that she could make the car turn
around and drive the other way. That she could have Benny back.
Because there was Joe. Her relationship with him was the most
confusing thing of all.

For a while she'd stopped thinking about their marriage and
whatever Joe might be feeling about it. There simply hadn't been
the time or the energy. After Baby was born and they were booking small-time tours, they were too busy working and traveling to
worry about love or relationships or anything but making sure
Baby was clean and fed before they fell into bed at night. But then
they'd started to reach their goal. That had happened, as many
things in show business did, by sheer luck.

About a year after the gig in Shell Point, when she and Joe were
two years into their marriage that wasn't one, Joe was booked as a
disappointment act on a big-time circuit. Suddenly, they were
touring major cities: Joe played Chicago, Winnipeg, Vancouver,
Seattle, Portland, Oakland, San Francisco, Denver, and Detroit,
and then the tour doubled back to Chicago again. He was working
in plush houses, the act was booked for one or two weeks at a time,
and he and Ellie and Baby could afford to stay in nice hotels.

It was easier to work on the monologue when they were staying in the same place for a few days; they didn't have to write as much new material for every show. And Joe himself was becoming looser and freer onstage as his confidence grew. The young man who had insisted on having every second of his act locked down now liked to wing a few jokes. Once, in Detroit, the audience had kept him onstage after he'd finished his regular routine, and he'd managed to ad lib for another twenty minutes.

It was during this period when things were easier that Ellie started to see Joe in a different light. It was as if she'd finally had time to relax and notice the way other people reacted to him. Other girls. The women on the tour seemed to be realizing that Joe was a comer. Suddenly he'd become attractive to the pretty flash dancers and the beautiful magician's assistants and cute acrobats who waited for him to come offstage and regularly invited him to come along for the cast's late-night suppers after the show—suppers Ellie skipped because she had to take her sleeping daughter back to the hotel. "But you go ahead," she'd say to Joe. "You need to unwind." And then she'd be angry when he went.

Something else had changed too. Now that they could afford a two-suite room, Ellie often bunked in with Baby. It wasn't something she and Joe had planned or talked about, it just seemed to happen. Ellie wasn't sure how she felt about it. Sharing a bed had always been slightly awkward in spite of their best efforts to downplay it. But there had been a warmth and intimacy to it too. Ellie found herself wondering if Joe missed it. She began watching him more closely when they were with the others in the company, and she made an unpleasant discovery. When all those girls flirted with Joe, he was flirting back. And he was going out to those late-night suppers.

Unpleasant as it was, it was to be expected. Joe was a man, and since she was treating him like an older brother, there had to be other women somewhere in his life. Whatever he had done in that way, he was discreet—so far. But eventually he would have to be tired of this bargain they'd made. Maybe he already was. After all, they had agreed in the beginning that this marriage would not last forever. It had been easy to forget that with all the writing and rehearsing and packing and unpacking, but now that they were doing an easier tour, maybe Joe had had time to think as she had. And maybe he was thinking he wanted to move on. If so, Ellie was not going to stand in his way, no matter how it felt.

She waited for a night—one of the increasingly rare ones—when he came back to the hotel room after the show. Ellie watched Joe put Baby to bed and lean over to kiss her good night. Ellie felt herself swallow hard—the child was going to miss him so much. But that couldn't be helped. A bargain was a bargain. When he turned around, she began the speech she had been preparing for days.

"Joe, when we got married, we said it was just until I was doing okay. . . ." She thought she saw his face tighten. She understood. This was not something she wanted to face either; they had grown accustomed to each other. There was comfort in that. But she wasn't going to back out. "I'm all right now," she said bravely. "What I mean is, I can be. I can take care of myself." She was trying to find the right way to say it to him, which was ridiculous because she was doing it for his own good. "I'll always be grateful—"

"Who is it?" he shouted at her. The explosion, coming from placid, careful Joe, was shocking. Then he looked at Baby's crib. "Who is it?" he asked again, more softly.

"What?"

"It's that son-of-a-bitch Benny. You've seen him."

The white car parked in the sunshine flashed into her mind, but there was no way Joe could have known about that. "What are you talking about?"

"The reason why you're leaving."

"Me?" Now it was her turn to explode. "*You're* the one who's been following that girl around like a puppy!"

"What girl?"

"The one who works with the violinist in the novelty act, they're third on the bill. I don't even know her name. . . ."

"Marie. She's married."

"So are you." He gave her a look. "But you're not . . . we're not . . ." She stammered and felt her face flush red. "We don't . . ." she tried and failed again.

"No. We don't," he said steadily—but his face was getting red too.

"And if you want to . . . leave me . . . so you can . . ." She stopped again. "Joe, you've done more for me than anyone I've ever known. I want you to be happy. I want you to have everything you want."

He gave her a strange little smile she couldn't read. "I was about to say the same about you." Then he looked away. "So you haven't heard from Benny?"

The white automobile flashed into her mind again. But there had been no words exchanged. "No."

"And there hasn't been anyone else?"

"No." She had to wait a second. "You?"

He picked his words carefully. "Not in any way that counts." Then he had taken in a big breath. "So if neither of us . . . what I mean is, why do we have to change things? I don't see the reason."

"No," she'd said, and relief flooded her. "No, I guess there isn't any. Not now. But someday—"

"Today isn't someday. Today is today," he'd said. "And today, everything is fine. Right?"

"Right."

But there would be a someday. Because he hadn't said there had been no one for the past two years. In fact, he'd implied there had been, it just hadn't counted. But the time would come when he would want to be loved in a way that did count. And when that day came, some smart girl would see what a catch he was. And she— the smart girl—would have a whole heart to give him. She wouldn't dream sometimes of a man with sky-blue eyes and a mop of bright blond hair who had given her red roses and a daughter who looked so very much like him. The girl would love Joe and only Joe. But in the meantime . . .

Joe had moved to the window to look out over the city. Being on a high floor above the other buildings was another benefit of making a larger paycheck. Ellie moved to stand behind Joe and slipped her arms around his waist. She felt his body tense as he turned around.

"Ellie, you don't have to . . ."

"Yes, I do."

He wasn't that much taller than she was, so it was easy to reach up so he could finally kiss her after two years. And after that one kiss, the rest came all too easily too.

She learned something that night: Any woman who hoped with even the tiniest part of her brain that one man could make her forget another was doomed to disappointment. That would not change. But she also learned that she didn't have to be madly in love to make love. There could be other feelings, like affection, warmth, and maybe even gratitude and familiarity. And those were good feelings. So from now on, she and Joe would be sleeping in the same bed. Even when they could afford a suite.

The gig as a disappointment act had been a turning point for Joe professionally. From that time on, he'd been booked into better houses and bigger cities. His reputation had built until he'd finally gotten the call to come to New York and play the Jefferson.

• • •

ELLIE HAD REACHED Fifth Avenue and turned uptown; ahead of her were the spires of St. Patrick's Cathedral. She wasn't one who prayed in a formal way, but she always felt when she went into a church that she should have her request worked out in a little speech, as a sign of respect for the Almighty. So she stopped now to gather her thoughts and make the best possible case for Joe.

AT PASTOR'S BOARDINGHOUSE, Joe walked to the door of Baby's room to look in on her while she slept. She'd had a late night; even though Joe wasn't performing until the following week, he and Ellie never went to bed before midnight, and Baby stayed up with them. If they weren't careful she'd become a night owl who slept until noon.

Baby didn't seem to mind that her days and nights were topsy-turvy, although sometimes Joe worried that a youngster needed a more orderly schedule than they were able to give her. And she needed space. Whenever they arrived in a new town, Ellie tried to find a park where the child could run, but when you were doing two shows a day and spending hours writing new material, there wasn't much time for parks and playing. Baby spent most of her days in hotel rooms and dressing rooms. He and Ellie should talk about that. They should start making plans for the child's education and her future. But he didn't want to have that conversation. Because then he and Ellie would have to talk about their own future, and he was too afraid to do that.

Joe shook his head. This was not the time to be thinking about difficult things like his marriage, not while the Jefferson opening was looming. He and Ellie were both nervous enough already, although he hid it better than she did.

Ellie couldn't sleep when she was wound up about something, which was why she'd gotten up early this morning and left without telling him where she was going. He knew anyway; she was off to light a candle for him at St. Patrick's. Ellie wasn't a practicing Catholic. Her pa had not been a churchgoer, and she and Joe usually caught up on their rest on the Sundays when they weren't traveling. But Ellie's mother had taken her to mass faithfully and had believed in the power of candle-lighting. So in moments of great need—like now—Ellie turned to her mother's tried-and-true faith.

Baby was stirring in her crib. Joe was glad she was waking up. She didn't care that next week he'd be starting the most important engagement of his life. She didn't know his entire future hung on it. She was going to be hungry and she'd want her breakfast.

ELLIE HAD COME to a stop in front of St. Patrick's Cathedral. She looked up at the lacy twin spires reaching into the sky like something out of a fairy tale, a magical place where miracles could happen. When Ellie went to church, it was because she needed miracles and magic. Perhaps that was wrong, she was sure church-going people would say so. But she was pretty sure God understood. She started up the stone steps to the heavily carved front door. She'd planned what she was going to say when she lit her candle: *Please, dear God, let Joe kill at the Jefferson.* Nice and simple.

CHAPTER 30

Joe waited while Baby struggled to put on her shoes—at three she was a determined little thing, whose favorite expression was an emphatic "Do it myself!" It could take quite a while before she'd finally turn her blue eyes up to him in a silent appeal for help. So he waited. The truth was, her independent streak gave him a kick. She was so like her mother.

After she was dressed, Joe took her hand, and together they walked to a coffee shop called Neely's on the corner of Broadway and Forty-fifth. Mrs. Pastor served a full breakfast at the boardinghouse, but this morning he was feeling antsy and wanted to go out.

Neely's was cheap and good, and it catered to a show-business crowd of managers, bookers, and performers who worked in all areas of the industry: variety, vaudeville, and legit. The place was open from 6 A.M. until after midnight—and Neely could be talked into staying open later if a show had opened and the performers wanted to continue celebrating after the cast party had ended.

Having breakfast at a theatrical watering hole was not what Joe would have chosen to do if he'd known of another place to go. At some point while he was downing his coffee, he knew some well-meaning soul would congratulate him on his upcoming engagement at the Jefferson, and his nerves would tighten even more. However, he ran the same risk at the boardinghouse. Gossip was a favorite pastime in show business.

Joe pushed open the glass door with *Neely's* written in gold and black cursive across the middle and walked inside. "Chocolate ice cream?" Baby asked, as they waited to be seated. She'd recognized the place from a previous visit when she'd devoured a double scoop. She was such a bright little thing! And she was growing up so fast soon they'd have to stop calling her Baby and find a new nickname for her. "No ice cream morning," Joe told her. "How about some flapjacks?"

Suddenly, he was aware that someone was watching them. He turned to encounter the sky-blue eyes that matched those of the little girl whose hand he was holding. Benny was sitting at a table with three of the biggest bookers in the business. Benny was now one of their number; he'd finally climbed to the position of power he'd always wanted.

Now he was staring at Baby. Joe watched Benny's face go white and his eyes darken as if he was stunned by what he was seeing. It couldn't have been news to Benny that Joe and Ellie had married and she had had a child; thanks to the show-biz grapevine he'd have heard about that. But the similarity between himself and the little girl must have been a shock—particularly for a man with Benny's large ego. Sensing a danger he couldn't articulate, Joe pulled Baby toward the door of the coffee shop.

"No," she protested. "Flapjacks!"

"We'll get some from Mrs. Pastor," Joe urged. "You like her flapjacks."

She agreed, bless her, and they were able to leave. He felt Benny watch them go.

JOE AND BABY were sitting in the boarding house dining room when Ellie came back. Baby was trying to eat a flapjack and was happily smearing herself with maple syrup, but Joe's soft-boiled egg had congealed in the shell untouched. Swallowing food was an impossibility.

"You're back," he said as Ellie bustled up to the table and sat down.

"I went to St. Patrick's." She threw a quick look at him and another at his uneaten breakfast. "I lit three candles for you in the Lady Chapel."

"You think I need that much help? Thanks a lot."

"Oh, good," she said cheerfully. "The candles are already working."

"What is that supposed to mean?"

"When you're grouchy before a performance, you always knock 'em dead."

Joe didn't tell her that his bad mood had nothing to do with knocking them dead at the Jefferson. He didn't mention the near encounter he'd had with Benny at the coffee shop. He told himself it was because he didn't want to upset her, but he knew that this wasn't the real reason. Ellie had never gotten the man out of her system; that was why Joe was afraid to talk about their future. Sometimes he thought it was a stubbornness in her makeup—she had given Benny her whole heart, and she refused to accept the fact that it wasn't enough. But at other times Joe thought maybe there was something in all those songs that said that each of us has only one true love. Maybe Benny *was* the only one for Ellie, and there was nothing anyone could do about it. It was the kind of sentimental notion he usually found silly, but there had to be some explanation for the way Ellie clung to her memories.

In the beginning, Joe had hoped that time would do the trick. Once she was away from Benny, she'd realize how deeply selfish he was—and Joe would be right there, working and living with her and helping her to raise her child. Proximity and time would bring her to her senses. And for a moment it had seemed as if that was what had happened. When Ellie put her arms around him and reached up for their first kiss, he'd thought he'd won her. But he'd realized quickly that he hadn't. Perhaps it was her stubbornness— or perhaps the love songs were right and Benny was the only man for her.

There were times when Joe told himself he was through. He couldn't go on like this; he didn't need this woman who was still hanging on to a dream. But then she'd wake up at the crack of dawn to light candles for him at St. Patrick's, and he'd know he wasn't through at all. At such moments, he'd have to ask himself if he was the stubborn one.

And there was Baby—his little girl. She *was* his; to hell with what anyone said. But if people were to see her standing next to Benny—or, worse, if Ellie were to decide that she wanted to end the marriage—how could he live without that child?

Baby was sitting next to him, and as if she could read his thoughts she gave him a smile that was sticky with maple syrup. And he knew that he could go on like this. He could do it forever if he had to.

"Thank you for lighting the candles," he said to Ellie. He was going to put the near run-in with Benny out of his mind. It had to happen eventually. At least they'd gotten the first encounter out of the way.

CHAPTER 31

After breakfast, Ellie and Joe took Baby to Central Park. "We might as well let her play outdoors as much as we can now," Ellie said to Joe. "When we start working she'll be cooped up again." By the time they went back to the boardinghouse, the daily mail had already been delivered. Joe brought Baby upstairs while Ellie went into Mrs. Pastor's parlor to see if she and Joe had gotten any letters.

"There, nothing from the post office, but there is a note for you," the landlady said. "A boy brought it over from the Keith office."

"It must be for Joe." She felt a little pinprick of apprehension. The Keith organization had promised that one of its bookers would be catching Joe's act at the Jefferson. Had something happened and the man wasn't coming . . . ? She closed her eyes and tried not to think about the past three years of brutal hard work. *If the Keith scout doesn't show, I don't know if I'll be able to stand it*, she thought.

"It's not for him, it's for you," said the landlady.

"It can't be." But then she realized: Benny worked for Keith's. And of course he'd know she was in town with Joe. *And Benny hasn't married anyone yet.* The stupid thought flashed through her mind before she could stop it. She took the note from Mrs. Pastor.

Ellie—not Ellie Masters, just plain *Ellie*—was written on the front of the envelope in Benny's big, loopy handwriting with the forward slant. She tore it open.

He wanted her to meet him the next day at a restaurant called Manaletta's on Forty-fourth Street. It wasn't a usual show-business haunt; she'd never heard of it before. So Benny wanted to be discreet. Her heart was beating too fast, and she felt light-headed. She sat on the velvet love seat in Mrs. Pastor's parlor and tried to make her mind grasp the meaning of the words in the note. *Benny wants to see me. After all this time. After he drove away from me in Shell Point.*

She wanted to see him too. She had to see him. There was no question; she would go to the out-of-the-way restaurant, and she would have lunch with him tomorrow. The only decision to be made was, should she tell Joe? She and Joe had an understanding— that hadn't changed—so there was no reason not to tell him. But agreeing to something with your brain didn't mean that your feelings went along with it. She sat in Mrs. Pastor's parlor for what seemed like hours, trying to figure out what to do. It was the opening at the Jefferson that finally decided her. With that ahead of him, Joe had enough to think about. There was no need to add to it by telling him she was meeting Benny for lunch. She stuffed the note into her pocket and started up the stairs to their room.

I'll tell Joe I'm going to do some shopping. He knows I've been wanting a new coat. But then I'll have to tell him I didn't find one I liked. Or I'll have to buy one. I hate lying to Joe!

That was when she realized that in three years she'd only done it once—when she didn't tell him about Shell Point. And that wasn't a real lie, it was more like keeping a secret from him. Everyone had secrets, didn't they?

Baby was in her room playing; Ellie could hear her murmuring the way she did when she was deep in make-believe. Joe was reading a newspaper; even though it was too soon to work on the monologue, they both read every line of every newspaper every day. It had become a habit for them—one of many they'd slipped into together, she thought. Joe looked up and smiled at her, a familiar smile she'd seen so many times. And before she could begin telling the lie she'd rehearsed, she heard herself say, "This came for me today," and she took the crumpled note out of her pocket and handed it to him.

It seemed to take him a long time to read it, but it was probably only a minute or two. Finally he handed it back. "Do you want to go?" he asked.

"Yes." And then, even though they had an understanding and they both knew that she was free to do this, as he was free to do whatever he wanted, she heard herself add, "I'm sorry."

Something flickered in his eyes when she said that, and for a second she thought he was going to ask her not to go. But they had an understanding. Or maybe it wasn't because of the understanding, maybe he was truly all right with it. Whatever the reason, he took another pause and then picked up the newspaper again. "Well," he said, "if that's what you want to do, you should do it." And he started to read.

THE NEXT DAY she wore her everyday dress for her lunch with Benny; she brushed her hair and pinned it in a simple updo on the top of her head. There was no need to fuss, she told herself. And besides, she didn't want Joe to catch her primping—even though they had an understanding. But Joe had been out of the room all morning with Baby. By the time Ellie was ready to go, he still wasn't back. She was grateful to him for that, although she didn't want to think too much about why he'd done it. She didn't want to feel that she was hurting him, but she also found she didn't like the idea that he wasn't concerned, at least a little. The odd thing was, she missed him. It had been a long time since she'd had to do something momentous on her own, and she found herself wishing she could ask him for advice. Not that there was any need for advice. All she was going to do was have lunch.

Manaletta's was a small restaurant that occupied the bottom half of a four-story brownstone. The doorman told her Mr. George was waiting for her in the dining room on the second floor. She climbed the stairs, pushed open the door, and couldn't resist a gasp of delight. The room was a riot of color. Its walls were covered with murals depicting a garden full of flowers and trees, and green velvet curtains were draped in luxurious swags over the bow window. The shades on the chandeliers and the wall sconces were flowers made of tinted glass, so the light that shone through them onto the white tablecloths was colored like a rainbow. But even more beautiful than the spun-glass flowers were the vases and baskets of real red roses that crowded every available surface. And standing in the center of the room with a red rose in one hand was Benny. He was smiling the same confident smile that had always convinced her that everything was going to be just grand, and if anything he was even more handsome than he'd been four years ago. The double-breasted coat of his bespoke suit was tailored to show off his broad shoulders, and the pants clung fashionably to his narrow waist and long legs. There was a softness in his strong features now, as if success had worn away the sharp edges. His mop of blond curls wasn't parted and pomaded anymore, so tendrils fell down onto his forehead. "Good," he said softly. "You haven't bobbed your hair."

"No," she said. "I didn't know I was supposed to."

He laughed at that. "Oh, I've missed you, Ellie. Nobody says things like that." His bright blue eyes were glowing with tenderness.

She found she didn't want to see the expression in his eyes. She looked around the room instead. "Do we have this place to ourselves?" she asked.

He nodded. "I reserved the whole floor for us. Is it too much?" Then he added quickly, "Don't answer that. If it is, I don't want to know. Will you sit down? I've ordered lobsters, and we have champagne. And for dessert, hot fudge sundaes."

"You've thought of everything."

"I tried."

"Why?"

"Could we please sit down?"

She sat and waited while he poured the champagne. He raised his glass. "I haven't thought of a toast. I'm just glad you're here," he said, and they both drank the sparkling, bittersweet wine. She'd never had champagne before. She thought it lived up to its reputation.

"I've kept track of you," he said. "I knew you'd had the child— a girl." She nodded. "I know every town you and Joe played. I drove out to Connecticut once because I knew you'd be there."

"At Shell Point. You didn't get out of the car."

"You saw me." She nodded again. "I just wanted to look at you. And her." He sipped his champagne. "There's no way to say this except to admit I was wrong four years ago. I was scared, Ellie. We were both so young. I couldn't see how we could take care of ourselves and a baby. I thought what I was telling you to do . . . was the only way. I wasn't ready for you. Or her. Not then."

"And now?"

"Now I am."

There had been so many times when she would have given anything to hear him say that. And to see the light in his eyes as he looked at her. "How come?" she asked.

She watched him pull his thoughts together. No wonder he was a good booking agent. He could sell anything. "It's taken me all this time to do what I set out to do," he said. "I've made something of myself. I couldn't have done that with a family. I know that was selfish of me—"

"Yes."

"But now things are different."

"And you want me back."

"I always wanted you. There's no one like you. Not for me."

"You never sent me a letter. You came to see me once in four years—and drove away without talking to me."

"I'd walked out on you, Ellie! What was I going to say to you after that? I thought you'd spit in my face. . . ." He paused. "I didn't plan to do this . . . to see you again. I planned to forget you."

"What made you change your mind?"

"I saw your daughter—my daughter."

That was a surprise. "My daughter? Where did you see her?"

"She came into Neely's with Joe yesterday. It was only for a minute." He studied her face. "He didn't tell you."

"No." So Joe kept secrets from her too.

"When I saw her, I thought . . . Ellie, we could give her the best of everything."

"We?"

"We could be a family, you and I and our little girl. It should be the three of us. I know we're getting a late start, and I know that's my fault. Let me make it up to you."

"You saw her for a moment in a coffee shop and now you're telling me you want us to be a family?"

"I think I've been wanting it for a long time. Seeing her just made me realize it. I have so much to give you now. Not just money, although there's plenty of that. I can give you both a real home. She can live with her real father."

He was sincere now; this wasn't a salesman's spiel. He meant this.

"We'll move out of the city, to a house where she'll have trees and grass," he said, and his eyes were shining. "What kind of life does she have running around the country with you and Joe? What will you do in a couple of years when she's ready for school? Teach her yourself like all the other mothers do on the road? Stick her in a boarding school somewhere when she gets older? That's not what you want for her—it can't be."

It wasn't. Not when she really thought about it. She tried to imagine Benny's big house with the grass and the trees. Then she thought about her little girl living in cramped hotel rooms, where she had to keep her voice down and couldn't run. Baby thought the upper bunk of a railroad sleeper was a proper bedroom. Ellie looked up and saw that Benny was watching her.

He seemed to read her mind, but then he always had. "We'll have the white picket fence and the dog and cat, all for her. And you and I—think about being together again. Think about the good times we'll have. I've never had as much fun with anyone else as I've had with you, Ellie. You're the only girl I know who knows that you can fix anything that's gone wrong with a hot fudge sundae."

But could you? Didn't it take more than hot fudge and roses to fix things that had gone wrong?

"I love you, Ellie."

"I'm married," she said.

"You're not in love with Joe. You never were. He was in love with you from the beginning, but it was never a two-way street."

When she heard Benny say it, she knew it was true. She'd suspected that Joe was in love with her, and she'd worried about it, but she'd put it out of her mind because she had to. And then so many other things had happened. "Yes," she said. "Joe was always in love with me."

"Of course he was! He married you to get you out of a jam. He wouldn't have done that if he didn't love you."

"No. He wouldn't."

"And you're grateful to him. He helped you when you needed him, and you'll never forget that. I understand. But that's not love, Ellie. That's not what you and I had."

He was right, it wasn't.

"Joe should have a woman who loves him for real. He deserves that. And we can have it again too, because it's still there between us. That feeling doesn't go away. You know that."

"Yes," she said.

"You and I deserve a chance to be happy. At least, you do. And I'll make sure you are."

"So everything will work out for the best for everyone?"

He took her hands in his. "Why not?"

She looked down at the hands that had held hers as they walked down the streets of the pretty little towns four years ago. She looked at the slender fingers that had caressed her when they made love. Then she looked up at his confident smile. "You're right, Benny," she said. "I'll always be a little in love with you. But I don't like you. You'll never be my friend."

The smile disappeared, and he jerked back his hands. But she didn't care about Benny anymore, because the confusion she'd been feeling for so long was finally over. She felt like she was watching a mist lift and float away, leaving a clear, sharp-edged world.

"You see, I've been very lucky," she said. "I'm married to my friend. I didn't intend to do it that way, but it happened, and now . . . I love him."

He pushed away from the table and turned away from her. When he turned back his face was red with anger. This temper was something different. He'd always wanted to get his own way, but now he expected to; that was new. And maybe a little frightening.

"She's my child," he said. "Do you think I'm going to stand by and let a nothing like Joe raise her?"

"I don't see how you can stop it," she said, as steadily as she could.

"Do you have any idea of what I can do to you and Joe? All I have to do is put out the word, and he'll never work again."

"Joe has a great act—"

"Great acts are a dime a dozen. I'm one of the biggest bookers in the business. I have friends, Ellie. People who want to do me favors because I can do them favors. You don't want to go against me."

"Do you think I'm afraid of you?" she asked, and hoped he wouldn't see that suddenly she was. "Do you think Joe will be afraid?"

"I think Joe loves show business. I think all he's ever wanted was to be a headliner. And he knows how the business works. So you go back and tell him what I said. He's no fool. He'll understand."

AND SHE DID tell Joe. After she'd left Benny sitting at the table in the pretty restaurant with his bottle of champagne that no one was going to drink and his lobster lunch that no one was going to eat. She went back to the boardinghouse and she told Joe what Benny had said.

CHAPTER 32

"You told him I was your friend?" Joe said.

"My friend who I love."

He rolled it around in his mind for a second. "All right," he said. And he kissed her. Which led to another kiss. Which led to the bed, which was interrupted by Ellie, breaking away. "Baby," she said, and pointed to the child, who had wandered into the room.

"We have to do something about the way we live," Joe muttered.

"Benny wants to be a part of her life, Joe."

"For the moment. Until something new and more exciting comes along. Then he'll forget about her."

"But he doesn't know that. Right now, he thinks he wants her. And me."

"A ready-made family. Benny always was on the lookout for a shortcut."

"He can hurt us."

"Only if we let him."

"How can we stop him?"

"I'll have to reason with him."

Ellie didn't believe anyone could reason with the new, imperious Benny. But the next morning, Joe announced that he was going out for a while, and she knew he was going to talk to Benny.

JOE LEFT THE boardinghouse and turned south on Broadway. He'd heard via the ubiquitous grapevine that Benny was living at the Hotel Astoria, which was right around the corner, but Joe had another errand to run first—down on Fourteenth Street. He paused for a second and looked up. The famous lights of Broadway weren't shining from the theaters now, but the names of the stars—those who had made it big enough to play this street, which was the biggest of the big-time—were up on the marquees. There they were, spelled out in foot-high letters above the traffic of everyday mortals. Joe turned his gaze down to the street swirling around him. He'd always loved New York City, and for as long as he could remember he'd dreamed of taking it by storm. When he was a kid he'd hung around the Knickerbocker Hotel dining room and Rector's Restaurant to watch the stars sail in for supper after their shows had come down. He had imagined doing that himself one day. He'd pictured himself casually handing off his coat to the hat-check girl and laughing at the jokes told by the maître d' as he was escorted to his regular table. The Knickerbocker Hotel was an office building now, but he'd planned to take Ellie to Rector's after his act opened at the Jefferson. He'd been saving up for it. But he wouldn't do it now.

Joe took one last look around him. He knew what he had to do;

that decision was already made. But once it was done, there would be no turning back. He'd known this since yesterday, when Ellie came back from her luncheon. After she'd left the hotel room to meet Benny, he had paced around the room for so long it was a wonder he had not worn the pattern off the rug. He'd made bargains with God during the hour and a half that she was gone—something he had not done since he was a child—vowing to do whatever God required, if Ellie would just come back to him. And then she had walked back in. She'd stood framed in the doorway for a moment while she pulled off her gloves, and seeing her standing there he'd known he would go back on every promise he'd ever made to let her go easily if she wanted to leave him. He would fight for her and their daughter with everything he had. But then he'd learned that he didn't have to fight, because she was staying. Because she loved him. And then she'd told him about the threats Benny had made. That was when he'd known what he had to do. Joe started walking south on Broadway.

He had finished his business and was back uptown by lunchtime, so he did a quick check of the spots he'd heard were Benny's favorites and finally ended up standing in front of Neely's glass door. He peered through the big front window of the restaurant and saw Benny sitting at a table with a group of friends. There was no point in going inside and making a scene, so he moved to the side of the building and leaned against it to wait until Benny came out. But Benny had seen him through the window, and he came outside right away.

"I suppose you want to see me," Benny said.

"Yes."

"We need to get some things straight."

"I agree."

"I told Ellie and I'm telling you. I'm not going to let you raise that little girl. She's my daughter."

"That's not what her birth certificate says."

"Oh, for God's sake, you know the truth!"

"But no one else does."

"All anyone has to do is look at her to tell she's mine. She looks like me."

"I think my daughter looks like her mother; Ellie has blond hair and blue eyes. But I think Baby's going to be short—like me. You're how tall? Over six feet, aren't you?"

"The women in my family are small."

"What a coincidence." Joe had been resting his back against the building, and now he leaned forward. "Here's the way it looks to me, Benny. Ellie and I will both lie. We've been married for four years, and people are used to thinking of us as a couple. If you try to claim our little girl is yours, you'll look like a fool. And you won't like that; you know you won't." Joe paused. "You can't prove you're the father. Give it up."

"You think I'm going to let you get away with this?"

"If you're smart."

"How are you going to support them? Because I promise you, if you do this to me you won't work again."

"We'll be just fine."

"Doing what?"

"None of your business."

"You won't be opening at the Jefferson next week, Joe."

"I know. I went there this morning and canceled." Joe turned and started walking back toward Pastor's Boardinghouse.

"She'll never stop loving me!" Benny called after him. "I know her. She'll get tired of you, and she'll want—" He never said what she'd want. Because that was when Joe turned back and punched him.

• • •

"YOU STARTED A fight with Benny in the middle of Broadway?" Ellie demanded. She'd grabbed a chunk of ice from Mrs. Pastor's ice box and was chipping it into small pieces to make a pack to press on Joe's rapidly swelling eye. "Are you crazy?"

"Been wanting to do it for four years."

"But you canceled the Jefferson. Do you know what that means?"

Joe stood up and walked to the window. He looked out at Forty-fifth Street for what seemed to Ellie like a very long time. "We're out of show business," he said. He kept himself turned away from her. He didn't want her to see his face.

"But you were just getting started," she said. "Joe, you don't have to quit. Benny can't keep you from working forever."

"No. But he can make it tough for a while—I don't know how long. We'd be on the small small-time—maybe even on a couple of Death Trails—playing tank towns, five shows a day. Staying in dirty rooms, doing the long jumps, worrying about the next meal. You know what it's like. If it was just you and me, we'd take it. Wait it out until something broke again. But we have a little girl." He still hadn't turned to look at her.

"You're quitting for her and she's not—" Ellie started to say, but he stopped her.

"Don't tell me she's not mine. I've already heard that today." He finally turned. "And Benny is right. Anyone who looks at her and knows him will see the resemblance. Do you want that for her, all that gossip? Do we want Benny playing father of the year—when it's convenient for him?"

"No."

"If we're in the business, we're going to keep running into him. We need to live somewhere out of the way."

"But you're so good in the act—"

"I can live without it. But not being with you?" He looked into her eyes. "Ellie, I'll never tell you I can't live without you. I could if I had to—and you could live without me. But I just don't want to."

It wasn't the kind of declaration of love you wanted to hear when you were young and foolish. But it had been a long time since Ellie had been that. Joe would never sing a corny love song for her, or buy her a silly present he couldn't afford. But he'd always been there with whatever she needed, starting with the first time she'd met him, when her pa gave her the black eye.

Ellie picked up the bowl of ice, dumped it in the basin, kissed Joe on the back of the neck, and started out of the room. Joe turned to see her opening the door.

"Where are you going?" he asked.

"To get you a piece of raw steak. You're going to have one hell of a shiner."

CHAPTER 33

"What did Joe and Ellie do next?" I asked Chicky.

"What time is it?" Her voice on the phone sounded groggy.

"I'm not sure. I just finished writing the last section and there aren't any more tapes. You said you were going to make more, but you never gave them to me."

"It's five in the morning, Doll Face."

"Okay. That sounds about right."

"I don't do early morning anymore. In case you haven't heard, I'm very old."

"You didn't tell me the end of the story. I don't know what happened after Joe and Ellie quit show business."

Chicky took a moment. "Do you know how to operate a car, Doll Face?"

"I can drive six to the ground, and I once took a Bentley out on the Four-oh-nine in LA during rush hour. The car had not been adapted yet for the American market, so the steering wheel was on the right. Why?"

"Because I can get us some wheels and there's something I want you to see."

THAT WEEKEND, CHICKY and I drove an ancient Honda— courtesy of the grandson of one of the Swinging Grandmas—up the Taconic Parkway to Millertown, New York.

Millertown was established as a port on the Hudson River when New York was still a colony, long before the hey-let's-go-dump-tea-in-Boston-Harbor movement. The town consists of two main drags running parallel to the river, and a couple of side streets that intersect with them to form the ubiquitous northeastern town square, with the requisite white clapboard churches flanking it, along with a minuscule fire station and a tiny town hall. There are other streets that intersect with the intersecting streets, so that a small residential area radiates out from the square. The train used to stop in Millertown, but it doesn't anymore, and whatever industry kept people in the area employed has long since vanished.

Chicky had given me this history on our trip north, so when we reached Millertown I was expecting to find one of those sad little villages whose time has passed. Not so. It took us fifteen minutes to find a parking space, and once we hit the sidewalk it was clear that the place was thriving. There were cute little clothing and home goods shops, art galleries, several antiques stores, and the old railroad depot had been turned into a school that proudly bore the name MASTERS ACADEMY. I figured this was the engine behind the town's prosperity.

"Academy of what?" I asked Chicky.

"That's the next part of the story."

"Which you are not going to tell me until you are good and ready."

She patted my cheek. "You've come to know me so well. Look to your right." We were standing in front of a building with a neon sign above it that read MILLERTOWN DINER. It looked like one of those boxcars you see in antique postcards; it was small and squatty, painted lime green, and loaded with immaculately maintained chrome trim. A plaque proudly displayed on the front door identified it as one of the few remaining Silk City diners still standing in the country. According to the brief history written on the plaque, these diners, which were popular in the 1920s, were inspired by railroad dining cars, and today they are considered to be architecturally significant. This one was a historic landmark.

"Come on," Chicky said, and led me inside.

The booths on either side of the diner were full. Every seat at the counter was taken. The three chairs in the small waiting area were taken too. "People still love this place," Chicky said happily. She turned to a kid who was manning the ancient cash register. "Hey, Pabir," she said, "how's your granddad doing?"

"Omigod," said the kid. He rushed around the counter and he and Chicky hugged and did some how-are-you-it's-been-forever dialogue; then he turned to the kitchen and unleashed a cascade of a language I didn't understand, which was followed by a man and two women racing out of the kitchen to hug Chicky some more.

The older of the two women was wearing a cook's work apron over a sari, and Chicky introduced her as the wife of the man who had purchased the diner from her back in the fifties. "Samir retired a couple of years ago," Chicky explained. "But Aditha is still coming in every day to make the pies." As everybody beamed, I glanced at the old-fashioned dessert case, where my eye was caught by a clone of the killer lemon-meringue pie Chicky had baked when Show Biz and I had our party.

"And Grandma makes the curry too, the best you ever had," Prabir assured me.

"I want to show Doll Face the Wall," Chicky said. She led me to the back of the diner, where there was a glass case full of pictures hanging on a wall. The photos were arranged chronologically, starting in the late twenties, and they all featured Joe Masters on a platform in a spotlight, with a mike in his hands. Standing nearby in each picture was Ellie. As far as I could tell, this show, or whatever it was, had been a yearly event in town for quite a while. As time passed, Joe's hair had started to recede and he had developed a bit of a paunch. But in the last picture Ellie was still a slim beauty with just a touch of gray in her reddish-blond hair.

"This town is where I grew up," Chicky said to me. "My folks moved here after they quit vaudeville."

"After Joe canceled the gig at the Jefferson," I said.

"You've got a good memory, Doll Face."

"I just wrote a book about them."

"So you did." She gave me a fond little chuckle. "When my parents came here, they didn't have much money—just what they'd saved to get them by for a few weeks if they were laid off. But the old couple who owned this diner wanted to retire and Pop had made friends with them when he and Mom stayed in Millertown before. They let him buy it for almost nothing down and pay it off over time. It took twenty years. Mom and Pop learned to cook, and Mom turned out to be a damn good waitress. Pop made a great lemon-meringue pie. They added to their family and they were happy—as much as most people are—but they missed show business. It gets in your blood, and you never really stop loving it."

I turned to the wall of pictures. "It looks to me like they found a way to do something theatrical."

"Oh, yes."

"Miss Chicky, we have a table for you." Pabir was standing be-hind us.

"Good," she said, as she hooked her arm in mine. "Because when I tell you this next part, we're both going to need pie."

After we were seated and we'd ordered—pecan pie with vanilla ice cream for Chicky, lemon meringue for me—Chicky turned back to look at the wall. There was a dreamy expression on her face.

"Pop never talked about performing when I was a kid, but Mom knew he still missed the business, so she started having tal-ent shows, right here in the diner. Two or three times a year she'd put up a little platform in the back, right where the pictures are now. People would strut their stuff and Pop would be the emcee. The prize was whatever the house pie was for the day.

"They kept the shows going during the Depression and World War II, and on the side, to earn a little extra cash, they started giv-ing singing and dancing lessons—to kids, mostly. After the war, like I told you, some genius decided that Millertown didn't need train service anymore, which killed off the local economy. And now the town had an empty railroad station to get rid of. My folks rented it and opened a theater school there. The school turned out to be a big draw for this place. Kids from all over came to take les-sons and perform in Mom's talent shows. Some people said that school saved Millertown.

"Between running the school and the diner, my folks worked hard. But we could always tell they loved it. And of course they had us to help out."

"Us?"

"Their kids."

"Plural? As in, younger brothers and sisters?"

"Only one sister. And she was older than I was."

"But Ellie was pregnant when she married Joe. How . . . ?"

"I was born five years later and named Eleanor, after Mom. Benny's daughter, my half sister, Joanna, had been named after Pop; he was very proud of that." She took a beat. "When Joanna got too old to be called 'Baby,' her new nickname was 'Annie.' "

"Annie? But that's—"

"Yes, Alexandra named your pooch after her mother. Annie was your grandmother's name. I'm your great-aunt."

CHAPTER 34

You know the feeling when you're walking down a flight of stairs and it's dark so you can't see very well, and you think there's one more step—but there isn't? As your foot reaches for something solid, it can feel like the whole world is in free fall. That's how I felt when Chicky dropped her bombshell.

"My dog is named after Benny and Ellie's daughter?" I said stupidly.

"Yes."

"Her name was Joanna."

"Because it was a feminine version of Joe."

"But everybody called her Annie."

"It seemed to fit her better. My family was big on nicknames."

"And she married my grandfather, and she had my mother, and my mother named my dog—"

"Doll Face, enough with the dog."

"But it's like one of those murder mysteries where the big clue has been in plain sight all along and no one noticed it. Annie sleeps in my bedroom. She eats her cookies there. And you're telling me—"

That was when Pabir showed up with our pie and then hung around, waiting for us to give it a try.

I wolfed down a chunk of meringue. "Fabulous," I said, and gave him my best *Now go away* smile.

But Chicky loaded up her fork with pecan pie and ice cream very slowly and put it in her mouth very carefully. She closed her eyes and did a little swoon. "Ambrosia, Pabir" she said. They exchanged a few little pleasantries while I tried not to scream in frustration. He finally disappeared. Chicky reloaded her fork.

"Are you telling me Joe and Ellie were—?"

"Shh, I'm soaking."

"If you don't talk to me, you'll be wearing that damn pie!"

Chicky gave me a big fake sigh. "Elder abuse is not cool, Doll Face." But I could see she was nervous about telling me the rest. That was what she did when she was afraid someone was going to be mad at her; she deflected. And who did that remind me of? Myself, that's who.

"Talk to me. Please."

"Joanna was Benny's daughter, I was Pop's. She was called Baby when she was little, then they nicknamed her Annie. Don't ask me why my folks were so big on nicknames; it was just something they did. I was called Tiny for a while, and then I was Cutie. They finally settled on Chicky, because—"

"Chicky," I broke in, "enough with the nicknames."

"Annie was your grandmother. Alexandra's mother."

"So the story I've been writing—"

"Is about your great-grandparents."

"And the Karras side fits in how?"

"Milos Karras was a truck driver working the Hudson River valley. He met Annie when she was waiting tables for my folks in the diner. They fell in love and got married, and Annie left Millertown. She was always the restless type. I used to put it down to Benny's bloodline, but then I turned out to be pretty restless myself, so who knows? Anyway—"

"Wait a minute. Did Annie ever find out about Benny?"

"My mom told her about him. But not until after Annie got married. I think she waited so long because she was afraid, if Annie wanted to meet Benny, Pop might get hurt. Mom always looked out for Pop that way. But Annie didn't want to meet Benny. She said Pop was the only father she'd ever want." Chicky paused. "That's one of the things I'm really grateful for. She said that to him just a couple of weeks before he and Mom died."

"Joe and Ellie died?" I heard the dismay in my voice.

Chicky heard it too. "You wanted a happy ending, didn't you?"

"Yes." Always.

"They had one for a while. But then there was a car wreck. It was her birthday and he was taking her out for a night on the town. They were only in their fifties. Way too young, you know?"

I remembered when *my* father died at fifty-six. "Yes," I said. "I know."

"I was pretty crazy after it happened," Chicky said. "I think I wanted to make time stand still. I tried to keep everything exactly the way it had been when they were alive."

I remembered how I had felt when Sheryl was dating and I was writing *Love, Max.* "I know," I said.

"I wanted to keep on running the diner and the school. It was as if I were keeping Pop and Mom with me, if I could do that. I didn't want anything to change."

"I know."

"But Annie had moved on. She wanted to sell. Her husband

wanted to start his own business and he needed the capital. And to be fair, I was having trouble trying to be the boss of two businesses. I was in over my head, but I couldn't face it.

"It got ugly between Annie and me—lawyers and the whole nine yards. But in the end, she won. The town offered to buy the school from us; the Masters Academy had put Millertown on the map, and they didn't want to lose it. Pabir's grandfather bought the diner. And I never forgave Annie.

"I started traveling, ran around Europe for a while, spent a few years in Hawaii, a few more in Mexico, the Pacific Northwest, you name it. I was so mad at Annie, I never came home to see her baby when it was born. When Annie died, I was out of the country and I didn't get back in time for the funeral. After that—I don't know, it just seemed easier to stay away. Before I knew it, your mother was a teenager. The last thing she needed was me coming into her life to play the loving auntie.

"I settled in Oregon for a couple of decades. But eventually you want to go home. The first week I was in New York, before I even moved into my apartment, I rented a car and drove up here to see the diner. Pabir's folks were still here." Her eyes were full of tears. "I can't tell you what that was like . . . seeing the school and the diner."

"I can imagine."

She wiped the tears away and shrugged. "The rest of the story you know." She started to signal for the check but I stopped her.

"Not so fast."

"What's left to tell? I fell and broke my hip. I moved to Yorkville House, decided to tell my parents' story, and found you. I got in touch. And here we are."

"Did you know who I was? When you read my ad?"

There was a hesitation. "Yes."

"Why didn't you tell me we were related?"

I thought she was going to give me a clever answer or try to avoid one altogether. She looked straight at me. "What would I have done if you didn't want to write the story?" She took a deep breath. "Or if you didn't like me? I'm not as strong as I appear to be, Francesca. Most people aren't."

"Didn't you think I should know who I was writing about?"

"I did think about that. But you were down in the dumps, and nepotism is bad for the soul. You didn't need to get a job because you were family; you needed someone to hire you for your talent."

"Someone who couldn't pay me."

"And look how beautifully you handled that! I'm so proud of you, Doll Face!" She beamed at me. Then she said softly, "I needed to give you time to know me. And to know Joe and Ellie. You were looking for a love story to write, and I gave you one—ours."

"Who says I wanted to write a love story? I'm the antiromantic, remember?"

"Nah. You're a true believer who got discouraged. And pissed off." She signaled again for the check. "Now, let's get out of here so you can go home and finish my book. At my age I don't have forever to wait for you."

CHAPTER 35

After that day in Millertown, I finished the book in record time. And I was more determined than ever to sell it. I mean, wouldn't you be after learning that you'd been writing your own family history? But first I engineered a meeting between Chicky and Alexandra, which was a whole lot less operatic than Chicky was afraid it would be. You've got to love my mother. She's got her faults, but carrying a grudge has never been one of them. You show her a little old lady who looks teary, and Alexandra melts. Besides, Chicky was family. In her own scattered way, Alexandra is a family person—as long as she doesn't have to wash their dishes. I mean, she did name my dog after her mother.

When I told Pete about the unknown branch of our family tree, he said, "We come from theater people? Well, you've always been a drama queen." Unfortunately, he was on the other side of the globe, so I couldn't get my hands on him.

But now I had this book to sell. I shared my fears with my loved ones.

"I know it's not going to be easy to find a publisher. I haven't written anything in four years," I said to Chicky.

"It's still the same problem: I'm trying to sell a book about people who lived almost a hundred years ago and worked in vaudeville—which most readers today can't even spell," I said to Show Biz.

"But I'm a much stronger person now than I was. I know how to handle setbacks. Sort of," I said to Alexandra.

"I'm going to fight for this," I told Sheryl on the phone.

"I'll never give up on this project," I said to Lancelot on our morning walk.

"Defeat is not an option for Francesca, aka Doll Face," I said to Annie.

The first step was to find an agent, since Nancy was doing the motherhood thing. I compiled a list of book agents who had made it a point to congratulate me when *Love, Max* hit big, and started making phone calls.

The first round of turndowns for Chicky's book—and my family history—were very nice. I think every agent used the word *charming*. They all wished me well in this brutally competitive market. Results: zip. I then turned to Plan B and contacted agencies where no one knew my name. Zilch. I turned to Plan C, and contacted agencies I'd read about on the Internet. Nada. Finally, I started sending the manuscript directly to publishers—and you can't characterize that as a plan; it's more like walking into a court of law when you've been accused of murder and saying you're going to be handling your own defense. The response to that effort? Zip. Zilch. Nada.

All those life lessons I'd been cherishing suddenly seemed like the kind of bad advice you get from television talk shows and astrologers. I was back to curling up in a fetal position in my bed—or would have been, if I hadn't been afraid that Show Biz would find me there. And I still had to walk Lancelot three times a day. I called Chicky to give her the bad news. She summoned me to her room, and soon I was sipping tea and munching cookies and trying not to cry.

"I failed," I told her. "I'm sorry."

"Do we have a good story, Doll Face?"

"Damn good." I bit back tears.

"Then I want you to see something," she said. She whipped out a TV remote and, after a few seconds of futzing with it, a segment of one of those shows that deal with the glorious world of entertainment popped up on her screen. "I saw this last night and I Tivo-ed it," she announced proudly. What she had recorded was an interview with two kids—a boy and a girl—who had been hugely popular on their teen-oriented nighttime television show and were now not only a romantic item but were looking for a project to do together.

"CeeCee and I want to stretch and grow as artists," said the young guy.

"And we have great chemistry," said the girl.

"Yeah, we want to take advantage of that while we're still hot for each other," said her male counterpart. "We've already inked a deal with a producer. Now we just have to find the right script."

"One that touches us here," CeeCee indicated her impressive cleavage and presumably the heart beating beneath it.

Chicky paused the interview and said, "Well, what do you think?"

"If I were CeeCee, I wouldn't be picking out an engagement ring just yet."

"I meant, what do you think about them to play Joe and Ellie? I've watched them on their show, and they can act."

"Chicky, what we have is a novel, not a screenplay."

Chicky waved that one away like she was swatting flies. "You'll rewrite it," she said.

"Even if I could do that," I went on, "I don't have any connections in television—or in show business. Those two actors are coming off a hit series. Everyone in the world will be swamping them with ideas for scripts. Do you know how hard it would be to get them to read a whole book? And ours hasn't even been sold."

"Oh, I don't think you should try to reach them. I was thinking you should get in touch with the producer. The one who has a deal with them." Chicky looked down at her hands. "Because you happen to know her."

For a second I was confused. "I don't know any—" I started to say; then I stopped. "Andy Grace," I said.

"Bingo."

"The last time I saw her, we were at a very public function and I was dumping very cold water on her."

"Yes."

"I also referred to her as a postmenopausal slut."

"Yes, I'm afraid you'll have some fence-mending to do."

"I'm not the one who has to mend fences. I didn't steal *her* husband."

"Leaving aside the question of how much you really wanted to hang on to the man, she's probably our only chance." She turned to the picture of Ellie and Joe on her wall. "I thought you wanted to honor them, Doll Face." She turned back to me. "Of course, if it's too much to ask—"

"Stop trying to play me."

"Damn, I'm losing my touch."

"No, I've just been watching you in action for a while."

"Okay." Then she looked at me very seriously. "Francesca, give it a try. What do we have to lose?"

I looked at her picture of Joe and Ellie on the wall—my great grandparents. I thought about all the good things that had come into my life since I'd met Chicky.

"It's worth a shot," I said.

Maybe we do learn life lessons after all.

CHAPTER 36

Jake was the one who finally set up the meeting between Andy and me. Our phone dialogue went like this.

HIM: *You want me to ask Andy to take a meeting with you? Why the hell would I do that?*
ME: *Because you remember me fondly?*
HIM: *Think again.*
ME: *Oh. (I make my voice quiver) Well, I'm sorry, Jake. Really so sorry. (There follows a section in which I do some ad hoc fake weeping, while Jake, who was never a bad person—just really, really shallow—attempts to console me.)*
HIM: *Francesca, I'll ask Andy. But I don't think it will do much good. That video of you . . . when you—*
ME: *Doused her?*
HIM: *It's still getting hits on the Internet.*

ME: *(unable to swallow a giggle) Really?*

HIM: *You think that's funny?*

ME: *No! Absolutely not! Can you smooth it over for me, Jake? I know I don't have any right to ask you, but could you? (Wistfully) For old time's sake?*

HIM: *(Big pause) It's not going to be easy, but I'll see what I can do.*

ME: *I don't know how to thank you.*

HIM: *Francesca?*

ME: *Yes?*

HIM: *Cut the bullshit.*

ME: *Okeydokey.*

He called back two hours later to tell me to buy my plane ticket.

THE SCENE WITH Andy was going to be difficult, I knew that. For starters, if Jake was right, my crack about her being a post-menopausal slut was still circling the globe. Any woman who took good care of herself the way Andy did was going to be pissed about someone mentioning that she was postmenopausal—the slut part probably hadn't bothered her all that much. And then there was the fact that I was still angry at Andy. As I'd said to Chicky, she had stolen my husband. And I don't care how evolved you are, no one can survive being replaced with their ego intact. Well, no one except my mother, the feminist icon. Most of us can't help asking all those What-does-she-have-that-I-don't? questions. And the answers we come up with at three in the morning aren't likely to make us real chipper.

But I had to be chipper—and conciliatory, if not placating—when I had my sit-down with Andy. So I have to admit I was pretty nervous on the trip to LA. To give myself strength, I reread the story I'd written about Joe and Ellie. And as I read, I finally knew what I wanted to say.

ANDY AND I met in her office, which reminded me of the sleek room Jake and I had once put together for my office in New York. She looked exactly the same way she had the last time I'd seen her—although drier. And she'd had her chin done.

"I want you to know there is no way in hell that I will produce anything you've touched," she said, after she'd closed the door behind me. "I'm only meeting with you because Jake asked me to."

"I know that," I said. "You're doing it for him, because you love him. You and Jake are perfect for each other."

I think that threw her a little. "You don't know whether we are or not."

"I knew him pretty well, and you were my friend. And you two being together—it's so obvious, I should have seen it from the beginning."

"I didn't take him away from you. No outsider can break up a relationship that's working."

"Absolutely not. That's why I want to thank you." That threw her more. "It took Jake four tries at marriage, and I don't know how many times you've given it a whirl . . . but the two of you finally got it right. And I'm not just saying that because I want you to read my project."

"Do you really think I'm going to believe that?" But there was a trace of doubt in her eyes. Maybe she could tell that I meant what I was saying.

"I don't care whether you believe me or not. You did me a favor. Jake probably wouldn't have left me if he hadn't had you to go to, and I never would have left him because I didn't know what a marriage should be like. We might have stuck it out. And that would have been too bad. Now what he's got is great. And I have a chance to find that someday. So, thank you." I put my manuscript on her slick glass coffee table. "This is a love story—a real one. You should read it. I think you'll like it." Then I walked out.

CHAPTER 37

"Where shall I put the hand wipes?" Sheryl demanded, as she bustled into the bathroom. "You can't put out finger bowls at a buffet. Which is why I always prefer a sit-down dinner party."

"Hand wipes?" I repeated vaguely. I was busy putting a pink daisy in my hair.

"Show Biz says he's serving barbecued ribs," Sheryl said patiently. "We have to have some way for people to clean their fingers." She turned to my mother, who had just come in. "What do you think, Alexandra?"

"Put a roll of paper towels on the sink, in here," my mother said.

"We've got over fifty guests coming," Sheryl said, in the tone of one explaining what green looks like to the color-blind. "There is no way you're going to fit all of them in this little powder room."

"Okay, everybody but Francesca out of the bathroom," Show Biz said, sticking his head in. Then he turned to me and added, "And you better get a move on. We're on a schedule; we've got to feed the crowd before the movie starts." He disappeared, and I raced into the bedroom to pull on my dress while Annie watched. That was when I noticed how easily the zipper was going up. Six dog walks a day and Show Biz's smoothies for breakfast seemed to have tightened my hips. And the best part was, I hadn't even known it. For the first time since I hit puberty, I hadn't been weighing myself every day. Or every hour. I'd been too excited about other things.

"Like the movie," I said to Annie. "As in *my* movie. The one I wrote. Based on the book, which I also wrote. About my family."

It had taken Andy two weeks to convince CeeCee and her boyfriend that Chicky's book was the project of their dreams. And it had taken me another two months to write the script. Then it had taken another eight months for the LA folks to shoot the movie, edit it, and do whatever else they do. Tonight it was going to air on television.

We had rented a flat-screen TV the size of a billboard and a ton of chairs, and Show Biz had ordered enough ribs to feed our entire zip code. Then, in his role as mine merry host, he had invited everyone Chicky and I had ever met to watch our movie with us. Sheryl, her husband, and Nancy had flown in from the West Coast. My brother and his family had flown in from Reykjavik (I still don't know what the hell he does there). Alexandra and Lenny had picked up Chicky at Yorkville House, along with the staff and all the ambulatory residents of the center, including the Swinging Grandmas.

"Paying off this extravaganza will probably take every dime I've earned for the screenplay," I told Annie, "but I don't give a damn. I'm soaking in the moment!" I took my lucky scarf—the pink chiffon with the ruffles—out of my drawer and wrapped it around my shoulders. "I'm ready for my close-up, Mr. DeMille," I said, to my image in the mirror.

"Looking good, Doll Face," growled a familiar voice behind me. I turned to see Chicky. She was wearing a green satin pants suit, and her golden curls were recently tinted and gleaming.

"You look like a million bucks yourself," I said.

She fingered her lapels, which were liberally sprinkled with sequins. "Just giving 'em a little glitz and glam," she said. Then she held out a thin rectangular parcel wrapped in brown paper. "I want you to have this, Doll Face," she said.

I knew what it was without opening it. "I can't—" I started to say. But she reached up to put her fingers on my lips.

"I want you to keep them with you," she said. "I think they will be good for you. Remind you of things you need to remember. And now I can pass them on to family."

So I took the package, unwrapped the picture of Joe and Ellie in the gilded frame, and I set it on my bureau.

"Tomorrow I'll get the super to hang it on the wall," I told Chicky.

"It'll look good there," she said.

And we went in to watch our movie.

Part of me wishes I could finish with a big happy ending tied up in a pink bow. On the other hand, the only way you really have an ending—happy or not—is if you're dead, so that's not a great plan.

Here's where my life is right now.

Our movie was good. It got nice reviews, and even though it was only a cable flick it did well in the ratings. As a result, Andy has thrown me some more work punching up other people's scripts. It seems I'm really good with dialogue. (And be proud of me, because when I went out to Hollywood I saw Jake, and it was obvious that Andy wasn't the only one who had had her chin done, but I didn't make one crack about group rates on surgery or adjoining beds in recovery. Honest, not one.)

I have a couple of ideas for novels I'd like to write. Especially now that Nancy has decided she wants to get back into the business and she's opening her own agency. So I'll probably start the old merry-go-round again. And I'll probably be work-obsessed, and there will be days when I'll forget to shower. But I may finish another book, so what the hell.

Meanwhile, I have two more dog-walking clients, a toy poodle and a Chihuahua. Lancelot isn't threatened by them because they're tiny so they can all walk together; he actually loves the company.

Mom and Chicky are getting to be even better friends, and Sheryl and Chicky adore each other.

Show Biz has found a fella. I was scared he was going to move out, but Jeff is a sous-chef who has been having trouble finding a job, so for the moment they're both living in the apartment. Someday Show Biz will go, I know that. I just hope it doesn't happen for a while. Until it does, Annie and I are soaking up the good times—and snarfing up the homemade cookies.

And now for the biggie: I've had a date. He isn't going to be the love of my life, but at least neither one of us ran screaming into the night. Sheryl says I'll find the right man, because now that I realize I'm high maintenance I'll know what to look for. Chicky says when you want something to happen, there's only one way to guarantee that it won't, and that is to quit trying. And yeah, I want it to happen. Meanwhile, I'll just keep wearing my pink ruffles and soaking. One thing I know, whoever I wind up with, he's going to have to be my friend. I learned that from Joe and Ellie.

Yeah, I'm still learning life lessons.

Acknowledgments

I don't know why so many wonderful people are in my life, but I'm finally old enough not to question it anymore and to just say thank you.

So, thank you first and always to Eric Simonoff, my agent and my friend. It just gets better the longer I know him. To the amazing Laura Ford, who edited this book with such smarts and humor. Publishing will miss you, Laura. Thank you to Caitlin Alexander who took over with this book, and gave its final stage such loving care and attention. Thank you to Libby McGuire and Jane von Mehren for faith and support that is truly phenomenal.

I am grateful to Robbin Schiff for the book cover, which makes me smile; to Dennis Ambrose, who continually bails me out and makes me look better than I am; and to Janet Baker for such a terrific copyedit. Endless gratitude, too, for Lisa Barnes, Caitlin Kuhfeldt, Kim Hovey, Kathleen McAuliffe, and Anne Watters, for making sure that the word about my books gets out there.

Thank you to Cynthia Burkett, whose continued friendship will always be a treasure in my life, and to the spectacular Robert

Reid, who made it a one-man mission to bring me into the twenty-first century with his own brand of brilliance, kindness, and generosity—and he makes a mean vegan "chicken" parmesan. Thank you to Gerry Waggett, Charlie Masson, Richard Simms, Margaret and Barbara Long, Ellie Quester, Emma Jayne Kretlow, Rachel Pollak, Ellen Tannebaum, the staff of the East Fishkill Library, especially Cindy Dubinsky and Kathy Swierat, the incredible Carolyn Rogers, Jane Ryan, who is still the world's best listener, and Melissa Crapser, whose goodness just does me in. And Charlie and Joshie will never forgive me if I don't mention the kind and caring Gil Anderson.

Thank you to those who will always give me a goal to aim for just by their lovely example of lives well lived: Phyllis Piccolo, Virginia Piccolo, Jessie O'Neil, and Albert Piccolo. Thank you to Christopher and Colin for making my life richer in ways I never knew were possible, and to Bee and Iris. And, as always, thank you to my sisters, Lucy and Marie, and my brother, Brad.

And I'd like to end with special memories of Mary Minnella. The world is not the same without you and your gift for happiness, Aunt Mary. We all miss you.

Looking
for a
Love Story

a novel

LOUISE SHAFFER

A Reader's Guide

A Conversation with
Louise Shaffer's Dogs

NOTE FROM LOUISE: Since the dog named Annie figures so prominently in Looking for a Love Story, *my two canine companions, Josh and Charlie, suggested rather strenuously that they should be a part of this interview. In fact, they thought they should* be *the interview. So here they are in their own words, telling everyone what it's like to live with an author. And, according to Joshua, giving humans a rare opportunity to explore our mutual existence from a canine point of view. I want it known that I take no responsibility for what will be said from this point on. Especially if it's Charlie saying it.*

RANDOM HOUSE READER'S CIRCLE (to two canines seated on a suede sofa that shows every hair that is shed and every bit of dirt that is dragged in by muddy paws): So you guys are going to give us an insider's perspective on Louise Shaffer the author.

CHARLIE: Josh and me, we call her "Mommy."

JOSHUA: Actually my correct name is Joshua. And technically speaking, Charlie's mother is a Loose Coated Wheaten Terrier and mine is an English Springer Spaniel—of impeccable pedigree.

CHARLIE: I knew he was going to bring up the pedigree thing.

JOSHUA: My breed has been around for centuries. We were the companions of kings. You can find us in portraits painted—

CHARLIE: (breaking in): During the time of Elizabeth the First—whoever she was.

JOSHUA: Only one of the greatest monarchs England has ever known.

CHARLIE: Like anyone cares.

JOSHUA: You are such a peasant.

CHARLIE: Who are you calling a pheasant? Do these paws look like wings to you?

JOSHUA: I said "peasant," dummy.

CHARLIE: You want to take this outside, Hot Stuff?

JOSHUA: Any time, Carpet Boy.

CHARLIE: You have no right to bring that up. The carpet thing was a mistake.

JOSHUA: Who eats the ornaments off a Christmas tree and then follows it up by chowing down on the carpet?

CHARLIE: I told you, my stomach was upset and the carpet looked like grass. I was just a puppy.

JOSHUA: You were an idiot. Our humans are still paying off your surgeries.

RHRC: Uh . . . guys—could we get back to the subject?

CHARLIE: Right. You want us to talk about Mommy.

JOSHUA: We call her that because it makes her happy.

CHARLIE: Go figure.

RHRC: What's it like living with an author?

JOSHUA: Most of the time, she's thoroughly presentable.

CHARLIE: Except for the week before a deadline.

JOSHUA: Yes, that's not pretty.

CHARLIE: Humans really should brush their hair every once in a while.

JOSHUA: And they shouldn't wear the same nightgown all day for a week.

CHARLIE: Also, it's better if they don't walk around the house talking to themselves.

JOSHUA: She usually does that when she's stuck on a plot point.

CHARLIE: Or when she can't make her characters do what she needs them to do to make the plot work. That can get scary.

JOSHUA: She'll walk into the middle of a room with this weird look in her eyes. . . .

CHARLIE: Like that duck in the Aflac commercials . . .

JOSHUA: And she'll talk to herself for a while, then she'll start answering herself. Sometimes she uses different voices.

CHARLIE: That's when you know it's bad.

JOSHUA: That's when Roger—he's her husband, but he doesn't make us call him "Daddy," thank God—hides the car keys.

CHARLIE: Sometimes she even forgets our dinnertime.

JOSHUA: And she does things like leave the refrigerator door open so certain people can inhale the smoked salmon she was going to serve at brunch before she canceled it because she was stuck on a plot point.

CHARLIE: I've always been partial to lox and bagels.

JOSHUA: A whole pound of lox? The vet was afraid they were going to have to pump your stomach.

CHARLIE: So I suppose you've never done anything wrong. . . .

JOSHUA: Now that you mention it—no. I can't think of a thing.

CHARLIE: Sometimes I really want to bite you.

JOSHUA: You're welcome to try.

RHRC: Guys? We were talking about Louise?

CHARLIE: Sometimes she can be really funny. Like when she tried to train us. Remember, Josh?

JOSHUA: Oh Lord, yes!

CHARLIE: She bought books.

JOSHUA: Hired a trainer.

CHARLIE: She spent a whole summer walking us around our cul de sac, going, "Sit! Stay! Heel!"

JOSHUA: As if.

(There are canine chuckles at the memory.)

CHARLIE (mimicking Louise): "Sit, boys!" "C'mon fellahs, stay. . . ."

(The chuckles have now turned into belly woofs.)

JOSHUA: Stop! Really. Or I'm going to have to go outside for a potty break.

RHRC: So I'm guessing the attempt at training wasn't a success.

JOSHUA: That depends on who you're talking to.

CHARLIE: We were happy with it.

JOSHUA: It was all a part of the learning process.

CHARLIE: For Mommy.

RHRC: That brings me to an interesting point. The whole dog-mankind relationship. Would you guys care to speak on that a little?

JOSHUA: Okay, here's the thing people need to know about any dog's relationship to his humans. These creatures—these humans—who have no sense of smell—

CHARLIE:—and lousy hearing—

JOSHUA:—and absolutely no understanding of how the universe works, come into our lives.

CHARLIE: The poor things don't know enough to drop whatever they're doing on a beautiful day, and go outside to sniff the sunshine.

JOSHUA: They don't know when it's time to stop worrying about the bills or their work, and roll in the autumn leaves, or throw a ball for us to catch, or just sit quietly and pet us.

CHARLIE: They're always worrying about what's going to happen tomorrow.

JOSHUA: Or what happened yesterday.

CHARLIE: So it's up to us, their dogs, to make them pay attention to today.

JOSHUA: Particularly if it's a good day. They don't seem to notice when things are going well.

CHARLIE: But they sure do complain when they aren't.

JOSHUA: Teaching them to say "thank you" can be a challenge.

CHARLIE: They're awfully stubborn.

JOSHUA: We just have to keep reminding ourselves that they aren't the brightest species on the planet.

CHARLIE: When you think about it, all they've really got going for them is the opposable thumb. Which is great for opening food cans. . . .

JOSHUA: But on a metaphysical level—not so much.

CHARLIE: Whatever that means.

JOSHUA: It means no matter how limited or flawed they are, we still love them.

CHARLIE: Well, duh, that's in the Dog's Credo. "Rule Number One: I swear to love my humans unconditionally."

JOSHUA: Yeah. Somebody's got to do it. (Turns to interviewer.) You need more?

RHRC: No, I think that does it. I'm going home to pet my dog.

CHARLIE: A suggestion? Give him some steak.

JOSHUA: He'll really appreciate that.

Questions and Topics for Discussion

1. Have you ever fallen in love with someone who didn't know the real you? Is it possible to be happy in that kind of relationship?

2. When Jake and Francesca finally have the Talk, she insists that she's not the one that wants out of the relationship, and he replies, "Yes, you do. You just don't know it yet." Is Jake right? At what point does Francesca realize that she's better off without him? Have you ever been devastated by the loss of something you didn't actually want?

3. What about Jake ("Shallow Guy") was so appealing to Francesca in the beginning of their relationship? What did he offer her?

4. How do Francesca's mother and father differ as parents? Sheryl?

5. Were you surprised at the friendship that blossoms between Alexandra and Sheryl? What do the two women have in common that brings them together?

6. Before the drink-throwing incident, Andy suggests that Francesca "look like a winner," even if she feels like a loser. Jake crows that "it's all about appearances . . . to hell with the real you." Do you believe that it's possible to "fake it 'til you make it"? Is future success more likely if you look the part?

7. How do Francesca's life lessons evolve throughout the novel? Can you plot her development through her favorite sayings?

8. Why does Francesca connect with Joe and Ellie's story so strongly? What shatters her writer's block?

9. When do you think Ellie finally falls in love with Joe? Can marriages that aren't grounded in love be successful?

10. What about Joe and Ellie's story mirrors Francesca's own?

11. Would you rather have a passionate love affair with someone unreliable, or a comfortable partnership with a friend you could trust with your entire being?

12. Francesca found a love story in Joe and Ellie. What kind of love story is she making for herself? Must a love story be about romantic love? How else can we star in our own love stories?

ABOUT THE AUTHOR

LOUISE SHAFFER is the author of *Serendipity, The Three Miss Margarets, The Ladies of Garrison Gardens,* and *Family Acts.* A graduate of the Yale School of Drama, she has written for television and has appeared on Broadway, in TV movies, and in daytime dramas, earning an Emmy for her work on *Ryan's Hope.* Shaffer and her husband live in the Lower Hudson Valley with several beloved rescue dogs.

www.louiseshaffer.com